JOHN GIELGUD'S
HAMLET

John Gielgud as Hamlet, New York, 1936

Photograph by Vandamm

John Gielgud's
HAMLET

A Record of Performance
By ROSAMOND GILDER

With Notes on
Costume, Scenery and Stage Business
By JOHN GIELGUD

OXFORD UNIVERSITY PRESS
New York Toronto
1937

PR
2807
G47
G468

16922

FOREWORD

' RASHLY, *and prais'd be rashness.*' It is Hamlet *himself who argues so, and since the rashness in question is concerned with him it seems not inappropriate to accept his encouragement, even at the cost of adding another volume to the legion already written on the subject of that much discussed young man. This book is, as a matter of fact, the result of a long cherished theory more generally accepted to-day than in the past. As Mr. Granville-Barker expresses it, Shakespeare in his plays was providing ' raw material for acting.' He should, therefore, be studied in the theatre rather than in the library, for his plays are best understood in terms of performance on a stage.*

There has been more scholarly ' throwing about of brains ' over Hamlet *than over any other play in the canon, or indeed over any other single work of man's play-writing genius. It has been endlessly analyzed, explained, torn to pieces, reconstructed, riddled and unriddled by philosopher and critic, historian and philologist, scholar and grammarian. Yet in this torrent of printed words one voice alone is silent, the voice of the commentator who is the final interpreter of Shakespeare and for whom the plays were created—the actor.*

By reliving in its own medium the Shakespearian miracle, the great actor, the poet-actor, pierces to the heart of the meaning of the playwright who was himself both actor and poet. The actor's creative interpretation explains, clarifies, illumines the text more vividly than volumes of scholarly elucidation. But his comment lives only in the brief hour of his performance. It is written in air, instantly gone, leaving nothing but the memory of an emotion in the minds and hearts of his audience.

Shakespearian criticism suffers a loss in that the records of the actual performances of great actors and actresses of the past are so meagre. A few discerning criticisms, a few passages in memoirs and biographies give fleeting impressions of outstanding interpretations, but there is little factual description. The editors of the Variorum Shakespeare comment on this lacuna, which is evident in the fact that of the 900 pages of their edition of Hamlet *only 25 are devoted to actors' interpretations. Yet every detail of the stage business of a performance by Garrick, Kean or Siddons is stimulating to the imagination and of absorbing interest to workers in the theatre.*

When I saw John Gielgud's Hamlet, the actor's power of creative interpretation was brought home to me once more, this time with consummate force. Here was a case in point: his performance established a comment on, an illustration of, the text. Was it possible to set down that interpretation in words, to fix in print that life which came into being on the stage, a life made up of sound and movement, of light, colour, costume, make-up and mood; of action and reaction between actor and actor, actor and audience; that life affected by the physical structure of the theatre, the psychological atmosphere of the day, the hour, the time and place? Could so dynamic a creation as Gielgud's Hamlet be conveyed in any other medium than its own? The answer is obvious, but the challenge was there and could not be avoided.

I have, therefore, attempted to set down a verbal portrait of a Hamlet of which Charles Morgan wrote: ' His performance is of such a rank as will entitle it to be remembered and debated for years to come.' ' The first Hamlet of our time,' W.A. Darlington called it, and added that ' There can have been few to equal him in the long history of the English stage.' My own reasons for believing that Mr. Gielgud's interpretation is of more than passing interest are given in the introductory chapter, in which I analyze its effect as a whole and discuss briefly some aspects of his technical approach. The details of his interpretation are set down in the scene-by-scene description of his performance which runs opposite the version of the text used in the London and New York productions.

Though I have written the account as a straight narrative, I have included in it all the information which a director's regie-book would contain, indications of movement and business, of emphasis, intention and mood. I have used the narrative rather than the prompt-book form because it conveys more vividly the sense of action in space which is so essential a part of the theatre commentary, as differentiated from the library commentary, on Shakespeare. The Hamlet of this description is, however, always John Gielgud, not an abstract, theo-retic or imagined Hamlet. It should be labelled ' Portrait of Hamlet-Gielgud as a Young Man, New York 1936–1937.' *If it is not a life-like portrait the fault lies with the painter, not the subject, for the whole intention of this delineation is its objectivity. I did not ask John Gielgud what he thought about Hamlet; I watched what he did on the stage and have set down here both what he did and what that doing meant.*

That this description of his interpretation is as nearly accurate as any restatement can hope to be may be judged by the fact that he has given it the validity of his collaboration. During a gruelling season of hard work he has taken time to read, advise, criticize. Finally, he has made the book alive by his own inimitable contribution. Though he has been wisely unwilling to discuss in print what he has so brilliantly stated in acting—his opinions on the psychologic, philosophic, dramatic and poetic content of the play—he has added by his notes and comments an essential theatre element to the picture as a whole.

The ultimate fascination of the theatre lies in the fact that it is made up in equal parts of poetry and greasepaint, of inspiration and box-office receipts, of dust and divinity. The draughts and electric cables back-stage, the glitter and coughing out front, the crowds in the gallery, the mob at the stage door, the dreadful occasions when someone forgets his cue, the ecstatic moment when everything sweeps heavenward in a blaze of inspired glory, of such is the kingdom of the stage.

Some of the flavour of that kingdom is brought to these pages by Mr. Gielgud's notes and comments, written between performances, on trains, in the dressing room, jotted down when Hamlet should have been resting but when John Gielgud, electrified by a new idea, would give him no peace. These reflections on the past, self-criticisms, advice to directors; these indications of a wide reading, of an eager and retentive mind, of a keen judgment and a sensitive intelligence, add an invaluable sense of back-stage living to this record of an outstanding performance.

John Gielgud played Hamlet *for months to packed houses in*

London and New York. His is an interpretation that has something vital to say, both now and in the future, to everyone who cares for the theatre. If this book can recreate something of that performance it will have served its purpose, for Gielgud's Hamlet has reaffirmed in no uncertain terms the fact that Shakespeare wrote for the actor and the stage, and through the actor on the stage Shakespeare and the theatre itself will continue triumphantly to live.

ROSAMOND GILDER

CONTENTS

" *Une œuvre de théâtre ne s'explique pas, elle se joue.*"
LOUIS JOUVET

JOHN GIELGUD'S HAMLET
By Rosamond Gilder

JOHN GIELGUD'S HAMLET

By Rosamond Gilder

FOR over three hundred and thirty years *Hamlet* has held the world in thrall. A stage success when it was written, the ' Standing Room Only ' sign records its drawing power today. It triumphs over time and change because, more than any other single creation of man's mind, it is a living organism, complex and passionate, ugly and exalted, defying final analysis and permitting each succeeding generation to re-create it in its own image. The theatre grapples with it continuously, dressing it in every conceivable garb, ancient, modern and imaginary. Every actor, man or woman, lusts for it. The scholars snatch it from the players and retire with it like quarrelsome bears into remote fortresses of words, definitions, factual and fantastic interpretations. Children feed their love of beautiful sounds on its music and wise men spend their lives analyzing the meaning of a single phrase.

Yet *Hamlet* survives them all, survives the fleshly tragedienne as well as the desiccated pedant, survives the experiments of directors, the fantasies of designers, the virulent attacks of the smart young things, the dullness of the classroom, the weight of legendary reputation. It survives because Hamlet himself has never yet been caught, because he springs from the pins with which the pedant would fix him on the dissecting board, breaks the mould in which the critic would cast him, and refuses to conform to any formula yet proposed by any one age or generation. The most self-explanatory and generally talkative of young men, he yet does not tell us clearly such major things about himself as his age, his mental health, his feelings about his sweetheart, his morals, his religious beliefs, his political opinions. A library of documentation has failed to reveal what he actually says at certain crucial moments, or what he does at others. By the happy accident that Shakespeare never wrote a well-made play, that he forbore prefaces and never bothered to edit his own texts, *Hamlet* remains flexible and alive, various and variable. To each generation it is a different thing,

13

and fortunate indeed is that generation which has its Hamlet made articulate for it by the genius of an actor who is kin both to the poet of Elizabeth's London and to the average man of his own day.

John Gielgud is such a Hamlet and by that he takes his place in the brief roll-call of the actors who have incarnated the Prince so completely for their day that they have become permanently associated with the part: Burbage for whom the role was written, Betterton who could make even his fellow actors' hair to stand on end, Garrick who held London in fee for years, Kean who revealed Shakespeare by flashes of lightning, Booth whose memory is cherished by our own parents and grandparents. The written records show that these men and the other great Hamlets of the past spoke directly and with no uncertain voice to the mind and heart of their own generation. In their presence the mystery of Hamlet was for the moment solved as it is solved to-day by Gielgud's performance. The creative genius of the actor, by its kinship with the creative genius of the poet, sheds a light on the text that the most fervid words, the most astute analysis of writer or scholar can never equal.

Two things must inevitably be said of any Hamlet worthy of his metal: this is Shakespeare's Prince—this is our own. Gielgud's fulfills both requirements—granting always that we can know either Shakespeare or ourselves! The play as he gives it is more nearly textually complete than we are accustomed to seeing it, and for this reason it is a more difficult, complex and startling Prince than the one, for instance, with which Booth fascinated and awed our forebears. Gielgud has been accused of not giving a unified impersonation. It is easy to see that the comment stems from a conception of the part based on versions delicately pruned to create the image of a princely youth of heroic mould who does, of course, exist in the text, but who is also doubled by a sardonic, virulent and cruel young man, a young man who talks bawdry to Ophelia, baits her father, sends his ex-friends to death without a scruple and kills without compunction once his blood is up. Hamlet, as

Shakespeare wrote him, was a Renaissance youth to whom philosophy, poetry and violence were familiar. He lacked a decent sense of modern stage conventions, of climax and dénouement, of time-relationships and the proper conduct of a plot. He has a way of not remaining consistent that is disconcerting to the theorist.

To unify and simplify the role, Booth, for instance, omitted the most unappetizing of Hamlet's comments on his mother's behaviour, such as the ' incestuous sheets ' of the first soliloquy, the ' most pernicious woman ' of the speech that follows immediately on the ghostly interview. He left out all the coarse banter with Ophelia and large sections of the closet scene which were apparently not considered fit talk for a prince and certainly inconceivable for a son. Shakespeare, however, did write these things, if we are to trust the quartos and folios, and Gielgud plays them as integral to the role, and with shattering effect on those who cherish an image of Hamlet as all ' sweet Prince ' in the modern and not in the Renaissance sense.

Shakespeare also provided Burbage with the Fortinbras soliloquy as well as the preceding soliloquies and the numberless elaborate set-pieces such as the speech to the players, and the graveyard passages. The Fortinbras soliloquy has usually been omitted, thereby depriving Hamlet of one of the telling facets of his multi-sided character. Another simplification has been to end the closet scene with the mood of reconciliation reached after storm and stress, in the rhymed couplet beginning ' I must be cruel only to be kind.' Actually, the scene at this point veers back again to the opening mood of violence and invective. By the elimination of this anti-climax a far smoother and more heroic Prince emerges from the text, but a Prince of less profoundly human proportions. Gielgud plays the scene through to the end, bringing it to a fresh and poignant climax with the one word ' mother ' thrown after the retreating figure of the woman who carries away his last anchorage, his last security.

Gielgud has chosen to play Hamlet whole because he can accept and understand him whole. The generation he has grown up in is one which knew in its childhood that nobility and brutality were not legends but common facts recorded for four years in daily torrents of blood and printers' ink. Modern psychology must be as much a part of his thinking as the Darwinian theory was of our fathers'. The Freudian aspects of Hamlet's character are not startling for those to whom the revelations of the psycho-analytical technique are an accepted part of thought and experience. He can see and understand as perfectly sound and accurate portraiture Hamlet's split personality, his mother-fixation, his sense of guilt, his battles that will not stay won, his desperate efforts to reconcile the conflicting elements in his psychic make-up, his tendency to unpack his heart in words, his heroism and cowardice, his final integration. Shakespeare saw, understood and by a miracle of grace set down the detailed portrait of the ' modern man ' of his day. Gielgud, speaking his words, fills them to the brim with the life blood of the ' modern man ' of ours.

II

GIELGUD's characterization is clear and convincing throughout, for though he shows a Hamlet, complex, moody—by turns furious and dejected, violent and indifferent—his concept is never blurred. He gives us at once, on our first sight of him, a picture of frustrated energy, of force held in check: force of grief curbed by lack of sympathy, force of filial love curbed by his mother's betrayal, force of ambition curbed by his uncle's usurpation, force of intellect curbed by surrounding stupidity. Hamlet sits frozen in grief, rage and futility. He has not been able to move forward from his father's death. His very natural grief, emphasized in Gielgud's performance, is denied its release in responsible action. He cannot take up the burden of his manhood, comfort himself by comforting his mother, heal the shock of his first severance from dependent childhood by assuming a role of leadership in family and state. His uncle has done more than pop in between the election and his hopes. Claudius has deprived him of the normal activities which would have permitted him to grow out of his state of shocked adolescence into maturity. In addition he has struck at his deepest physiological and psychological tie—his relation to his mother. Hamlet's profound trauma is disclosed in no uncertain terms in the virulent disgust of his first soliloquy.

To grief, frustration and psychic shock is added the burden of the ghostly visitation with its treble load of walking death, murder and revenge. Gielgud's performance gives a sense of an almost intolerable tension. Starting at the level of a sorrow which ' passeth show ' in the opening of the first act, waves of emotion mount in a continuous progression. In the following scenes they gather momentum, rise to a climax, break and subside only to start again with accumulated force toward another intensity, until finally in the closet scene the last crest is reached, the last crash carries all before it.

These successive climaxes, so characteristic of Gielgud's interpretation, are the outward sign of Hamlet's basic difficulty. The driving force of his emotion, his power to imagine, suffer, act, runs head on against the other motivating element of his nature, his contemplative, questioning, rational mind. The onrush of emotion is suddenly stopped, with the inevitable drop to profound despair and a sense of nullity, exhaustion. On the upward sweep Hamlet may be hysterical, on the downward drop morbidly depressed, but these are the alternations of mood resulting from a psychological conflict, not the manifestations of a diseased mind. Gielgud's Hamlet is not mad. His antic disposition is always a deliberate mask. Excitable and highstrung, occasionally dominated by a force within himself that he cannot master and does not know how to canalize, Hamlet erupts now and again into speech and action which startle even himself—but if that should be taken as an indication of insanity, who among us would escape the straitjacket?

Hamlet's problem as Gielgud presents it is not a matter of lack of will, courage or determination—' Sith I have cause and will and strength and means '—but of an unresolved discord within himself. The resolution of such a discord does not come about by taking thought, since thought itself is a causative factor. Rather it comes by a releasing emotional experience, either actual or relived in words. In Hamlet we see this release take place in the closet scene. Here, suddenly, the deadlock is broken by an action so instinctive that there is no time for thought, followed immediately by an outpouring in words of the very dregs of Hamlet's mind. This is the climax, the turning point of the play. From then on Hamlet is changed, though the transformation is not instantly evident. The Hamlet which Gielgud gives us by including the Fortinbras soliloquy is already on the way to becoming captain of his soul. By the time he has returned from the abortive trip to England, he is an integrated personality. Quiet, courteous, occasionally almost gay, with the tender lightness of those who, loving life, have accepted death, the Hamlet of the last scenes has discovered the springs of his own being.

Gielgud shows, however, that though Hamlet's conflict has been resolved and his way to action discovered, his personality is untouched. He flares into a rage at Laertes, throws an enigmatic taunt at the King, indulges in fantastic quibbles with Osric, talks philosophy with Horatio as of old. But through all this he walks forward, his eyes open on a foreseen and calamitous end. In every gesture, every intonation, every quiet word and relaxed pose, this Hamlet is a contrast to the tense, tormented creature of the first scenes. Emotion and will are at last fused. When this happens to any one of us, such inner power as exists is released. In Hamlet that power is great, for it is intellectual and spiritual as well as physical and emotional. He is sure of his strength, because he is healed within: ' I do not fear it, I shall win at the odds.' But—there is also the prescience of disaster. As Gielgud turns to Horatio and speaks the two words ' Let be ' with complete, quiet acceptance, the human race seems for a moment redeemed from its hopelessness. The theatre, which is poet-actor-artist in one, has made manifest before our eyes that noble particle which leavens the lump and makes hope possible.

Hamlet's psychological graph is but one element in the rich

texture of his theatrical being. It must inevitably be the warp upon which any characterization is woven, since action, tone, tempo, mood and every detail of reading, every item of business, costume and make-up are based upon it, but it is only a part of the living whole, a largely unconscious part of the actor's apprehension of the role. It is Gielgud's ability to grasp this basic structure and express it in terms of a convincing theatricality that makes his performance illuminating. He combines the power to convey subtle movements of the spirit, delicate shades of thought, the inner workings of mind and heart, with a knowledge of theatrical technique and an ability to go ' to 't like French falconers ' and tear off ' a passionate speech ' with the best of them as occasion requires. He is not in the least afraid of the words he must handle, neither the poetry that pours in such beauty from his lips nor the invectives with which he attacks the foulness of the world and of those nearest him. He can fence with words as lightly and humourously as he can bludgeon with them.

He has above all an ever-renewed freshness of attack. In his hands Hamlet seems born again every night. He hears for the first time what is said to him, feels freshly his grief and bitter disgust, thinks through the torturing problems that beset him as though they had never been presented to him before. The movements of his thought and of his feeling are registered in expression, gesture, pause and intonation. Though listener and speaker alike may know to a syllable exactly what is coming, Gielgud's mastery of one of the cardinal technical mysteries of the actor's craft—' the illusion of the first time '—is so complete that he holds his audience suspended in breathless attention watching to see how his mental process or his emotional experience will evolve into speech or action.

He brings to the part a continuous flow of life. Thoughtful, philosophic and unhappy as this Prince may be, he is also keenly, almost painfully, alive. Though absorbed by his inner conflict he reacts to every impact from the unsympathetic world around him. This aliveness is expressed in every fibre of Gielgud's performance and is part of its dominant quality of young sensitiveness. For his

Hamlet is the revolt of youth at the destruction of its faith in truth and decency and love. His Hamlet is also youth itself, with its intolerance, ruthlessness, arrogance and self-absorption. Gielgud is willing to play him both nobly and angrily, extenuating nothing of his harshnesses but painting so clearly the picture of his outraged purity, his sorrow and his spiritual isolation, that Hamlet becomes in his hands the prototype of all lost and lonely souls, as well as a prince most royal, the 'unmatch'd form and feature of blown youth.'

III

THE outstanding elements of Gielgud's playing are its power, its subtlety, its variety, its physical beauty in movement, mask and voice. Slight and young as he seems, his Hamlet has a formidable force. 'Beautiful, bad, and dangerous to know' Caroline Lamb said of Byron. And the Hamlet who rouses himself from his first mood of brooding melancholy gives just this impression of latent menace. Gielgud moves on the stage with swift strength. He is a master of his body, using it with a consummate technical precision. *Hamlet* is so often discussed as a psychological and philological problem that the fact that it is a play and as such a matter of movement in space is sometimes forgotten. Gielgud does not forget it.

His Hamlet is three-dimensional as well as mobile, effectively related to the planes and solids about him. In the more active scenes it is a pattern of fluid movement, in moments of stillness a visible expression of mood. From his elaborate pose during the opening scene when he sits exuding disgust for the King, through the intricacies of the play scene when every event is commented by the soaring action of his black figure, to the moment of relaxation when, standing beside Horatio but, as ever, quite alone, he sees the coming end, Gielgud runs the gamut of action and reaction, of movement balanced against pause. This feeling for spatial relationship is like the painter's or the sculptor's instinct for composition. In an actor it is most effective when it is joined as in Gielgud with an accurate sense of timing. Throughout the play this expert handling of tempo and movement is evident, giving the observer, often unconsciously, the sense of satisfaction derived from watching a dance movement or an acrobatic performance.

The pattern of his action is carried through to every detail of his use of costume and properties. Whether he inherited the trick from his actor-forebears or learned to swing cloak and sword in his drama school days, his ability to handle all the adjuncts of his trade add immeasurably to such dramatic moments as that in which he flings off his friends and with them his enveloping cloak to follow the Ghost on the parapet, or when he reveals himself— ' this is I, Hamlet the Dane '—from a swirl of folds in the grave-yard scene. In the details of living at Elsinore he is entirely at home. He wears his clothes, either formal or antic with equal ease, handles a book or a snuff box, a handkerchief or a rapier, with authority, using them to underline the thought or action of which they form an integral part and not merely to give himself something to do. He is chary in his use of properties, even omitting such time-honoured accessories as the tablets on which Claudius' villainy is usually inscribed and the miniatures in the scene with Gertrude.

If his body as a whole is trained, his face and his hands are equally under the control of a guiding dramatic intention. The theatric effectiveness of the tragic mask which has served the Terry family so well is raised to extraordinary power and delicacy in Gielgud. Finely modelled throughout, the bony structure of his face has a ruggedness and prominence which gives it on the stage a hawk-like force and aggressiveness. His profile cuts through space. In such a scene as the one in which Horatio and the two soldiers tell of the visitations of the Ghost, or in the various scenes with Rosencrantz and Guildenstern there is a sweep as of a scimitar when he turns sharply from one to the other. Again and again as the light catches his face, its architecture shows that this Hamlet is a man of action, its expression that he is a man of thought and acute sensitivity.

A dramatic mask is a vehicle to convey the working of mind and emotion. It is theatrically worthless unless it is transparent. In this quality Gielgud is well endowed. Every thought or intention he wishes to express on the stage is written in his face before the words are spoken. It is possible to watch the successive ideas which pass through Hamlet's mind as he receives, holds uncomprehendingly for a moment and then finally grasps the astounding news of his father's ghostly return. He says only two words during this heartshaking interval, yet between his polite, abstracted and slightly bored ' Saw ' to the incredulous, explosive ' Who? ' with which he challenges Horatio's statement he has travelled the whole road from personal grief and self-absorption to the threshold of death and disaster.

Gielgud's ability to listen, always a sign of mastery on the stage, is continuously fascinating. It reaches a climax in the scene with the Ghost, where, with almost no lines to speak he seems to carry on a dialogue of truly unearthly horror. His occasional strangled exclamation, his gestures of protest and revolt, reinforce the succession of shattering emotions his face records. His whole body is intent. Here too, his hands, strong, expressive, flexible, help to build the crises. He uses both hands with equal and unconscious ease. Though sparing of anything approaching gesticulation, he will point a line, underscore a phrase, emphasize an idea, by a perfectly timed turn of finger, thumb and wrist, gestures which range all the way from the delicate irony of the ' moult no feather ' remark addressed to Rosencrantz and Guildenstern to the sombre brushing of dust and corruption from his fingers after he has returned Yorick's skull to the gravedigger.

The supreme weapon in the actor's arsenal is his voice. Bernhardt, physically reduced to a thing of pity, could still enthrall with the magnificent cascade of her speech and Duse's voice will ring forever in the ears that have heard it. Gielgud brings again to the stage something of this lost beauty. The range and quality of his voice is not more remarkable than his control of its possibilities. Even more than his face it registers the constant movement of his mind so that a single phrase, even a single word or exclamation, can convey a whole range of experience. The demands of Hamlet on the voice are formidable. Not only does he talk continuously for hours, but again and again throughout the play the actor is called on for what is actually a spoken aria, a building of tonal harmonies to greater and greater heights. In such elaborate passages as ' what a piece of work is a man! ' the vocal music has the quality of mounting chords, each phrase rising above its predecessor in majestic progression, yet the effect is never oratorical. Rather, Hamlet seems himself caught up in the excitement of a mental adventure in which his own words engender a sort of poetic intoxication.

The tonal quality of each of the four chief soliloquies is markedly different, since each is based on a different mental and emotional climate—anguished in the first, frenzied in the second, searching in the third, determined in the fourth. All of these speeches, however, require an equal technical force and control, as, in fact, does the entire gigantic role. Ultimately such force depends, as in singing, on the proper placing of the voice and on breath. The smooth transition from one register to another, the dramatic use of head tones, the absolute control of the breathing apparatus which permits a rising emphasis with increase of volume at the end of a long phrase, are indications of Gielgud's proficiency in the use of this essential element of technical equipment.

Though highly individual in timbre and quality, his voice is free of mannerisms, devoid of that rotund quality which the reading of Shakespeare so often engenders. Fatigue will occasionally make it husky or an irresistible impulse toward experimentation lead to the use of vocal pyrotechnics, but this is quickly disciplined. His voice is unusually clear of such impedimenta. It is an instrument delicately attuned to his intention and responsive to his will.

The various registers are used throughout the play in connection with various types of thought and action, though probably not schematically planned. The meditative, sorrowful or philosophic mood generally uses a lower register supported by a stronger breath than, for instance, the scenes of feigned madness or the light give and take with the ' good lads ' from Wittenberg. In the use of resonant head tones lies the effectiveness of his occasional outbursts of sound and fury. This strong, hard note is struck in moments of high excitement, as in the Hecuba speech, the close of the nunnery scene, the climax of the rant at the grave of Ophelia. It is one of the many stops Gielgud can sound at will. These tonal and quantitive variations are so closely woven into the pattern of his playing that the need for some sort of musical notation becomes evident to anyone attempting to make a record of his performance.

This is particularly true when discussing the fundamental problem in Shakespeare, the reading of verse. How, for instance, is it possible to convey in words the effect of Gielgud's delivery of ' To be, or not to be ' beyond the bare statement that the quality of voice, the sound of the words, the poetic and emotional content of the passage were one in sensuous and spiritual beauty? The prompt-book from which the detailed description of Gielgud's performance has been made is marked throughout with indications of where he paused, the approximate length of those pauses, where he changed from one register to another, where the inflection rose, where it fell, the weight of certain words, the relative tempi of certain passages, the stress on a vowel or consonant, where the rhythm was retarded, where it was speeded. Yet all this means nothing except to those in whose ear the living voice has rung. Phonograph records of speeches are even more unsatisfactory. The essential movement is lacking. They may recreate a memory; they cannot create a fact.

Gielgud's reading of verse is based on the dramatic and intellectual content of the line and tuned to the poet's deepest rhythm, the rhythm of the play itself. *Hamlet* as a play has already advanced both from Shakespeare's own early essays in dramatic writing and from the more ornate and elaborate style of his contemporaries. Rich and intricate as the pattern is, it is not so frequently embroidered with passages of poetic rhetoric as is *King Richard II*, for instance. The formal rhythms of the lines themselves are often shaken by the force of the emotion they contain, or again, a change of idea or direction breaks a line in two to start in mid-stream on a new tempo as in the speech to Horatio before the Gonzago play begins.

Most important of all, Hamlet himself, as Shakespeare has created him, is a man of words, a poet, often to his own despair. In Gielgud's reading, the creative poetic process of thought is felt throughout. The rhythm of the verse, and of the prose as well, is present as a strong sustaining pulse. The pauses accentuate the process of thought but do not break this underlying beat. Granville-Barker in his preface to *Hamlet* makes the statement that the verse in this play will always respond better to a dramatic than to a prosodic analysis. Gielgud approaches the problem from this angle and it is his dramatic analysis that gives his reading its sustained power and authority.

The various elements of Gielgud's craftsmanship are the means by which he obtains his objective, the projection of his characterization across the footlights. Yet no analysis of technical methods can explain the result. The ability to convey to the audience, often without words, the total being of the character which the actor is at the moment impersonating is the basic ingredient of all great acting. It has to do not only with technical skill but also with inner conviction. Gielgud's power of projection is strong; his concentration, the freshness and conviction of his attack, are matched by his gift of conveying his emotion directly to each member of his audience. He can, as one New York critic expressed it, ' fling his feeling across the footlights stirring the emotions of the audience, establishing and maintaining a tension—in them—that leaves him free to go on building to superb and superbly simple climaxes.' It is no wonder that an audience so moved comes again and again to see a performance which in beauty and distinction is not unworthy of the theatre's greatest masterpiece.

THE HAMLET TRADITION
SOME NOTES ON COSTUME, SCENERY AND STAGE BUSINESS
BY JOHN GIELGUD

THE HAMLET TRADITION

SOME NOTES ON COSTUME, SCENERY
AND STAGE BUSINESS

By John Gielgud

Ellen Terry describes Henry Irving's appearance as Hamlet minutely in her memoirs, and speaks of it as if it were revolutionary and original at the time he produced *Hamlet* at the Lyceum in 1874. The pale face, disordered black hair, simple tunic edged with fur: ' No bugles, no order of the Danish Elephant—he did not wear the miniature of his father obtrusively round his neck.' Perhaps she was thinking of Fechter, who played Hamlet with Ellen's sister Kate (my grandmother) as Ophelia. He was a fair Dane, and a print I have of him in the part certainly looks elaborate, though vaguely Nordic and barbarian.

If Irving's Hamlet broke one tradition, it certainly started another, which has varied but little in continental or American representations of the part from that day to this. Of an earlier date is the famous portrait by Lawrence of John Philip Kemble with his hat of plumed feathers and long cloak. There are curious prints of Macready, Forrest and others in which the miniature is usually predominant, if not the bugles. Following Sir Henry, his son, H. B. Irving, naturally copied his father's make-up and costume, and looked extremely like him. Forbes-Robertson, who had played continually with Irving, also wore much the same attire. Booth wore cross-garterings instead of plain black tights. Salvini, Moissi, Katchalov, Kainz, from the continent—and, of course, Sarah Bernhardt; Booth, Sothern, Hampden in America; and in more recent times Tree, Wilson Barrett, Ainley, Barrymore, Martin-Harvey, Milton, Swinley and Tearle—all these famous Hamlets conformed more or less to the traditional appearance of the prince. Tree wore a fair wig and beard, in which unkind people said he looked like a German Professor, and Wilson Barrett was extremely décolleté. Basil Sydney in America, Colin Keith-Johnston in

London and Moissi in Vienna played the part in modern dress.

The first production to make a stir in England in sixteenth century costume was that of the late J. B. Fagan at Oxford in 1924. This was an amateur performance by the Oxford University Dramatic Society in which Gyles Isham made a great success as Hamlet. The costumes were of the Dürer period, and the men wore puffed sleeves, short surcoats and slashed tights. The Ophelia was not assisted by a hat with a very long and ridiculous feather (in the play scene); otherwise the costuming was strikingly effective.

The late William Poel presented *Hamlet*, among many other Shakespeare plays; for the first time in Elizabethan dress. His experiments began as early as 1881. An even earlier attempt had been made by Benjamin Webster in 1844. Since Poel's productions the method had been followed at the Old Vic and elsewhere on various occasions. The first time I played Hamlet (1929) at the Vic, Harcourt Williams used this period for his production. The most practical drawback to it is that the women are not sympathetic dressed in farthingales, which seem to be stiff and ugly in an emotional or pathetic scene, nor are the men helped in tragic or exciting scenes by the short cloaks and bolstered trunks of the period. Besides, the actors find these clothes very hot and tight to act in.

The archaeological period—Saxo Grammaticus—which is the traditional theatrical and historically accurate period for the play, has the opposite disadvantage. The women look like virgin heroines from grand opera, with plaits, girdles and straight dresses with key-pattern borders, and the men are hampered and made absurd by war-like studded breastplates, thongs and winged helmets, contradicted by skinny arms and smooth faces, or ' dreadfully attended ' by voluminous wigs and beards. Gertrude and Claudius are liable to resemble the King and Queen in a pack of cards, and Polonius, in a pale blue gown, very long beard, and white staff of office, is boring before he has even opened his mouth. The key-pattern is sadly echoed in the scenery, climbing around doors, pillars and arches, and the furniture, in trying to be primitive, usually looks uncomfortable and lonely, in spite of the skins draped hopefully about. The period can be strikingly handled as in the recent *Hamlet* of Leslie Howard, which I am told was beautifully set and costumed by Stewart Chaney, but I have a very real and vivid reminiscence of H. B. Irving's archaeological production—the first I ever saw. I suppose I was about twelve at the time, and it made an unforgettable impression upon me. In this performance, Ophelia, played by Lady Forbes-Robertson, was introduced, dripping, on a bier at the end of the Queen's willow speech, to make an effective curtain—a very favourite Edwardian device to gain applause.

To return to Hamlet and his clothes. There is no doubt that the traditional costume of the Prince is becoming, loose, and comfortable—three essentials for such a long and exacting role. Long hair is apt to be more difficult to wear on the stage nowadays than short, but otherwise the dress is admirable to look at and easy to act in. Personally, however, I have always had a feeling that it is almost too much steeped in tradition, and therefore I have never worn it in the part. I like the more definite lines of the sixteenth century dress, which I have always worn (with slight modifications—as my own production was set in 1520, and the one in New York in 1620!). I feel the Renaissance costume suggests the scholar, the poet, the prince, the courtier, and the gentleman; that it is more youthful and at the same time more sophisticated than the Gothic Peter Pan of the traditional theatre. Probably if I had ever played in the cooler and more comfortable Saxon dress I should change my opinion.

Modern commentators seem to think that much should be made of Hamlet's appearance and costume after he feigns madness. Mr. Granville-Barker even thinks he should wear colours in this middle section of the play. This innovation has never, I believe, been tried, partly, perhaps, because we actors know that black is becoming and dignified, and partly because the sympathy of the audience towards Hamlet on account of his love for his father's memory would be jarred by such an emphatic deviation from mourning. There is also the practical question of effort. Hamlet is

on the stage nearly all the evening, and a change of costume is an
added labour for the actor. I have tried changing into a violet and
grey travelling dress for the last act, thinking it would be a great
innovation, and no one even noticed it (this was at the Old Vic).
As to the 'mad' scenes, it is dangerous to overdo a fantastically
disordered appearance—and almost impossible, in any costume, to
follow Ophelia's detailed account of ' stockings foul'd, ungarter'd
and down-gyved to his ankle,' without continually distracting the
audience. An old print shows one actor who attempted this,
Henry E. Johnstone (1777–1845). One stocking is half way down
a muscular leg, the other definitely ' ungarter'd, ' but the expression
on his face is quite calm.

Ophelia's costume in the mad scene presents another vexed
question of tradition. Walter Lacy, Henry Irving's adviser on his
Shakespearian productions, undoubtedly voiced Irving's own
opinion when he said to Ellen Terry who planned a black dress
for the mad scene: ' My God, Madam, there must be only one
black figure in this play and that's Hamlet! ' So in Irving's production and many others before and since, we have the white robe,
tousled hair, and generally conventional appearance of Ophelia,
with or without her flowers, which would pass equally well for
Margaret in the last act of *Faust*. She has variously been played
since in black, red and yellow. Mr. Granville-Barker thinks she
should have a lute in the first half of the scene, and in the second
part herbs picked from the garden which she delivers to the other
characters as at a funeral. It was apparently the Elizabethan custom
to distribute them so and it would certainly be appropriate and
effective. Played by an actress in an Elizabethan dress (but not
necessarily in a farthingale) carelessly worn and soiled with mud
and dirt, her hair dressed wildly but not altogether loose, Ophelia
might become a stranger and more poignant figure than she usually
presents in theatrical usage.

Two other points in costuming: now that audiences are intelligent enough not to feel that ' there must be only one black figure
in the play ' there is no reason why both Ophelia and Laertes too

should not wear black for their father. Not only does this mark the similarity and contrast of the two revenge stories, but it is particularly effective, in my opinion, in the final scene of the duel, when the two young men stand pitted against one another, fighting to the death for a similar cause. There is one other innovation I have never seen attempted on the stage, which is suggested strongly by the text. In the closet scene, the Ghost should appear ' in his habit as he liv'd,' i.e., in a cap and nightgown—or some kind of crown and robe—in contrast to his war-like appearance on the battlements. I believe the effect would be a fine one in so domestic a scene, and that Shakespeare intended it. It seems to be an impossibility to design ' silent ' armour for the Ghost, and consequently he is always dressed extremely vaguely and underlighted almost out of all recognition, and therefore cannot make the impression intended in any of the scenes in which he appears. I consider this was a bad failing in my own production, as well as in every other I have seen or appeared in, and I commend it as one of the important details worth study and solution in any future performance of the play.

As regards scenery: it is important, of course, in this play, that the sense of pictorial richness and sensuous decadence of a Renaissance court should be somehow combined and contrasted with the feeling of a ' war-like state,' where ghosts and horror haunt the battlements by night; where armies are marshalling for war, graves give up their dead and a barbaric Northern feeling of cold and grimness cuts across the luxurious court life of the murderous poisoner and his shallow Queen. A pretty big problem, this, for any scene designer and director. The unlocalized setting, originally conceived and devised by Gordon Craig, and carried out by him with varying success in Stanislavsky's Moscow production in 1911, has of course influenced later productions tremendously. There was a violent reaction against the old-fashioned realistic settings. In Martin-Harvey's production, and in Arthur Hopkins' *Hamlet* designed by Robert Edmond Jones for John Barrymore, and later in my own, the influence of Craig was apparent. The chief danger

in these unlocalized settings is the temptation to use steps and platforms to excess. The groupings and static pictures are greatly
assisted by this means, but audiences quickly tire of looking at
actors continually leaping up and down stairs that lead nowhere.
The solidity of such settings enforces a minimum of variations. If
the interiors are impressively majestic, the scenes of the battlements
and the graveyard are seldom equally convincing. Finally, the
necessity of using drop curtains, near the front of the stage (in a
totally different stage convention) for short scenes during which
furniture is being moved on the main stage, is most unsatisfactory.

ACT I—Scene i
The Sentinel's Platform before the Royal Palace
[1] *(Act I, Scene I)*

THIS, one of the finest and most famous of all Shakespeare open-
ings, is usually unimpressive on the stage. There are many technical reasons for this. Audiences will not be punctual, and, knowing
the play well enough to remember that the principal characters
do not appear until the second scene, fidget inattentively and do
not encourage the atmosphere the actors need. In order to help
the appearance of the Ghost, the stage is usually very darkly lit,
and the scenery is either a drop-cloth, to allow of an easy and quick
change of scene, or else a permanent set, which the producer
bathes in deepest shadow, so that it may look different when used
as an interior a few moments later. In addition to these drawbacks,
the actors are all ' small part ' men, with the exception of Horatio,
and seldom capable of expressing by their voices and emotional
power the great range and quality of the poet's invention.

The scene has been played high on a rostrum, down on an apron
close to the audience, with wind, bells, clocks, twinkling stars and
music to heighten the effect. (The cock crowing, by the way,

1. These notes are arranged according to the scene sequence of the London and
New York productions printed in this volume. The act and scene notations
given in parentheses are those of the standard editions.

which I tried in my own production, had never to my knowledge been used before, and was remarkably atmospheric.) But the tremendously dramatic and staccato opening, the dramatic rhythm of the scene as it varies so markedly between the two entrances of the Ghost and moves towards its beautiful and poetic close, these beauties have not been apparent in performances I have seen.

With one exception: the production, in German, in which Alexander Moissi played in London in 1929, which was, I believe, an old one, originally Reinhardt's. The company was not outstanding, and there were many strange and ineffective innovations, but this opening scene was played better than I have ever seen it before or since. On a flat stage the soldiers waited, warming their hands over a brazier of coals. They were not raw young actors, but old and bearded veterans, whose terror at the sight of the martial figure of their old master, coming from such simple men of obvious physical hardihood, was moving and convincing in the extreme. Their trust in the wisdom of the young student Horatio seemed real and probable—he was cleverer than they and would interpret their fears. The disturbed feeling of imminent wars and horrors lurking about the castle communicated itself immediately to the audience, and, when Horatio spoke the famous lines about the dawn, his own relief and its effect upon the other actors made one feel as if a great curtain of darkness which had hung over them during a long sleepless night had rolled away at last to let in the fresh air of a cold morning and another day.

One wonders how this scene can have been played effectively when it was originally written. A noisy, fidgeting, mostly standing audience, no darkness, afternoon sunshine streaming on to a tidy little platform. But then we must remember that to know the play beforehand is a great loss for us today. It cramps our imaginations and our enjoyment of the thrilling drama of the scene, while demanding at the same time far greater conviction in the playing of it. No doubt first class actors and simple production (with enough light to see every expression clearly) is all that is really needed to make it as effective as it should be, and so seldom is.

Notes: ' Who's there? ' I wonder whether Francisco is not meant to mistake Bernardo for the Ghost.

The cutting of the long speech of Horatio which is customary in the modern theatre has the disadvantage of making the second entrance of the Ghost far too quick upon the first, which does not therefore take the audience by surprise as the author seems to have intended.

' I'll cross, it though it blast me.' Horatio sometimes moves across the path of the Ghost on this line; alternatively he holds up the cross-hilt of his sword and makes a cross in the air with it towards the Ghost.

Scene 2

The Council Chamber in the Castle
The First Soliloquy; the scene with Horatio and the Soldiers
(Act I, Scene II)

COMMENTATORS seem to agree that this represents the first privy council meeting held after the accession of Claudius as elective king. The more traditional stage usage has always been to place it in a throne room or a hall in the castle with the monarchs on their thrones, a crowd of soldiers, ladies and attendants, and Hamlet seated on a stool apart or standing sadly below the chairs of state. Henry Irving, in stricter obedience to the text, had a long procession, at the end of which came Hamlet. Ellen Terry says, ' The lights were lowered at his entrance, another stage trick,' but this must have been cunningly contrived, and seems rather a curious artifice to resort to so early in a play which is often hampered in performance by too many dark scenes. On the other hand, I once saw a Hamlet who made a ' star ' entrance, centre, just before his uncle's first line to him; this made his first aside a little unconvincing, to say the least of it, and, as he was also accompanied by a burst of limelight, he evidently thought differently from Irving.

In the Barrymore-Arthur Hopkins production the curtain rose in darkness, and sibilant whispering and laughter opened the scene, until the court was discovered lolling in amorous groups on a stage built up in masses of steps and at the top of them a great curtained arch. This first effect was most imposing, but the setting remained unchanged throughout the play, and the steps and arch became monotonous when used in many scenes. Harcourt Williams, in his Old Vic production (1929) had the Queen and her ladies sewing and the King entering in cloak and gloves, as if from hunting. This was original, as well as being alive and vigorous.

The design of Gordon Craig for his Moscow production with Stanislavsky in 1911 has been often reproduced, and I have always been greatly impressed by it. Hamlet is sitting wearily in the foreground by a dark pillar. He is separated from the court by a barrier of mysterious shadow which cuts across the front of the stage, embracing the slight figure of the Prince. Beyond rises a brilliant pyramidal group of heads growing to a peak formed by the figures of the King and Queen, wearing huge cloaks, the folds of which seem to envelop the whole court. Actually at Moscow I believe the actors representing the courtiers put their heads through holes in the cloak (Komisarjevsky employed a slightly similar device recently in the trial scene of his Stratford production of *The Merchant of Venice*). How the exit was managed as the scene progressed and the cue was reached I have never been able to discover. The drawing is extraordinarily dramatic and right in feeling, but it seems to me rather an idea than an actual practical stage arrangement. What attracts me most in it is the placing of Hamlet, the contrast of light and shade, and the focusing of attention on the King and Queen at the rise of the curtain.

I followed this scheme of grouping in my own production in 1934, but at an angle to the audience instead of straight, with courtiers ranged in a semi-circle before the thrones and hiding Hamlet from his mother and uncle. The exit of Laertes caused a slight change in the positions of some of the courtiers and opened a space through which Claudius became suddenly aware of the presence of Hamlet. Then as Hamlet spoke his first lines the courtiers naturally turned to look at him, and the scene continued as the Queen came down from her throne to speak to her son, turning the whole focus of grouping and attention at the right moment in the scene (and not before) to the other side of the stage and to Hamlet himself.

Guthrie McClintic (in New York in 1936) placed the scene in a council chamber, and the King and Queen were seated behind a table. The court left the stage before the King addressed Hamlet, and the scene thus became a domestic argument between the three principal characters. This had a certain effect of concentrated development of the story, but I cannot help feeling that the formality of address used by Hamlet and the flowery tone, half rebuking, half avuncular, of Claudius' speeches have greater point and effect when uttered for the benefit of his admiring and sycophantic courtiers. There is also a legitimate stage effect in a ' grand exit ' at the departure of the King and Queen (and perhaps entrance, too, as the scene begins). They can sweep from the stage to music and trumpets, the courtiers bowing and curtseying before they follow, until the solitary figure of Hamlet is left alone on the big empty stage looking bitterly after them as he begins his first soliloquy. I think, however, that the privy council treatment, done more elaborately, with other councillors, like Polonius, sitting around the table, might be very admirable.

First soliloquy. I find this the most exciting of the soliloquies[1] to speak, partly because it seems to set the character once and for all in the actor's and the audience's minds, and partly for its extraordinary, forthright presentation of information as to the whole plot, matched unerringly in the march of the words and the punctuation of the sentences. Executed correctly, it has no possible

1. In this speech I very much wished to use the word ' sullied ' for ' solid.' It is now agreed upon by most of the commentators as the correct reading, but fearing I should be accused either of altering the line because I am thin, or else of pronouncing ' solid ' with an Oxford accent, I gave up the idea. ' Faint and scant of breath ' in the last scene has also luckily been blessed with academic warrant as well as physical appropriateness in my own case.

pauses except at the natural places marked for taking breath or
when there are full stops. A short break seems to be demanded
before ' Frailty, thy name is woman! ', and another more definite
one before the last two lines which sum up the whole speech.
Otherwise thoughts and exclamations succeed each other in the
most vivid and natural manner, so that it is impossible to falter
either in speaking or thinking. One is driven on at a naturally
steady pace—in spite of a certain intensity of feeling which at
first makes one tend to dwell upon some of the lines at greater
length than others.

The following scene in which the soldiers come with Horatio
to tell Hamlet of the Ghost has always been my favourite in the
whole play, and I knew every word of it by heart long before I
ever dreamt I should have the chance of playing the part. I also
knew by heart the vivid description in Ellen Terry's memoirs of
how Irving played it, and tried to follow him in every detail from
the first. It may seem lazy for an actor to copy ' business ' or
readings from other actors, but I do not believe that one should
ever discard tradition without first examining its purposes and
inspiration. Quite recently, in London, I saw a production of
Julius Caesar in which the murder scene was ' improved ' by a
curtain in which Calpurnia was discovered kneeling in heavy
mourning (which she must have ordered very quickly) at the side
of her husband's corpse! This business had been invented by Tree,
who was famous for such touches of originality. (At the first
rehearsal of his *Othello* he is supposed to have said to Roderigo—
Ernest Thesiger—' We enter at the back in a gondola—and
I thought it would be effective if you were hauling down the
sail! ')

Unfortunately, audiences love striking pieces of business and
showmanship, and remember them long after they have forgotten
the play in which they occurred. In Shakespeare, when they are
pictorial, attractive to the audience and make a personal effect for
the actor too, they are difficult to resist. Irving was a great actor,
and people who saw him will tell you that he was a genius at this

kind of thing, and used it sincerely, originally, to the best advantage, but all the stars who followed him, particularly Tree, tried to outdo him in their lavishness and inventiveness.

Irving's famous invention of Shylock's return over the bridge after the flight of Jessica—Irving, I believe, never actually reached the door before the curtain fell—has been copied and elaborated out of all recognition. Shylocks have knocked once, twice, ten times, rushed in, rushed out again, cried out, called through the house, rushed off down the street in pursuit. Tree topped them all by finding a handy pile of ashes on the doorstep and pouring them on his head. Nowadays, if the Jew does not return at all, people ask why the great moment has been cut. It became the ' star ' episode of the part because it was conceived by a fine star actor— and Shakespeare never meant it to occur at all!

Invented business such as this is obviously an interpolation. Audiences love it, but it is a bad concession to the picture stage and falling curtain, which Shakespeare never imagined, and underlines and elaborates a situation which the dramatist purposely touched on very lightly—and to us it smacks of the ' problem picture ' so popular in the Royal Academy Exhibitions of twenty years ago. Therefore there is little or no excuse for borrowing it or for inventing similar business at the same point in the text, though I am sure if I had seen it when Irving himself did it for the first time, I should have admired it as part of his invention, and, magnificently carried out, it must certainly have contributed to the brilliance of his performance as Shylock.

But when I read how, as Hamlet, Irving greeted Horatio, warmly but still abstractedly, still in his dream when he said ' My father, methinks I see my father—' how he half heard Horatio's line ' My lord, I think I saw him yesternight—,' the dawning of intelligence on ' Saw. Who? ' breaking into flashing realization as his face blazed with intelligence from ' For God's love, let me hear! '—on to the quick doubts and suspicions in his questions and his touching appreciation of loyalty in saying farewell to his friends —then I find a guide to the playing of the scene which seems to me still so perfect that I have never veered a step from it ever since I first rehearsed the part.

Ellen Terry says that at the last couplet of the scene,

> '. . . foul deeds will rise,
> Though all the earth o'erwhelm them, to men's eyes.'

Irving's acting appalled by its implication of rising rage and horror, and this description, too, helped me to realize how those few short words bind the end of the scene together. The understatement of the court scene, the dull bitterness of the soliloquy, the rising excitement of the scene with the men, all of this is caught together in these words and leads the actors and audience unerringly towards the subsequent revelation of the Ghost and the setting in motion of the whole machinery of the play's action.

I am always glad that we have few actual records, in films or gramophones, of the great ones of the past, though this feeling may seem to run contrary to what I have just been saying of the inspiration given me by the description of Irving's performance. I cannot help thinking that the greatness of all fine acting lies to some extent in its momentary creation before an audience, that the inspiration (and the ' copy ' of the inspiration which in many consecutive performances actors give by means of what we call technique) is partly contributed and guided by the audience present at any particular performance. The effect of an acting moment may be one of unforgettable vividness, but it passes immediately and merges into another, which the actor has carefully prepared and arranged so that his performance may proceed harmoniously and in a certain line with his development of the character and the progress of the play's action. Afterwards the spectator may remember and record certain vivid impressions, but probably if he goes again to see the same performance—indeed, even if he sees rehearsals and watches a performance every night—he will never again receive exactly the same impression. The temperament of the actor must vary, to a greater or less extent, according to his own mood and the mood of the other actors and of the audience.

But, just as a great teacher trains his pupils to adopt a correct method of study, and leads them towards the most sincere approach to an appreciation of style, so, it seems to me, an aspiring actor should be able to study these essentials from watching his masters in the craft. It is not from a great actor's mannerisms, or some brilliant but fundamentally personal expression of voice, gait, or carriage that he will learn, but from the master's approach to character, and from every moment in his performance in which he reveals or clarifies the text. These moments, I am sure, are only evident to one who has actually seen a stage performance. A great actor, even if he is not playing his best, is more interesting to me ' in the flesh ' than his shadow, however well made up and lighted; and his voice, however husky, or even bored, has more life in it than a reproduction, no matter how cunningly reproduced by machinery. The mechanics of cinema and gramophone advance too quickly. The films and records of Bernhardt and Ellen Terry are ridiculous and inadequate curiosities today—and who knows that future generations will not laugh at the records of Caruso and Chaliapin and the plangent masks of Garbo, Dietrich and Gable. Some idea of an actor's performance may be conveyed to a third person by a brilliant and expert description or critique, written or told by an eye-witness, but I do not believe that any mechanical reproduction can recreate an acting performance that one has never seen (though it may be an interesting reminder or a valuable curiosity) whereas a description may suggest it most vividly and encourage those who come after to use it creatively without any spirit of imitation.

Hamlet is, of course, the greatest play of tradition in our language. Nearly all the great players (and many not great at all) have attempted to make history in it by touches of originality— from Garrick overturning the chair in the closet scene to Edmund Kean kissing Ophelia's hair, from the deathshield of Forbes-Robertson to the plus-fours of Sir Barry Jackson's production in modern dress. I see no possible harm in reading about all these traditional or sensational innovations, and borrowing or discarding them as they seem to fit the character, the play, and the meaning of the text, as long as one does this sincerely and without losing sight of one's own original study and characterization. It is curious to find, however, that the fuller the text used the less is it necessary to waste time resorting to business to illustrate the meaning or clarify the effect upon the stage. On the other hand business has often to be invented by actors to cover the gap in thought made by a bad cut; often it takes no longer to speak the cut line than to carry out the business or to make the pause that replaces it.

Tree, in trying to rival Irving's method without such good taste, and rearranging the text to allow of sumptuous tableaux and pageantry, found it necessary to cut extensively. The Victorian editors had already done their worst by publishing versions of the play ridiculously bowdlerized, and with long and inaccurate descriptions of scenery of which Shakespeare never dreamt. Tree was an eccentric character actor, and relied on brilliant make-ups and stage effects far more than on any real interpretation of Shakespeare. He and others started a fashion for hearty laughter, back-slapping, worked up entrances and effective curtains, which substituted pictorial show for real dramatic speed and the marvel-lously dramatic contrast of scene against scene, which lasted until the Granville-Barker productions just before the war.

Remnants of this style of Shakespearian acting have survived with some actors right up to the present day. The picture stage with its curtain, the successful use of elaborate scenery, lighting, and incidental music went to the heads of the Victorian and Edwardian theatre managers, and their audiences revelled in them too. They responded gladly to the ' inexplicable dumbshows and noise ' which Shakespeare knew they loved so well. Today we have much to be grateful for. The circus and cinema can always be relied upon to out-herod Herod and we are forced back, in the theatre, to the realization that nobody looks at the scenery, how-ever fine, after the first minute or two, but that acting—voice, characterization, movement—interpreting a fine play correctly will still hold an audience enthralled for hours on end. More time and hard work at rehearsals are of greater use than masses of money spent on scenery and costumes, and a producer who can handle actors is more valuable than a pageant master. Granville-Barker, Robert Atkins, Sir Philip Ben Greet, William Poel, and others like them have done immeasurable service in rescuing the text from the ravages of the star actor-managers, and proving in performance how amazingly Shakespeare catered for his stage with its limited means of presentation and for nearly every actor in his plays, even in the small parts, if they are given their proper importance by the director and acted correctly by the performers.

Scene 3

Polonius' House. Ophelia, Laertes and Polonius
(Act I, Scene III)

OPHELIA, as Ellen Terry has observed, only ' pervades ' her early scenes, and they are therefore notoriously difficult both for actress and producer. Compare her first appearance with that of Desdemona, who is talked of long before she appears, so that the audience is impatient to see her, and whose strikingly gracious entrance onto a stage full of men is such a beautiful moment in the Senate scene. Cordelia, too, is a lonely and unforgettable figure—almost like Hamlet—in the great scene at the opening of Lear, and when she speaks for the first time the whole interest concentrates upon her immediately.

But not so with Ophelia. Too much else has to be set forth in the first scenes of *Hamlet*. Though we meet her father and brother in the court scene, and they are marked for us in two or three telling little speeches, there is no slightest mention of Ophelia until we see her in a first scene which gives her little opportunity to be anything but a charming sister and an obedient daughter. But her first two appearances follow scenes of great dramatic power and emotion, and hers are apt to suffer by contrast. The audience is inclined to relax rather than stiffen in attention, especially as she usually finds herself in the modern theatre before curtains or a drop. It always seems to me that the audience reacts to such scenes very much as children do. They attend with difficulty to what is going on in a front scene, knowing that something splendid is being prepared behind the curtain, and subconsciously longing to see what it will be. In spite of this handicap Ophelia's first scene is a justly famous and beautiful one, and makes a brilliant pendant, in its triangle of father, son and daughter, to that of the uncle, son and mother in the preceding scene.

Polonius is a grateful and rewarding part for a good actor, and has been conspicuously successful with audiences, particularly since the brilliant performance of A. Bromley Davenport in the modern dress *Hamlet* of Sir Barry Jackson in 1925. Before this the part was usually cut extensively, and the admittedly difficult combination of wisdom and sententiousness was not appreciated or properly characterized. People are still confused by the speech of advice to Laertes with its worldly wisdom and the moral precepts put into the mouth of the ' tedious old fool ' and ' foolish, prating knave ' of the later scenes. Davenport was the first to combine the elegance and admirably diplomatic manner of the court official with the selfish but strict attitude of a loving parent. This was his outward appearance. He used it to conceal his true character which revealed itself as that of an inquisitive, pompous, spying old fox, who had surely bought his position with the new king by tactfully forgetting his allegiance to the old.

There has always been much speculation, particularly among actors, as to whether Hamlet and Ophelia were lovers before the opening of the play. Mr. Granville-Barker has remarked on how useless it is to imagine that Shakespeare characters have lives apart from those they lead in the play. Though it is certainly true that we gain little by day-dreaming about the mothers of Desdemona or Cordelia, the question of Hamlet's relationship to Ophelia is very important to the actress who attempts to portray her—especially as Hamlet is too busy to mention the poor girl (even to Horatio) except in the scenes when he is actually confronting her. He makes sly digs about her to Polonius, and rants at her graveside, but in the soliloquies and sane moments, to his mother even, not a word.

The lines about conception and the fishmonger and the bawdy songs in the mad scene are the main reasons for supposing that Hamlet has been Ophelia's lover, but Dr. Dover Wilson has explained the first, to my satisfaction at any rate, in his remarks on the entrance of Hamlet in his first ' mad ' scene of which I shall speak later. Mr. Granville-Barker, however, does not take this view of the fishmonger scene, though he does not hold any brief for the lover theory. All we know for certain is that Ophelia says ' he hath importun'd me with love in honourable fashion' and further that he had ' given countenance to his speech . . . with almost all the holy vows of heaven.'

In the nunnery scene, Hamlet exclaims: ' I did love you once ' and ' I loved you not,' ' you should not have believed me.' Then he proceeds to rail at her as though she were a harlot, but it does not seem justifiable to make her one. If Ophelia is lying to her father in her first scene the effect of her lying to Hamlet in the nunnery scene would be lost, and her innocence and purity as the thwarted ideal of his love spoilt entirely in its place in the play. As to the bawdy songs, psychoanalysis would nowadays seem to be so generally understood that any modern audience accepts them as the result of repression or wish fulfillment rather than reminiscence. We are told that the purest women often use bad language under anaesthetic. The Victorians and Edwardians, who might have taken another view of the meaning of Ophelia's songs because of their stricter upbringing, naturally never heard the lines, as they were always cut on the stage and often not even published in the books. Above all, for the purposes of acting and production, an Ophelia guilty of a concealed love affair is even more difficult for the actress to suggest than an Ophelia innocent of anything but the best intentions. The actress has a difficult task in any case, and nothing she has to do or say in this short scene, or indeed in any other, is clarified or explained by an interpretation based on her guilt.

SCENE 4

The Sentinel's Platform. The Ghost Scene
(Act I, Scenes IV and V)

THE two scenes on the platform should, I believe, be played together as they were in our New York production. The dropping
of the curtain between them is most harmful to the continuity,
and though the applause may be tempting, the difficulty of starting
the following scene after the break soon dispels the charm of that.
In the old days much play was made by the scene painters with a
more remote part of the platform for the second part of the scene—
cairns, gnarled trees, and Horatio's ' dreadful summit of the cliff
that beetles o'er his base into the sea,' were painted and built in
detail. Leslie Howard played the scene in a crypt and Moissi by a
large cross in a churchyard which the Ghost leant on, looking
like a very large turnip on top of a nightshirt (but rather terrifying
all the same) growling out revengefully, while Hamlet sat on a step
below, and jumped like a jack-in-the-box at the word ' murder! '

The difficulties in the acting and production of these scenes are
manifold. The Ghost must be unearthly yet revengeful, sad and
yet inspiring, not too sorry for himself, nor yet too human in his
resentment. I was not myself impressed by the much praised Ghost
of Courtenay Thorpe, with Barrymore, nor have I ever seen the
part played altogether to my satisfaction. In spite of the elaborate
care with which he is described in the text, he is never dressed in
full armour, and his vanishing is usually poorly contrived in a blackout. (But perhaps a too successful effect by Mr. Maskelyne might
be too distracting and sensational. One never knows.) I imagine
that his disappearance down a trap—which would, I suppose, be
laughed at by a modern audience—gave point, long lost today, to
the lines about the ' cellerage ' and ' old mole.'

In our American production, the voice was done with a microphone and loudspeakers, the actor being of course behind the scenes
and another silent one walking on the stage. Though this was
most effective for the first ' Mark me ' and the ' Swears ' under

the stage (which often used to make the audience laugh in London, but were very impressive in New York) the house was quickly aware of the microphone device. It was impossible to hold the audience with it for long speeches, so later it was cut out and the lines spoken ordinarily from the wings. Even this was not as effective, to my mind, as a real actor would have been. He should, also, I think, be lit clearly and not over-disguised facially, as an audience cannot be interested in a mask-like face for very long.

Hamlet has a terribly difficult task in this scene, made twice as difficult by familiarity with the story, which robs the whole scene, with its purposely delayed climax, of half its effectiveness for actors and audience alike. The long speech on seeing the Ghost, which I have always spoken kneeling, is very difficult to build up with correct breathing, pace and emphasis in the right places. It needs a good deal of voice yet must be at any rate begun and finished with awe—and yet too much whispering in the dark hereabouts in the play gets on the audience's nerves. The line, by the way, that got a safe laugh every night in the tryout in America was ' something is rotten in the state of Denmark.' This did not seem very helpful for the scene, and so we cut it out. It is evidently a comic phrase to Americans!

I do not know how the tradition started of Hamlet saying ' O, horrible! O, horrible! Most horrible! ' It belongs of course to the Ghost, and though I have taken it, thinking to do something very effective with it, I have always regretted it afterwards, and would like to play with a Ghost who could utter it as it ought to be uttered. Irving is said to have made a great effect with it as Hamlet, and could no doubt have made an equally great one if he had said it as the Ghost.

I think the main difficulty of the Ghost is the timbre of voice needed for the part. The scene is not usually rehearsed or played sufficiently in cooperation between the two actors. A director might, I think, get an extraordinary result by sound alone, but it is an impossible scene to play in and direct as well. It may be that I seldom please myself in it, and so I think it more ineffective because it is technically so difficult. I should like to see and hear Leon Quartermaine play the Ghost; he has to my mind the perfect voice for the part, combining dignity and sweetness with emotion and authority, as well as a spiritual remoteness.

I have also an idea that it might be good to double the Ghost and Claudius—very effective, their physical likeness, from my point of view as Hamlet—but the qualities of voice and character needed for the two parts are so different that it would need a superb actor to differentiate between them without confusing the audience. Malcolm Keen read the Ghost's lines in New York and also played Claudius—but as he did not appear on the stage as the Ghost this was not quite the same thing.

I do not know whether I invented or acquired from someone else the business of seeing the Ghost from the expression of Horatio's face and then turning slowly and looking at it before ' Angels and ministers of grace ' but I do know that this came off very well in London. For some reason I could not make it so convincing in New York. I have never written on the tablets, because I could not manage them and a pencil and a sword all at the same time. I have always used ' the table of my memory ' and banged my head at ' So, uncle, there you are.' School-children always thought this funny, and I have to cut it (or do it very quietly) at matinees!

I copied from H. B. Irving—not that I remember it myself, but read it in a criticism—the putting of my cloak around Horatio at the end. I added to it by leaving my own cloak when I rush from the men in the beginning of the scene (how actors have chosen to play such an emotional scene in a cloak throughout baffles me completely) and having Horatio put his around my shoulders because I was shivering. This is effective and not as elaborate as it seems in describing it, though possibly it falsely emphasizes the ' curtain ' when Shakespeare intended a quick exit, and then the next scene following immediately. Effects of this kind, if not too complicated, are to some extent, I think, demanded by a picture stage and descending curtain, though I fear we actors like them particularly because they bring applause more surely than a simple exit. When I directed a production of *Romeo and Juliet* in which the front curtain came down only once, and one scene followed another in a different part of the stage—with even blackouts reduced to a minimum—I found it far less necessary to build up the ends of scenes with any device to encourage applause. Sometimes, indeed, several scenes would pass without any, and this certainly did no harm to the play, though unfortunately it always depresses the actors.

Scene 6

The Council Chamber in the Castle. Hamlet and Polonius;
the arrival of the Players; the Hecuba soliloquy
(Act II, Scene II)

When one studies and considers *Hamlet* through a great number of consecutive rehearsals and performances one realizes perhaps some of the things which account for its perennial popularity with actors and audiences alike. The scenes themselves are audience-proof. By this I mean that if they are played theatrically for all they are worth they will always hold the house. But audiences at this play are apt to be composed either of people who know nothing of Shakespeare or *Hamlet* except what their parents and school-teachers have told them, or else of students, scholars and ' Hamleto-manes ' for whom every moment in the play is important not only for its own sake but for its significance with regard to the rest of the action and the psychological relation and development of the characters.

People who love the play and have studied it closely can frequently interpret motives in an actor's performance of a part of which he never dreamt himself. Conversely, with such a complicated character as Hamlet, the actor may try his utmost to convey a certain meaning and yet never be sure that he has conveyed it clearly to the people in the audience, some of whom are admiring the poetry, some watching a pet theory of their own, some comparing the performance with others they have seen, some not attending at all.

The director, therefore, or so it seems to me, must take a very firm hand and do his best to help the actor to give and the audience to receive the same meaning at the important moments in the play. Perhaps this is to under-estimate the average intelligence of the average audience, but all theatrical representation suffers when actors and audience are not properly fused; and in this particular play the fact already mentioned—that the scenes themselves are audience-proof—often makes it appear that this fusion has come about when really there is little except ordinary theatrical contact.

To develop this argument a little in relation to Hamlet's first appearance when he is feigning madness: the lines with Polonius about the fishmonger and conception are archaic and to a modern audience vaguely connote rudeness, bawdry, suggestiveness, etc. But they will always be funny when spoken in the theatre (by which I mean they will get laughs and ' go ' with an audience be- cause the actors instinctively say them rightly, even if they do not completely understand them). Yet at rehearsals, actors and directors always try to reason out this scene. Dr. Dover Wilson has evolved a clever theory that Hamlet's entrance should take place some lines earlier than when the Queen's ' but look where sadly the poor wretch comes reading ' heralds his appearance. Both in my own production and in Mr. McClintic's I have tried different cues for the entrance in the hope that Hamlet's overhearing the last lines of Polonius to the King and Queen would make clearer the lines in his scene with Polonius as well as his subsequent treatment of Ophelia in the nunnery scene.

One or two people have noticed this treatment, but on the whole I do not think it clarified the meaning sufficiently to warrant the trouble we took with it at rehearsals. I was also afraid that the audience might mistake my meaning or wonder what was happening (whether one had made a mistake and come on too early) and, while they were speculating thus, miss what followed. I was continually struck with the feeling when playing this scene that if Shakespeare had meant Hamlet to overhear something, he would surely have made it clear in the text. The play has much spying in it, and two or three of the most vital moments in subsequent scenes are built around this device, but in each case it is Hamlet who is spied upon. I think it unlikely that Shakespeare would weaken this characteristic feature of his play by making Hamlet spy on, or overhear, any other character before the more important point of his enemies ' spying on him had been definitely registered with the audience.

Mr. Granville-Barker draws attention to the long stretch in this part of the play in which the actual plot is not touched on at all. From the entrance of Hamlet until he says to the Player: ' Can you play The Murder of Gonzago? ' the plot does not move forward at all. The variety of the dialogue and wealth of theatrical invention is so extraordinary that I had never noticed this important point either in acting or producing the play. Reading Mr. Granville-Barker's stimulating essay I was greatly helped by his remarks, forcing myself to decide on certain definite moments in the scene in which Hamlet must remember his mission of vengeance and is shocked to find how easily he has been forgetting it. Yet, though I tried to make these moments clear in my by-play, for an audience seeing the scene there is so much else for them to watch and to listen to—so much beauty and wit, action and counteraction— that this point, so very important to the actor playing Hamlet, does not really matter greatly to the spectator.

I cannot quite decide in my own mind whether Hamlet asks the Player emphatically for a passionate speech, thinking at that moment of his own lack of passion, or whether Shakespeare is simply writing towards his climax with unerring instinct, suggesting it in advance, as a composer might use a warning note before introducing a great theme in a symphony. I have been struck later in the play by the lines:

> ' . . . bless'd are those
> Whose blood and judgment are so well co-mingled
> That they are not a pipe for fortune's finger
> To sound what stop she please.'

coming only a little while before the scene with the recorder. This seems to me something of the same kind. At any rate, Mr. Granville-Barker has led me to much greater ease during the recital of the Player's speech by his remarks on the subject. ' The unnerved father falls ' would surely strike Hamlet as a vivid reminder of his own forgetfulness; and ' Aroused vengeance sets him new a-work ' serves finely as the first point of his determination to clear the room and unburden himself to the culminating ' O! Vengeance.'

I shall never forget the tremendous effect of this scene in the Moissi *Hamlet*, of which I have spoken before. The First Player was, perhaps, the finest actor in the company—an enormously tall man, over six feet, with deep-set eyes and black hair and beard. He played the part as high tragedy and at the end of the speech on Hecuba he veiled his face with his cloak thrown over his forearm and fell headlong on the stage. This was extraordinarily moving, and beautifully carried out. It showed, as usual, what can be made of the smaller parts of Shakespeare and how greatly it helps the central character when they are played, as they so seldom are, to the full extent of their possibilities.

If the Player has done his work well, Hamlet's comments need only echo the audience's thoughts, and how much more moderately and easily expressed than if Hamlet must ' tear a passion to tatters ' to convince himself and the audience of something they have not really seen. In Moissi's production also, Hamlet left the stage at the end of the Hecuba soliloquy, and, as far as I remember, received just as much applause at this point as any other Hamlet. For some reason I have never been able to bring myself to do this, though of course it is what Shakespeare intended. I suppose I was hypnotized by the famous business of Irving, when, as the curtain falls, he is seen writing madly on his tablets. One cannot help feeling that

> ' the play's the thing
> Wherein I'll catch the conscience of the king '

should be the signal for the greatest applause in the play. When I have played the part on first nights I have never been able to believe that I could succeed in it until this applause has come. At later performances, however, I have been and still am, irritated by my actor's desire to make such a ' curtain ' of it. If we could bury the play for twenty years we might perhaps feel it mattered less how certain parts of it would be received than whether the great speeches would be correctly interpreted in their own place in the play.

I have spoken a great deal in these notes about stage business and the Victorian and Edwardian traditions of Shakespeare which I deplore in the theatre. At the same time I know only too well that my own performance has been cluttered with these things. I have never been either sufficiently experienced or sufficiently original to dare to direct or play *Hamlet* without including a great deal of this kind of theatricalism for fear of being unable to hold the interest of the audience by a more classical and simple statement of the written text. As in music, it needs the greatest artist to perform most simply and perfectly the greatest composition.

Scene 7

The Great Hall in the Castle. ' To be, or not to be ';
the Nunnery Scene
(Act III, Scene I)

I REMEMBER in the Moissi production, the German text of which I could not follow, that I was surprised by ' To be, or not to be ' coming so quickly on top of ' O! what a rogue and peasant slave am I.' This contrast had never struck me before, because there had always been an act wait between these two scenes, and then another before the play scene. When we first rehearsed the play at the Old Vic it seemed obvious that the best place to have the only interval was after the nunnery scene rather than before it. Apart from the time lapse which is suggested in the text there is also the practical consideration of preventing people coming in late and slamming down their seats during ' To be, or not to be,' whereas if they miss the whole of the advice to the players (which, however, is hellishly difficult to play under such circumstances) they will have lost nothing of the main progress of the plot.

Apart from this, I realize now that the effect of despondency in ' To be, or not to be ' is a natural and brilliant psychological reaction from the violent and hopeless rage of the earlier speech. If it were not such a famous purple patch which everybody in the audience waits for all evening, it would seem perhaps more perfectly placed for the character than it does. I imagined I created a great innovation by walking about in this speech and was extremely proud of the way I slipped in the opening words, trying to make not too long a pause before them and to get underway before the audience was quite sure it really was the big speech. But of course this defeated its own ends in time. When I did the play in New York I became self-conscious in the walking and after a few nights Mrs. Patrick Campbell, who came to see the play, implored me to cut it out as she said that watching the movements distracted from the words and destroyed the essential sense of composure necessary for the full effect of the lines.

The familiarity of this scene is an utter curse. Several times a week one is distracted by the knowledge that the audience is repeating one's lines after one—frequently one can hear words and phrases being whispered by people in the front rows, just before one is going to speak them—indeed, Leica cameras and the quoting of famous passages aloud are two of my worst phobias in a performance of *Hamlet*. This particular speech in itself is such a perfect thing that if you have executed it correctly you are apt to feel complete and satisfied at the end of it, but not ready to go straight into the rest of the scene. Like so many other great speeches in this play, it has to be studied, spoken, re-studied and re-spoken, until one can combine in it a perfect and complete form of poetry and spontaneous thought and at the same time use it only as a part of the action. The character and the value of the speech lie in the fact that it leads on to the next part of the scene, just as it must grow out of the previous action. Of course, the better one speaks it and the more completely one can win the audience by a good delivery of it, the more difficult it is to join it to the subsequent conversation and interplay with the other characters.

The scene with Ophelia has never really been explained to my satisfaction in any book I have read or performance I have seen. I have certainly never been able to decide positively for myself its general meaning or the particular meaning of many of the lines. I cannot be convinced by the traditional business of Hamlet seeing the King and Polonius before saying ' Where's your father? ' nor am I sure when Hamlet says ' I loved you not ' that he should immediately belie his words with affectionate by-play behind Ophelia's back. This is another of Irving's legacies which I inherited at an early age. (Moissi, by the way, took out a big white handkerchief to cry in before Ophelia even came on the stage.) It seems to me reasonable to suppose that Hamlet suspects from the very first that Ophelia has been set on to spy upon him. ' Are you honest? . . . ' That is why I have been inclined to favour Dr. Dover Wilson's theory of overhearing Polonius' ' I'll loose my daughter to him ' in the other scene, though against this I feel that so much time has elapsed between the two occasions that I doubt if an ordinary audience seeing the play for the first time would notice the connection.

' Why wouldst thou be a breeder of sinners? ' has led some commentators to suppose that Ophelia might be pregnant, and bolsters the theory already discussed that Hamlet and she had been lovers. The prevalent opinion seems to be, however, that the idea refers to his mother. This applies also to the later references to women painting their faces. The lines in which Hamlet accuses himself seem to me most poignant if they are spoken as if pleading with Ophelia to admit that she is not telling the truth. He is giving her every chance to speak out by showing her that he has just the same weakness as she. The scene is such an extraordinary mixture of realism and poetry that it needs elucidation. It maddens me to think that the author, were he here today, could so easily enlighten us as to the way it should be acted. The fact that like the other great scenes in *Hamlet* it is full of theatrical effect and is sure-fire with the audience does not make it any less of a problem for both the actor and the director.

ACT II—Scene 8

*The Great Hall in the Castle. The Advice to the Players;
the Play Scene*

(Act III, Scene II)

The advice to the players is always slightly embarrassing for the actor because he feels the audience is only waiting to catch him doing all the things he has told the players not to do. One of the most curious and amusing things about *Hamlet* is Shakespeare's mania for what one might call double suggestion. For instance, he invites an audience to watch an actor pretending to be a Prince apparently weeping real tears for his father, and a few scenes later he shows them the same actor being impressed by the mimic tears of another actor weeping for Priam's slaughter. He invites them to watch the actor who is playing the Prince discourse on acting and to see a play acted within a play. He asks them to mock at the damnable faces of Lucianus and the next instant to be thrilled by the terror of the King; to grieve with Laertes at his sister's grave, and yet to sneer a few moments later at the violent ranting of the two young men. The effect of contrast is echoed in the characters themselves—in the two sons avenging their fathers, the two princes waiting for their kingdoms, the two brothers, poisoner and poisoned, and the two women, shallow, weak, victims of circumstances and tools of men stronger than themselves.

The question of the dumb-show and the whole content of the play scene has been most exhaustively discussed by Dr. Dover Wilson. His views are fascinating, but I do not think that in carrying them out to the letter the conduct of the scene itself would gain, particularly for the average spectator. Well or badly played, well or badly cut, this scene has been and always will be one of the most exciting ever invented, although the great climax ' Give me some lights. Away! ' has never been staged with any great invention.

Presumably, in the Elizabethan theatre, the King and his Court were brought on by attendants with torches. These retired during the action of the play, and at the King's cry they re-entered and the Court left the stage, surrounded by this blaze of light, leaving Hamlet and Horatio alone. It is difficult to imagine that this was effective without artificial light, but perhaps torches flickering on the inner stage, which was out of the full sunlight, may have provided some illusion. Today fire regulations are so strict that it is extremely difficult to devise anything really effective with naked lights on the stage. They are not allowed either in London or in New York and a sore problem is added to the trials of the modern producer of classical plays.

Sarah Bernhardt is supposed to have snatched a torch from an attendant and held it to the King's face on 'What! frighted with false fire? ' and Moissi did much the same with a large candelabra. Shakespeare, however, said ' Suit the action to the word, the word to the action,' and as such fire is hardly false it seems a paradoxical gesture, though no doubt theatrically telling. Irving, I believe, created the business of lying on the floor with the manuscript in his hand and of squirming on his stomach across the stage. He also played with a fan of peacock's feathers which Ophelia let drop, and which he tore to pieces as he lay exhausted on the throne, and flung away on the words ' A very, very—pajock.' I do not know where the tradition originated of tearing up the manuscript—this has often been followed.

Macready, in this scene, waved a white handkerchief two or three times at the entrance of the King and the Court. I have never been able to discover on what particular line he did it, but apparently it was a signal for applause from the audience in the same way as was the famous business of Edmund Kean in the nunnery scene when, having left the stage, he electrified the house by returning, tiptoeing across the stage, and kissing Ophelia's hair. I always wonder how he accomplished this without her noticing it, and what she was doing while it was happening. At any rate, it brought down the house. And so did the handkerchief business of Macready, until the American actor Edwin Forrest attended the performance one night, and hissed at this particular piece of business.

Macready's diary is full of the incident and the rows and taking of sides which ensued on the subject, both in England and America.

The recorders scene was one of Irving's great triumphs, but many subsequent Hamlets cut it out. Personally, I would rather sacrifice almost anything else in the play, while admitting frankly that the breaking of the recorder at the end of it—taken also, I think, from Irving, though I am not sure—is pure theatrical business and not justified by the text. Unfortunately, I succumbed to it at the Queen's Theatre—not having done it originally at the Old Vic—and found the resulting applause, and chance of cutting several seconds playing time in a version that was inclined to run too long, too strong a combination to resist. When I played the soliloquy that followed, ' Tis now the very witching time of night,' the scene would pass entirely without applause. This soliloquy, with its curious references to Nero and Hamlet's thought of matricide (never touched on anywhere else in the play), is one that does not go with an audience—at any rate, when I have played it—any more than the following one of the King at prayers. Perhaps the speeches are too frankly Elizabethan in feeling, or it may be that they have less poetic appeal than others. In any case they are very difficult to deliver and unrewarding to play. Sir Philip Ben Greet wrote me that it was impossible to break a recorder, as it was then made in one piece, not screwed together like a modern flute. I replied, undaunted, that it was the most effective piece of business in the play and that people always liked it. I fear I am an inveterate ham, and shall never be the conscientious interpreter of Shakespeare that I should like to be.

In the Harcourt Williams production at the Vic Polonius came with a candle, which I took from him, pointing with it to the cloud, which made these lines frankly fantastic. I carried the candle through the rest of the scene, on into the King's room, and finally into the Queen's closet, where I set it down on a table. This gave a certain sense of continuity which I liked, but it did not fit into the stage management of subsequent productions.

Both Rosencrantz and Guildenstern, as well as Polonius, are

frightened by Hamlet's behaviour at the play and anxious to get him to his mother as quickly as possible. I am sure it is this feeling of being hustled that makes Hamlet delight in ridiculing them and in forcing them to leave him to come in his own time. This situation is a sort of pendant to the early part of the scene when they had announced that the King would see the play and Hamlet had hurried them off to summon the players. It could easily be stage-managed so that the audience would notice this excellent parallel stage effect.

I wonder, by the way, why the court of Claudius and Gertrude is always portrayed by actors representing young men and women. Gertrude must be nearly fifty, and in spite of the vanity of Queen Elizabeth, who certainly liked young people about her, it is surely more probable that a corrupt court under the influence of a king such as Claudius would include a great many older people. If I ever direct the play again I should like to have supers representing old councillors and ladies-in-waiting of about the Queen's age. The appearance of these in all the court scenes would suggest the complacent stupidity and mature decadence of Claudius' entourage. Hamlet, Horatio, Ophelia, Laertes, Rosencrantz and Guildenstern would stand out by contrast as the rebellious young people of the play. It would also be a change to indicate that Polonius did not run the entire affairs of Denmark single-handed. On the other hand, the modern custom of casting a younger woman for Gertrude greatly enhances the effect of the part and the meaning of the story. In the old days, the part of Hamlet being usually played by older men, his mother naturally became the property of the ' heavy ' actress in the company, and the result was not advantageous to the play.

Scene 9

A Room in the Castle. The King at Prayers
(Act III, Scene III)

Mr. Granville-Barker points out that the effect of this scene lies in the fact that the audience knows that Claudius cannot pray.

Therefore, if Hamlet had known that the King was not in a state of grace he would have killed him. Of course this is brilliantly true. But how can it be shown to an audience and how can the scene be arranged so that Hamlet's long speech may seem natural and yet audible? I should like to try an effect which I venture to think may have been the one achieved in the Elizabethan theatre. Kneeling on the stage is a conventional symbol for prayer, but kneeling at a prie-dieu immediately suggests prayer itself. It seems to me that if the King knelt at the front of the stage on the floor and not at a prie-dieu or altar, and Hamlet appeared above (the upper stage of the Elizabethan theatre—a balcony or rostrum would serve the same purpose in ours) the kneeling figure would convey to Hamlet the idea that the King was praying, but the King's face, which the audience could see clearly, would belie the attitude of his figure. Hamlet could not actually reach Claudius without coming down onto the stage. His pause and his subsequent speech would seem naturally to check him from doing this. He could then pass on along the upper stage, the King would rise and speak his final lines, leaving by a side door. The inner curtains could then open to disclose Polonius with the Queen, and Hamlet would enter as if he had traversed a passage and descended a staircase—as he would actually have to do—behind the scenes.

Played as it usually is today before a drop curtain, the scene with Claudius is extremely difficult for the actor. He is so close to the King that, even when the words are whispered, the audience is aware of the falseness of the convention and thinks it very odd that Claudius does not hear. The sentiments of the speech are intensely Elizabethan and therefore do not appeal much to a modern audience. As Mr. Granville-Barker says, the play is much more deeply concerned with what will happen to the individual after death than with any question of the momentary pain and violence of the act of dying. Today a lingering illness and the ugly attributes of the deathbed are what many of us fear the most, whereas the physical fact of sudden death must have been so continually present to the Elizabethans that they were inclined to consider the matter with greater philosophy than we do.

I am proud of a piece of business I invented in this scene—the only one I think that I can call entirely my own. I did not want to wear a sword in the play scene, as it is an impossible appendage to violent movement, but it is essential in the killing of Polonius in the scene with the Queen. In London the sword was carried before the King in the play scene, and at the beginning of the following one he was seen taking off his crown and robe but keeping the sword by him as if afraid to be left alone without it. Hamlet finds the sword lying on the chair, picks it up to kill the King, and at the end of the speech goes off with it in his hand to his mother. The King rises from his knees, finds the sword gone, and the discovery of its loss ends the scene on a legitimate note of excitement, and softens, to a certain degree, the rather trite-sounding rhyming couplet with which it closes.

Many critics believe that this scene is really the crux and climax of the entire play, but perhaps because I have never felt that I played it effectively, or that it was staged to the best advantage either in my own or other productions, I have not been able to agree with them. The following scene and the killing of Polonius is to me, as an actor, the climax of Hamlet's long inaction. The whole of the subsequent tragedy springs from this later moment. Besides, it is this physical act that seems to break the spell of doubt in Hamlet's mind and unloose his stream of repressed anguish and revenge.

SCENE 10

The Closet Scene
(Act III, Scene IV)

IT is a terrific strain to open this scene at the pitch which the text demands, but it is essential to carry the mood of the play scene through the four or five scenes that follow it and maintain the feeling of a consecutive time-lapse. I realized from a description of Bernhardt's cry ' Is it the king? ' when her sword was held above her head making her whole figure into a great interrogation mark (as, I think, Maurice Baring has described it) the tremendous theatrical effect of the killing of Polonius. The lines which follow have to be most carefully presented by the actors so that the audience may not miss the significance of both characters at this point. The Queen's line ' As kill a king! ' has to convey to the audience not only her horror at what Hamlet has just tried to do but her dawning knowledge of what he implies Claudius has done. Hamlet has to understand in a very few seconds, and convey clearly to the audience (1) that he realizes his mother did not know Claudius was a murderer, (2) that she set someone to spy on him behind the arras, and (3) that it is evident from her cry that it is not, as he imagined, Claudius whom he has killed.

I am constantly receiving letters asking me whether the Queen was an accomplice of her husband's murder. This is, I suppose, because the actresses who have played the part recently—Martita Hunt and Laura Cowie in London, and Judith Anderson in New York—have played her with real fire and sensuality, whereas in the old days as I have said she was played as the heavy woman— nothing more. It seems obvious to me, and I should have thought to everyone else (but one is never done with speculation in *Hamlet*), that Shakespeare meant her to be an adulteress, shallow, hand- some, but not in the least wicked in the sense of being a murderess. Mrs. Campbell said to me, ' The point about Gertrude in the closet scene is not that she didn't know Claudius was a mur- derer, but that she doted on him so much that she wouldn't have minded if he had been.' This seems to me feminine and shrewd.

The business of the pictures, which to judge from old prints was done at one period with portraits on the wall and later with miniatures around the necks of the characters, is another vexed point of theatrical tradition. Many recent Hamlets, myself in- cluded, have dispensed with both. But Mr. Granville-Barker, to my surprise, advocates the miniatures. I suppose they are really warranted by the text, but I never dared to use them for fear that they would lead me inevitably to the elaborate business of dashing down Claudius' picture and stamping on it at the line ' A king of shreds and patches! ' This, I imagine, was the point at which Garrick knocked over the chair, which was supposed to be very effective. This is the point, also, where, it seems to me, the Ghost should appear in ordinary dress and not in armour.

The arrangement in New York was criticized in one case because Hamlet was between the Ghost and his mother. The Queen should be in the middle, it was said, to get the full effect of her inability to see the Ghost. On the other hand, if Hamlet is in the middle, there is a fine effect when the Ghost bids him speak to her and he addresses her over his shoulder with a movement of his arm, but still not looking around, his eyes fixed on his father.

The text seems to warrant a chair in this scene for the Queen to sit on, but I have always thought there should be a bed as well. In London we used curtains which hung in the middle of the stage, suggesting a bed. One half of the stage represented the King's room and the other the Queen's. The King knelt in prayer at one end of the bed and the Queen was discovered kneeling at the other. This gave a sense of atmosphere, but without too definite localization. In New York we had a real bed and no chair. I imagine it was very effective when I leaped on the bed and stabbed Polonius through the hangings, but on the other hand it was necessary for the Queen to sit on it and as somebody said, a Queen would never sit on a bed—it makes her look like a housemaid! Another difficulty is that later when the Queen is going out of the room and Hamlet begs her not to go to his uncle's bed, a real bed on the stage may encourage the audience to indulge in speculation as to the sleeping accommodations of the palace. This scene and the scenes that follow could probably still be played best on an Elizabethan stage, with the inner stage arranged with hangings for the killing of Polonius. The action in the scenes before and after could then continue on the forestage, backstage, and above, in quick succession.

SCENE 13

A Plain in Denmark; the Fortinbras Soliloquy
(Act IV, Scene IV)

THE scene with Fortinbras and his army seems certainly to require a change of scene, yet the modern picture stage fails as usual, just at the moment when it should be most useful. A really striking setting might be possible with a revolving stage, but though we planned in London to use the entire extent of the permanent set for this one scene, lighted and angled at a different point from any other, we found when we came to the dress rehearsal that this particular arrangement was not good. We had to fall back on curtains as we did also in New York. Of course the soliloquy is most easily spoken close to the footlights, but it would also be of enormous value to suggest space, open air, and nature in the background after the madness and scurryings of the dark scenes in the palace.

I did not see Chaney's Viking ship in Howard's production, which I am told was a fine innovation for this scene, but there is a drawing in Craig's *Toward a New Theatre* called ' Enter the Army ' which I should love to see carried out in the theatre. If the audience could be somehow persuaded that they could see an army marching as clearly as Hamlet does, it would be an excellent cross-current in the action of the play. But when one's mind begins to dwell on masses of soldiers and banners, one knows at once the danger of turning a production of the play into the kind of pageant that no doubt the pageant-master producers and Hollywood would be glad to make of it. If Hamlet is forced to conjure up in his imagination an army on the march, and succeeds in doing so, the audience may be readier to believe in its existence than if it were really there. I am told that Tyrone Guthrie arranged the scene brilliantly in his recent production at the Old Vic with Fortinbras above on an eminence, in shadow, while Hamlet spoke on the stage below—and that Herbert Menges devised a brilliant effect with music to heighten the mood as the scene closed.

SCENES 14 AND 16

The Great Hall of the Castle, and the Council Chamber. Ophelia's Mad Scene

(*Act IV, Scenes V and VII*)

THIS is the point in the play where Hamlet at last gets ten minutes in his dressing room, so perhaps I am not very well fitted to discuss it in detail. Once Ophelia has done her two showy pieces the house becomes inclined to polite indifference until the gravediggers appear. But the King and Laertes have a difficult scene to play here which never seems to be very effective and is always severely cut, which probably does not make it any easier. And perhaps it is not possible in any play of Shakespeare's to avoid two or three stretches, usually in the fourth act of the standard editions, that are less interesting than others.

The Victorians often set this scene in a garden or exterior of some sort, presumably to help the idea of Ophelia's flowers and the Queen's description of her drowning. Needless to say, pastoral scenery is of little avail in illustrating Shakespeare's text. The entrance of Laertes with the mob is obviously more effective played indoors, and I am told it was one of the great successes of lighting and stage management in the Norman Bel Geddes production of *Hamlet*, in which Raymond Massey played.

Technically, the most difficult part of the scene is the entrance of the Queen to tell of Ophelia's death. Laertes' ' Drown'd! O, where? ' has defeated many actors, and if the Queen is a good character actress she finds it difficult to fit the willow speech (as it is called by actors), which is a sort of cadenza, into the rest of her performance, to which it seems to have no particular relation. Here, I think, there is no doubt that a bit of the old grand manner is required. The actress must be given the stage and know how to take it and not attempt to make a realistic effect with her lines. After all, if one examines it carefully, the whole situation is absurd, for if the Queen or anybody else had seen the drowning in such detail, obviously something would have been done to prevent it.

Shakespeare merely uses the Greek messenger method of describing an important incident happening off-stage, and no producer can hope to make the incident more convincing by arranging it realistically for the actress.

SCENE 15

Hamlet's Letter
(Act IV, Scene VI)

I HAVE always retained the letter scene with Horatio as it gives some sense of continuity. The actor has a difficult time at about this point in the play for after being in attendance on Ophelia, we see him receiving Hamlet's letter and then when we next meet him he is with Hamlet in the graveyard knowing nothing of Ophelia's death. Here again it is no good trying to build the character too realistically in sequence. Shakespeare uses him all through the play in whatever way he wills, as a foil to Hamlet and the other characters, but he is so tactfully and rightly put in the foreground when Shakespeare needs him that the audience accepts him exactly as is intended and believes all that he stands for in Hamlet's eyes.

SCENE 17

A Churchyard. Hamlet's Return; Ophelia's Funeral
(Act V, Scene I)

HERE a serious technical problem is presented to the scene designer. There is no time for an interval before or after—yet he must have a practical set, a grave, a glint of sky, besides some other suggestion of an exterior. Beerbohm Tree indulged in a spring landscape with blossoms, sheep scattered on the hills, and flowers which he picked for Ophelia's grave. In the Reinhardt-Moissi production the scene was played at night by torchlight and Ophelia was carried on in white robes on an open bier. This was all very well. Unfortunately there was no trap, and having set the bier above the grave, the men fought over her, were parted, the Court retired, and poor Ophelia was left out all night for the daws to peck at, which seemed a little unchristian, to say the least of it.

A most impressive version of this scene was given in the modern dress *Hamlet*, for I suppose all of us (unless we are Irish) have a rooted aversion to modern funerals. The black, brass-handled coffin, wreaths, boots and mourning veils lent a sordid reality to the scene which I found quite unbearable. The gravedigger was, in this production, played by Sir Cedric Hardwicke and he gave a brilliant performance on the lines of his old countryman in *The Farmer's Wife*. Ralph Richardson in another Old Vic performance also gave a memorable reading. The part does not seem to amuse an audience very much as a rule, but children love it and roar at the jokes and the business of the skulls, which seems rather surprising. George Nash, who was the clown in our American production, is certainly the best gravedigger I have ever played with. Without resorting to ten waistcoats or any of the old business, and with a very cut version of his lines, he contrived, it seemed to me, to present a most Shakespearian and delightful rendering of the old fellow.

Hamlet and Laertes should surely not fight in the grave, for the moment they disappear from view it is impossible to see clearly what is happening and the effect on the stage is bound to be ridiculous when they are separated and have to climb sheepishly out again. The lines do not really demand it anyway.

SCENE 18

A Corridor. Hamlet and Osric; the Challenge
(Act V, Scene II)

MARTIN-HARVEY, who played Osric at the Lyceum, says that Irving seemed to be surrounded by an aura of death in this scene. It is a very difficult passage to play, especially when the audience is flagging, and the actor out of breath from the rant in the graveyard which immediately preceded it. The necessary cuts always make one feel as if something had been left out, but even played in full there is an abrupt transition of mood and action. Again the necessary front scene demanded for the striking of the churchyard and the setting of the final scene cramps the actors for space and bores the audience, who begin to cough and look at their watches. The description of the pirate ship and the changing of the letters comes too late for the audience to be interested in it and the actors always feel, however the scene is cut, that it is difficult to settle the house so that it will be attentive for the last stretch of the play.

A good Osric does much to remedy this, and I have been very lucky in those who played the part with me—Alex Guinness in London and Morgan Farley in New York. Mr. Granville-Barker has an interesting theory about Hamlet's attitude in this last part of the play, and I think there is much to be said for his suggestion that he should be keen, ruthless, his mind made up. But with this must be weighed the half affectionate, half philosophical mood of the scene with the gravedigger, of his words about Yorick, and his touching farewell to Horatio. These moments win such obvious sympathy from the audience that no doubt this is apt to encourage the actor at the end of a long part to play for pathos and sentiment more than he should.

The fatalistic vein in which he speaks ' It is no matter . . . A man's life's no more than to say " One! " . . . If it be not to come, it will be now . . .' these are simple moments which, when spoken sincerely, will move almost any audience. But the general attitude of the character all through these last three scenes is extremely difficult to reconcile with the violent and often more showy passages in the earlier scenes and the actor has to take the line which he feels is most justified by his reading of the text and his whole conception of the character.

Scene 19

The Great Hall. The Duel; the Death Scene
(*Act V, Scene II*)

THE final scene is apt to be a little ridiculous unless everybody concerned is very careful. Irving made his one really ill-judged cut in this play here, and left out Fortinbras altogether. The rest of his acting version is well arranged and compares favourably with his other Shakespearian texts, which were maltreated and bowdlerized to a shameless degree. Recent productions have made the fight tremendously pictorial and built the whole scene around it, especially in the productions in which Raymond Massey and Laurence Olivier played. As I am not a good swordsman I have never myself attempted more than is absolutely necessary. Frankly, also, I haven't the energy for it at the end of such a long and exhausting part. But the better the fight is done, of course, the better for the scene, and if the stage can be arranged for different levels to be used for the duelling the effect is proportionately greater.

I have always fought with rapier and dagger as the text seems to demand. Moissi, to my amazement, after an elaborate but quite anachronistic eighteenth century fight with foils (in a Gothic production) took the poisoned sword by the blade with both hands, and stabbed the King in the back! The guards, in diagonally striped cloaks, then closed in in three groups covering the bodies of the King and Queen and Laertes, making a background for Hamlet himself to die against. This was too much of a stunt and I prefer my own arrangement of the scene, in which the Queen and Laertes died on big thrones, one on each side of the stage close to the footlights, and the King in a big cloak and crown was pursued up to a centre platform where he fell in a swirl of red folds. There were still steps below for Hamlet and Horatio to play their final scene, and Fortinbras and his army in grey cloaks and banners came from above over a kind of battlement and dipped their flags at the final curtain.

Forbes-Robertson died sitting on the throne with the King's crown set on his lap, and was then borne off on locked shields. Leslie Howard also, I believe, was carried off in a great procession to end the play. The poisoning of the Queen is difficult to manage and Mr. Granville-Barker has a fine idea that she should really play her death scene on the ground like the pictures of the death of Queen Elizabeth, suffering and moaning in her ladies' arms, and not die until Hamlet says ' Wretched queen, adieu! ' I had never noticed what he so brilliantly points out—that the King, being a professional poisoner, was unable to resist using a device a second time, as so many great criminals have done. It is indeed ironic for Hamlet to realize at this moment that his mother has died just as his father did, and undoubtedly the King should have poison in a ring and the audience should see him pour it into the cup. In Tyrone Guthrie's production the scene was produced for violent melodrama, and the Queen fell from a six-foot platform into the arms of the attendants.

The supers in the scene are an added problem, for one cannot think of actions which appear violent enough to express their horror at these tragic happenings without distracting from the main characters and the dialogue and action of the scene that follows. In London I had soldiers holding the people back, but in New York the courtiers left the stage altogether just before the King was killed. There is reason, however, to keep them on the scene in order that they should be in contrast to the corpses and also so that Hamlet may have someone to whom to address his ' You that look pale and tremble at this chance.' I should like, another time, to use the old councillors and ladies-in-waiting of whom I spoke in the play scene, for it would give point to Hamlet's lines if he could indicate this group of important people in the kingdom as those to whom Horatio would afterwards justify all that Hamlet has done.

Mr. McClintic invented for me the device of standing until the very end. I have never seen this done by anyone in the part and rebelled against trying it at first. It proved an admirable departure from tradition, for there are three recumbent figures on the stage already, and Hamlet in Horatio's arms is always faintly reminiscent of ' Kiss me, Hardy ' at the death of Nelson. The standing figure holds the audience's attention just as they are on the verge of reaching for their hats, and ' The rest is silence,' spoken standing, appears to gain greater simplicity and significance if the actor can still command the audience with his full height.

To sum up these notes, I would like to say this: I have been fortunate enough to make some success and reputation in this wonderful part and I have played it many more times in succession than I should have wished, to do anything like justice to the enormous complexity and the physical demands of the role. You will see that my mind has been torn in studying the part between a desire to walk in the traditions of the great ones and yet to carve out some interpretation that I might justly call my own. The result has only satisfied me spasmodically, and I think perhaps the only really original contribution that I have made to the history of the part has been to play it successfully when I was younger than most Hamlets have been. I do not believe that in this realistic age we are likely to see many more Hamlets played by men of forty or fifty years of age, at least I devoutly hope that I shall not be one of these. There are many parts for older men in Shakespeare, and I do not think that Hamlet is one of them.

It is curious that when I first played the part in 1929 I was supposed to have given my best reading and to have been a very modern Hamlet. Now that I have studied it for eight years, people have begun to say that I am a Hamlet in the classical tradition and I am not sure whether to take this as a compliment or not. I think it unlikely that I shall play the part again, and that is why I have attempted in these notes to describe some of the problems and questions that have occurred to me during fifteen years of reading, seeing, and thinking about the play. Few actors have time or training to be serious academic students as well and their interest is as much in practical theatrical usage as in the research of scholars, though I suppose a great director should be a great scholar and a fine actor as well. If only Mr. Granville-Barker would answer the prayers of us who love the theatre, and, instead of writing his brilliant treatises from far away, would come and work with us at the practical task of presenting Shakespeare in London and New York as he alone knows how it should be presented!

We have not many directors or actors with a strong bent for Shakespeare and even with those who have talent there is always the danger that too much work in Shakespeare may develop a bad acting tradition and defeat its own ends. If the modern generation in the theatre is to give its best in Shakespeare it must alternate performances of classics with performances of the best modern authors and the masterpieces of Chekhov, Ibsen, Congreve, Shaw. And, above all, a really fine performance of Shakespeare demands more than a bare three weeks' rehearsal. The cast needs a fortnight's work in the speaking alone, and beyond that there is all the preparatory work for the director, designer, musician, and stage-managers. Much of this can be roughly thought out beforehand, but how much better it could be if the play has time to grow at rehearsals, if costumes were planned for the actors who were to wear them, and the ' business ' of scenes discussed, developed, and finally arranged as they grew naturally from the actor's needs. English actors resent long rehearsals. Six weeks might induce them to become inventive and creative from very boredom. The director could study them, work with them, discuss with them, not merely impose his personality and order them about like sheep— and both would gain by natural contact and familiarity. This, I am sure, is one of the secrets of companies like that of the Moscow Art Theatre, and some of the famous continental repertory companies. The plays must be cast with as much care, particularly in the smaller parts, as if they were the work of a distinguished modern author, and the director must describe and discuss his attitude towards the play with the whole cast before beginning work on it. These councils of perfection are obvious, I suppose, to any intelligent person, but it is surprising how seldom they are carried out in the threatre. *Hamlet* is nearly always a success, but shall we ever see a really perfect production of it played, not more than three times a week, as the chief glory of a theatre's repertoire?

HAMLET

By William Shakespeare

*With a Scene-by-Scene Description of
John Gielgud's Performance*
By Rosamond Gilder

HAMLET

By William Shakespeare

Staged by John Gielgud

Settings and Costumes by Motley

CHARACTERS IN THE ORDER OF THEIR APPEARANCE

Bernardo	George Devine
Francisco	Peter Murray-Hill
Horatio	Jack Hawkins
Marcellus	Howison Culff
Ghost	William Devlin
Claudius	Frank Vosper
Laertes	Glen Byam Shaw
Polonius	George Howe
Hamlet	John Gielgud
Gertrude	Laura Cowie
Ophelia	Jessica Tandy
Reynaldo	Cecil Winter
Rosencrantz	Richard Ainley
Guildenstern	Anthony Quayle
First Player	George Devine
Second Player	Sam Beazley
Third Player	Alec Guinness
Fourth Player	Ian Atkins
Fifth Player	Richard Dare
Norwegian Captain	Peter Murray-Hill
Fortinbras	Geoffrey Toone
A Courier	Frith Banbury
First Gravedigger	Ben Field
Second Gravedigger	Lyon Playfair
Priest	Cecil Winter
Osric	Alec Guinness

Played in fourteen scenes, with one intermission

The Empire Theatre, New York
St. James Theatre, New York
October 8, 1936–January 30, 1937

HAMLET

By William Shakespeare

Staged by Guthrie McClintic

Settings and Costumes by Jo Mielziner

CHARACTERS IN THE ORDER IN WHICH THEY SPEAK

Francisco .... *Murvyn Vye*
Bernardo .... *Reed Herring*
Horatio .... *Harry Andrews*
Marcellus .... *Barry Kelly*
Claudius .... *Malcolm Keen*
Cornelius .... *Whitner Bissell*
Voltimand .... *James Dinan*
Laertes............................... *John Emery*
Polonius .... *Arthur Byron*
Hamlet............................... *John Gielgud*
Gertrude............................. *Judith Anderson*
Ophelia .... *Lillian Gish*
Reynaldo .... *Murvyn Vye*
Rosencrantz .... *John Cromwell*
Guildenstern......................... *William Roehrick*
The Player King...................... *Harry Mestayer*
Prologue............................. *Ivan Triesault*
The Player Queen .... *Ruth March*
Lucianus............................. *Whitner Bissell*
Fortinbras........................... *Reed Herring*
A Captain............................ *George Vincent*
A Sailor .... *William Stanley*
First Gravedigger .... *George Nash*
Second Gravedigger................... *Barry Kelly*
Priest .... *Ivan Triesault*
Osric................................ *Morgan Farley*

The Ghost's Lines are read by *Malcolm Keen*

Production Transferred to the St. James, December 21, 1936

THE SCENES

The place is Denmark

ACT I

INTERMISSION: 10 MINUTES

ACT II

HAMLET

ACT I.[1]

[1]

SCENE I.—*The Sentinel's platform before the royal castle.*
FRANCISCO *at his post. Enter to him* BERNARDO.

BERNARDO. Who's there?

FRANCISCO. Nay, answer me; stand, and unfold yourself.

BERNARDO. Long live the king!

FRANCISCO. Bernardo?

BERNARDO. He.

FRANCISCO. You come most carefully upon your hour.

BERNARDO. 'Tis now struck twelve; get thee to bed, Francisco.

FRANCISCO. For this relief much thanks; 'tis bitter cold,
And I am sick at heart.

BERNARDO. Have you had quiet guard?

FRANCISCO.   Not a mouse stirring.

BERNARDO. Well, good-night.
If you do meet Horatio and Marcellus,
The rivals of my watch, bid them make haste.

FRANCISCO. I think I hear them. Stand, ho! Who's there?

Enter HORATIO *and* MARCELLUS.

HORATIO. Friends to this ground.

MARCELLUS.   And liegemen to the Dane.

FRANCISCO. Give you good-night.

MARCELLUS.   O! farewell, honest soldier:
Who hath reliev'd you?

FRANCISCO.   Bernardo has my place.   [*Exit.*
Give you good-night.

MARCELLUS.   Holla! Bernardo!

BERNARDO.   Say,
What! is Horatio there?

HORATIO.   A piece of him.

BERNARDO. Welcome, Horatio; welcome, good Marcellus.

1. This version of the text of *Hamlet* is based on the Oxford University Press
edition of the tragedies (1935). There are one or two slight variations from
it, mainly those necessitated by the cuts. Sections which were not used in
either Mr. Gielgud's London production in 1934, or in Mr. McClintic's
New York production in 1936, are omitted entirely. Lines cut in London
but used in New York are marked with round brackets ( ); those cut in
the New York production but used in London are marked with square
brackets [ ]. In this way the words of both Mr. Gielgud's and Mr. Mc-
Clintic's versions can be studied here. The scene arrangement and numbering
is that of the New York production on which the accompanying description
of the action is based.

HAMLET

ACT I

SCENE I. *The sentinel's platform before the royal castle.*

The platform at Elsinore. It is very dark. Steps sweep up left and right to an upper level six feet above the main stage. On either side, back, two huge crenelated turrets rise into the dark. Between them, the night sky is grey and luminous. The sentry's helmet gleams as he stands on the upper platform, centre, and answers Bernardo who enters lower right and goes up the stairs to him. As Francisco leaves, coming down the left hand steps with that ominous ' and I am sick at heart ' on his lips, Horatio and Marcellus enter meeting him half way up. They are grouped here, Horatio seated on the edge of the centre platform, when the Ghost appears, right, where Bernardo had entered. Horatio rises and turns quickly, fronting the apparition. As it silently withdraws, Horatio follows it to the opposite side of the stage. Marcellus and Bernardo follow him and once more the men group themselves on the middle landing, right, discussing the state of Denmark.

The re-appearance of the Ghost, lower left, on the opposite side of the stage from its first entrance interrupts the talk. Horatio goes toward it, adjuring it to speak, but once again it moves away in silence. To the terrified men who attempt to stop it, the Ghost seems to appear in several places at once, first on one side of the stage, then on the other. After its exit the scene closes with a blackout on Horatio's words evoking the image of ' young Hamlet ' to whom these matters are of such concern.

MARCELLUS. What! has this thing appear'd again to-night?

BERNARDO. I have seen nothing.

MARCELLUS. Horatio says 'tis but our fantasy,
And will not let belief take hold of him
Touching this dreaded sight twice seen of us:
Therefore I have entreated him along
With us to watch the minutes of this night;
That if again this apparition come,
He may approve our eyes and speak to it.

HORATIO. Tush, tush! 'twill not appear.

BERNARDO.   Sit down awhile,
And let us once again assail your ears,
That are so fortified against our story,
What we two nights have seen.

HORATIO.   .   Well, sit we down,
And let us hear Bernardo speak of this.

BERNARDO. Last night of all,
When yond same star that's westward from the pole
Had made his course to illume that part of heaven
Where now it burns, Marcellus and myself,
The bell then beating one,—

MARCELLUS. Peace! break thee off; look, where it comes again!

Enter Ghost.

BERNARDO. In the same figure, like the king that's dead.

MARCELLUS. Thou are a scholar; speak to it, Horatio.

BERNARDO. Looks it not like the king? mark it, Horatio.

HORATIO. Most like: it harrows me with fear and wonder.

BERNARDO. It would be spoke to.

MARCELLUS.   Question it, Horatio.

HORATIO. What art thou that usurp'st this time of night,
Together with that fair and warlike form
In which the majesty of buried Denmark
Did sometimes march? by heaven I charge thee, speak!

MARCELLUS. It is offended.

BERNARDO.   See! it stalks away.

HORATIO. Stay! speak, speak! I charge thee, speak!   [*Exit Ghost.*

MARCELLUS. 'Tis gone, and will not answer.

BERNARDO. How now, Horatio! you tremble and look pale:
Is not this something more than fantasy?
What think you on 't?

HORATIO. Before my God, I might not this believe
Without the sensible and true avouch
Of mine own eyes.

MARCELLUS.   Is it not like the king?

HORATIO. As thou art to thyself:

Such was the very armour he had on
When he the ambitious Norway combated;
So frown'd he once, when, in an angry parle,
He smote the sledded Polacks on the ice.
'Tis strange.
MARCELLUS. Thus twice before, and jump at this dead hour,
With martial stalk hath he gone by our watch.
HORATIO. In what particular thought to work I know not;
But in the gross and scope of my opinion,
This bodes some strange eruption to our state.
MARCELLUS. Good now, sit down, and tell me, he that knows,
Why this same strict and most observant watch
So nightly toils the subject of the land;
(And why such daily cast of brazen cannon,
And foreign mart for implements of war;)
What might be toward, that this sweaty haste
Doth make the night joint-labourer with the day:
Who is 't that can inform me?
HORATIO.   That can I;
At least, the whisper goes so. Our last king,
Whose image even but now appear'd to us,
Was, as you know, by Fortinbras of Norway,
[Thereto prick'd on by a most emulate pride,]
Dar'd to the combat; in which our valiant Hamlet—
[For so this side of our known world esteem'd him—]
Did slay this Fortinbras; who, by a seal'd compact,
Did forfeit with his life all those his lands
Which he stood seiz'd of, to the conqueror;
                     Now, sir, young Fortinbras,
Of unimproved mettle hot and full,
[Hath in the skirts of Norway here and there]
Shark'd up a list of lawless resolutes,
But to recover of us, by strong hand
[And terms compulsative,] those foresaid lands
So by his father lost. And this, I take it,
Is the main motive of our preparations,
[BERNARDO. I think it be no other but e'en so;
Well may it sort that this portentous figure
Comes armed through our watch, so like the king
That was and is the question of these wars.]
HORATIO. But, soft! behold! lo! where it comes again.
                     Re-enter Ghost.
I'll cross it, though it blast me. Stay, illusion!
If thou hast any sound, or use of voice,
Speak to me:

If there be any good thing to be done,
That may to thee do ease and grace to me,
Speak to me:
If thou art privy to thy country's fate,
Which happily foreknowing may avoid,
Speak of it: stay, and speak! Stop it, (Marcellus.)

MARCELLUS. Shall I strike at it with my partisan?

HORATIO. Do, if it will not stand.

BERNARDO.   'Tis here!

HORATIO.   'Tis here!   [*Exit Ghost.*

MARCELLUS. 'Tis gone!
We do it wrong, being so majestical,
To offer it the show of violence;
For it is, as the air, invulnerable,
And our vain blows malicious mockery.

BERNARDO. It was about to speak when the cock crew.

HORATIO. And then it started like a guilty thing
Upon a fearful summons. [I have heard
The cock, that is the trumpet to the morn,
Doth with his lofty and shrill-sounding throat
Awake the god of day; and at his warning,
Whether in sea or fire, in earth or air,
The extravagant and erring spirit hies
To his confine.

MARCELLUS. It faded on the crowing of the cock.
Some say that ever 'gainst that season comes
Wherein our Saviour's birth is celebrated,
The bird of dawning singeth all night long;
And then, they say, no spirit can walk abroad;
The nights are wholesome; then no planets strike,
No fairy takes, nor witch hath power to charm,
So hallow'd and so gracious is the time.

HORATIO. But, look, the morn in russet mantle clad,
Walks o'er the dew of yon high eastern hill]
Break we our watch up; and by my advice
Let us impart what we have seen to-night
Unto young Hamlet; for, upon my life,
This spirit, dumb to us, will speak to him.

[MARCELLUS. Let's do 't, I pray; and I this morning know
Where we shall find him most conveniently.]

SCENE 2.—*The council chamber in the castle.* KING, QUEEN, HAMLET, POLONIUS, LAERTES, VOLTIMAND, CORNELIUS, Lords, and Attendants.

KING. Though yet of Hamlet our dear brother's death
　The memory be green, and that it us befitted
　To bear our hearts in grief and our whole kingdom
　To be contracted in one brow of woe,
　Yet so far hath discretion fought with nature
　That we with wisest sorrow think on him,
　Together with remembrance of ourselves.
　Therefore our sometime sister, now our queen,
　The imperial jointress of this warlike state,
　Have we, as 'twere with a defeated joy,
　[With one auspicious and one dropping eye,
　With mirth in funeral and with dirge in marriage,
　In equal scale weighing delight and dole,]
　Taken to wife: nor have we herein barr'd
　Your better wisdoms, which have freely gone
　With this affair along: for all, our thanks.
　(Now follows, that you know, young Fortinbras,
　Holding a weak supposal of our worth,
　Or thinking by our late dear brother's death
　Our state to be disjoint and out of frame,
　He hath not fail'd to pester us with message,
　Importing the surrender of those lands
　Lost by his father, with all bands of law,
　To our most valiant brother.
　　　　　　　　　　　　We have here writ
　To Norway, uncle of young Fortinbras,
　Who, impotent and bed-rid, scarcely hears
　Of this his nephew's purpose, to suppress
　His further gait herein;
　　　　　　　　　　And we here dispatch
　You, good Cornelius, and you, Voltimand,
　For bearers of this greeting to old Norway,
　Farewell and let your haste commend your duty.

CORNELIUS. ⎫
　　　　　　　 ⎬ In that and all things will we show our duty.
VOLTIMAND. ⎭

KING. We doubt it nothing: heartily farewell.
　　　　　　　　　　　　[*Exeunt* VOLTIMAND *and* CORNELIUS.)
　And now, Laertes, what's the news with you?
　You told us of some suit;
　What wouldst thou have, Laertes?

'*The Council Chamber*'

Designed by Jo Mielziner for the New York production of Hamlet

SCENE 2: *The council chamber in the castle.*

A tapestried room with double doors left and right on the facing wall. Three steps lead to the doors, and, when they are opened, the flight sweeps up and out into lobbies beyond. A council table in the centre has two high-backed chairs behind it. On the table books, parchments, a pewter ink-well, sand box and quill pens. The King's crown is on a form on the table; the Queen wears hers. The royal pair are seated in state behind the council table. There is a blaze of colour. Courtiers and attendants stand about, their attention riveted on the King in his showy glory.

On the extreme left, forward, is Hamlet—a black arabesque of silent scorn. His pose as he sits in profile to the audience expresses by its stiff and slightly mannered line his unwilling submission to a formal necessity. He is motionless with the immobility not of repose but of arrested movement. His face with its bold line of nose jutting abruptly from the slight declivity between his brows, its forward sweep of jaw, its strongly modelled cheek bone and eye socket, is a mask covering banked fires. For the moment it is drained of everything but its structural beauty, its grief and its bitter distaste of all that is going forward.

Prince Hamlet, attending against his will the first council meeting since his mother's marriage and his uncle's coronation, is dressed in protesting black, but richly and in the height of elegance, as becomes his position and reputation. The fitted doublet closing down the front with silver buttons, the puffed sleeves, knee breeches, black stockings and long folds of cloak are the basis of a costume that varies slightly through the play but retains always its Renaissance silhouette. The calix-like white collar sets off the head with its sweep of blond hair. At his throat, on this occasion, Hamlet wears a silver ornament. A silver chain is around his neck, his sword belt holds a jewelled, black-sheathed dagger. The cloak he wears this time is silken and hangs in long folds from one shoulder, looped up and caught at the waist on the opposite side. The ribbons

LAERTES.   Dread my lord,
　Your leave and favour to return to France;
　From whence though willingly I came to Denmark,
　To show my duty in your coronation,
　Yet now, I must confess, that duty done,
　My thoughts and wishes bend again toward France
　And bow them to your gracious leave and pardon.
KING. Have you your father's leave? What says Polonius?
POLONIUS. He hath, my lord, wrung from me my slow leave
　[By laboursome petition, and at last
　Upon his will I seal'd my hard consent:
　I do beseech you, give him leave to go.]
KING. Take thy fair hour, Laertes; time be thine,
　And thy best graces spend it at thy will.
　　　　　　　[*Exeunt all except* KING, QUEEN, *and* HAMLET.
　But now, my cousin Hamlet, and my son,—
HAMLET. A little more than kin, and less than kind.
KING. How is it that the clouds still hang on you?
HAMLET. Not so, my lord; I am too much i' the sun.
QUEEN. Good Hamlet, cast thy nighted colour off,
　And let thine eye look like a friend on Denmark.
　Do not for ever with thy vailed lids
　Seek for thy noble father in the dust:
　Thou know'st 'tis common; all that live must die,
　Passing through nature to eternity.
HAMLET. Ay, madam, it is common.
QUEEN.   If it be,
　Why seems it so particular with thee?
HAMLET. Seems, madam! Nay, it is; I know not ' seems. '
　'Tis not alone my inky cloak, good mother,
　Nor customary suits of solemn black,
　Nor windy suspiration of forc'd breath,
　No, nor the fruitful river in the eye,
　Nor the dejected haviour of the visage,
　Together with all forms, modes, shows of grief,
　That can denote me truly; these indeed seem,
　For they are actions that a man might play:
　But I have that within which passeth show;
　These but the trappings and the suits of woe.
KING. 'Tis sweet and commendable in your nature, Hamlet,
　To give these mourning duties to your father:
　But, you must know, your father lost a father;
　That father lost, lost his; and the survivor bound
　In filial obligation for some term

at the knees are black rosettes; his shoes, square-heeled and stub-toed, have heavy black tongues over the instep.

On his hands are one or two heavy rings, and from the crooked fingers of his left hand, which rests on his knee, hangs an accusing white handkerchief. Against the black cloak the hands arrest the eye. Strong, rather blunt of fingertip, instinct with life, they are the hands of a doer. Now they have taken on the frozen pattern of his pose.

For Hamlet, though present in the flesh, is absent in intention. He is not absorbed in his own world as we will see him later. Rather, on this occasion, he is present and absent simultaneously, proclaiming in that double act his thorough disapproval of all that is involved in the situation. The King's unctuous proclamation of his marriage, his bold and business-like discourse on the situation with regard to Fortinbras, his silken words to Laertes, do not penetrate the surface of the scorn with which Hamlet is armoured, the grief that lies below that scorn.

When the King, having dismissed the court rises and comes around the end of the council table, addressing Hamlet with ' But now, my cousin Hamlet, and my son,' the surface cracks. Hamlet realizes he must speak, must cope with this distasteful situation, must risk his welling bitterness to words. He dreads the impact of direct speech as a wounded man dreads the touch of a hand. As the King speaks Hamlet's face which has been so coldly empty is suffused with a mounting wave of emotion.

' A little more than kin ' is spoken quietly, but it is a venomed dart and the curling, almost-cruel lips frame it with deliberate, courteous malice. Decidedly this young man does not like his uncle, nor does he take the trouble to hide it. He has not moved from his stool but battle is declared—a battle of wits at present, which will end in a battle to the death. With the next line, the Queen has come forward also and Hamlet rises to his feet as he tosses his second contradiction over her head to the King. ' Not so, my lord; I am too much i' the sun.' The words roll out with the weight of suppressed scorn, the full, rich tones presaging the music

To do obsequious sorrow; but to persever
In obstinate condolement is a course
Of impious stubbornness; ['tis unmanly grief:
It shows a will most incorrect to heaven,
A heart unfortified, a mind impatient,
An understanding simple and unschool'd.]
              We pray you, throw to earth
This unprevailing woe, and think of us
As of a father; [for let the world take note,
You are the most immediate to our throne;
And with no less nobility of love
Than that which dearest father bears his son
Do I impart toward you.] For your intent
In going back to school in Wittenberg,
It is most retrograde to our desire;
And we beseech you, bend you to remain
Here, in the cheer and comfort of our eye,
Our chiefest courtier, cousin, and our son.

QUEEN. Let not thy mother lose her prayers, Hamlet:
  I pray thee, stay with us; go not to Wittenberg.

HAMLET. I shall in all my best obey you, madam.

KING. Why, 'tis a loving and a fair reply:
  Be as ourself in Denmark. Madam, come;
  This gentle and unforc'd accord of Hamlet
  Sits smiling to my heart; in grace whereof,
  No jocund health that Denmark drinks to-day,
  But the great cannon to the clouds shall tell,
  And the king's rouse the heavens shall bruit again,
  Re-speaking earthly thunder. Come away.

                    [*Exeunt all except* HAMLET.

HAMLET. O! that this too too solid flesh would melt,
  Thaw and resolve itself into a dew;
  Or that the Everlasting had not fix'd
  His canon 'gainst self-slaughter! O God! O God!
  How weary, stale, flat, and unprofitable
  Seem to me all the uses of this world.
  Fie on 't! O fie! 'tis an unweeded garden,
  That grows to seed; things rank and gross in nature
  Possess it merely. That it should come to this!
  But two months dead: nay, not so much, not two:
  So excellent a king; that was, to this,
  Hyperion to a satyr; so loving to my mother
  That he might not beteem the winds of heaven
  Visit her face too roughly. Heaven and earth!
  Must I remember? why, she would hang on him,

that is to come. There is a heavy fall on the final word, emphasizing the ironic quibble.

He listens unwillingly as his mother speaks, fearing that she will stir the deeper layers of a grief which he has held in check under the armour of a public attitude. As his mother's voice undermines his defences, reminding him both of his loss and her betrayal, his face loses its protective scornfulness. An expression of poignant sorrow, of heart-broken filial grief, softens its contours, the ' vailed lids ' quiver in an effort to control an upwelling storm of emotion. The ' Ay, madam, it is common ' is spoken with that careful control of breath which the immediate fear of bursting into tears at the sound of one's own voice makes necessary. As he speaks these five words the Prince of Denmark suddenly becomes one with every human being in the audience who has ever lost a being he really loved. It is indeed common—a shared experience, not to be smoothed over by any conventional acceptance. The quiet, almost broken phrase spoken over an abyss of grief binds the listener to this bereaved son in a sudden movement of human understanding.

The Queen's answer is characteristically obtuse and steadies Hamlet against the rising tide within. His anger at her callousness restores his equilibrium. He is able to speak, not with less emotion, for tears are in his eyes, but in a manner more suited to the occasion. A pause after ' I know not " seems " ' and then slowly the rich music of his speech begins, each phrase scanned with clarifying emphasis, each word, each syllable given its noblest stature, sculptured in the round, each sibilant driven with the force of controlled power. He stands immobile throughout until at ' These but the trappings ' he looks down, and, with his left hand, makes a weary, downward-sweeping gesture that emphasizes the deep melancholy of the final ' woe.'

The King, exasperated by these remarks, begins to harangue Hamlet who stands looking at him unmoving. The Queen goes up to Claudius with a placating gesture and turning toward Hamlet begins her plea to him to remain at Elsinore. As she speaks she leans against the King, an intimate gesture which makes her son's

As if increase of appetite had grown
By what it fed on; and yet, within a month,
Let me not think on 't: Frailty, thy name is woman!
A little month; or ere those shoes were old
With which she follow'd my poor father's body,
Like Niobe, all tears; why she, even she,—
O God! a beast, that wants discourse of reason,
Would have mourn'd longer,—married with mine uncle,
My father's brother, but no more like my father
Than I to Hercules: within a month,
Ere yet the salt of most unrighteous tears
Had left the flushing in her galled eyes,
She married. O! most wicked speed, to post
With such dexterity to incestuous sheets.
It is not nor it cannot come to good;
But break, my heart, for I must hold my tongue!

Enter HORATIO, MARCELLUS, *and* BERNARDO.

HORATIO. Hail to your lordship!

HAMLET.   I am glad to see you well:
Horatio, or I do forget myself.

HORATIO. The same, my lord, and your poor servant ever.

HAMLET. Sir, my good friend; I'll change that name with you.
And what make you from Wittenberg, Horatio?
Marcellus?

MARCELLUS. My good lord,—

HAMLET. I am very glad to see you. [*To* BERNARDO.] Good even, sir.
But what, in faith, make you from Wittenberg?

HORATIO. A truant disposition, good my lord.

HAMLET. I would not hear your enemy say so,
Nor shall you do mine ear that violence,
To make it truster of your own report
Against yourself; I know you are no truant.
But what is your affair in Elsinore?
We'll teach you to drink deep ere you depart.

HORATIO. My lord, I came to see your father's funeral.

HAMLET. I pray thee, do not mock me, fellow-student;
I think it was to see my mother's wedding.

HORATIO. Indeed, my lord, it follow'd hard upon.

HAMLET. Thrift, thrift, Horatio! the funeral bak'd meats
Did coldly furnish forth the marriage tables.
Would I had met my dearest foe in heaven
Ere I had ever seen that day, Horatio!
My father, methinks I see my father.

HORATIO. O! where, my lord?

HAMLET.   In my mind's eye, Horatio.

eyes drop. Then, to emphasize her words, she walks slowly toward Hamlet, putting her hand on his shoulder in appeal. With infinite weariness he gives her his promise, his voice low and unemphatic. He bends his head and kisses her cheek. The King, delighted with winning his point, leads Gertrude off left, while Hamlet turns and bows to them in formal salutation.

As the doors close behind them the mask of manners that has protected Hamlet's face drops. Grief, disgust, loneliness, weigh down the cadence of his voice. He walks slowly upstage, every step a burden. At the left end of the table he turns and stands for a moment looking out. ' Weary, stale, flat, and unprofitable '— each word drops to a lower level of misery.

His mood is such that tears again are in his eyes, on his cheek. With ' That it should come to this ' he drops down on the top step of the left doorway. The whole movement of the speech up to this point has been slow, dragging, without objective. As he begins to think of his mother there is an acceleration of tempo. A note of physical repulsion, almost of nausea, creeps into his voice when he speaks of the marriage. His face is curdled with distaste. The image of his idealized father— ' So excellent a king '—makes the thought of the satyr who has taken his place in that intolerable intimacy unbearable. ' Let me not think on 't ' he cries in agony, covering his face with his hand. A long pause, then again the grinding mind thinks on—cannot stop thinking. ' A little month ' and so on in mounting fury until with the ' incestuous sheets,' that ' nest of vipers,' he spits out all his horror. A pause, and, with the last two lines, he sinks back into his apathy and hopeless sorrow.

The door opens on the right and Horatio and the two soldiers appear. At Horatio's word of greeting Hamlet's face takes on the look of dread which several times during the play comes over him as he realizes his privacy is about to be invaded by an outside force. Before our eyes we see his spirit shrink from the coming contact. He would be left alone in his own world, but again and again importunate voices,—his uncle's, this courtier's, later Polonius'

HORATIO. I saw him once; he was a goodly king.
HAMLET. He was a man, take him for all in all,
  I shall not look upon his like again.
HORATIO. My lord, I think I saw him yesternight.
HAMLET. Saw who?
HORATIO. My lord, the king your father.
HAMLET.   The king, my father!
HORATIO. Season your admiration for a while
  With an attent ear, till I may deliver,
  Upon the witness of these gentlemen,
  This marvel to you.
HAMLET.   For God's love, let me hear.
HORATIO. Two nights together had these gentlemen,
  Marcellus and Bernardo on their watch,
  In the dead vast and middle of the night,
  Been thus encounter'd: a figure like your father,
  Armed at points exactly, cap-a-pe,
  Appears before them, and with solemn march
  Goes slow and stately by them: thrice he walk'd
  By their oppress'd and fear-surprised eyes,
  Within his truncheon's length; whilst they, distill'd
  Almost to jelly with the act of fear,
  Stand dumb and speak not to him. This to me
  In dreadful secrecy impart they did,
  And I with them the third night kept the watch;
  Where, as they had deliver'd, both in time,
  Form of the thing, each word made true and good,
  The apparition comes. I knew your father;
  These hands are not more like.
HAMLET.   But where was this?
MARCELLUS. My lord, upon the platform where we watch'd.
HAMLET. Did you not speak to it?
HORATIO.   My lord, I did
  But answer made it none; yet once methought
  It lifted up its head and did address
  Itself to motion, like as it would speak;
  But even then the morning cock crew loud,
  And at the sound it shrunk in haste away
  And vanish'd from our sight.
HAMLET.   'Tis very strange.
HORATIO. As I do live, my honour'd lord, 'tis true;
  And we did think it writ down in our duty
  To let you know of it.
HAMLET. Indeed, indeed, sirs, but this troubles me.
  Hold you the watch to-night?

and the others'—insist on demanding his attention and response. ' I am glad to see you well,' is spoken in a conventional tone of greeting, before he turns, to see by whom he has been addressed.

When he realizes who it is he leaps to his feet with a cry and a new Hamlet comes to light. The eager young face is suddenly illuminated. He walks toward Horatio with a swift free stride, his whole body alert, both hands out in greeting. By ' And what make *you* from Wittenberg ' he has reached centre stage and grasps him by the arms. Then over Horatio's shoulder he greets Marcellus and Bernardo with a word and a nod before returning to the same question he is to ask Rosencrantz and Guildenstern later. What should anyone do in this prison, his voice implies—but the voice is warm and gay and the smile winning as he welcomes a true friend in whom he has confidence. With the reference to drinking deep the clouds gather again. He looks toward the left where his uncle has just gone out talking of revelry, and his voice twists as he speaks of his mother's wedding. The ' Thrift, thrift ' is biting, but the crest comes in that exclamation which is a key to so much in the play that is often forgotten—Hamlet's belief in ' something after death.' ' Would I had met my dearest foe in Heaven ' is the most unwelcome, the most devastating conjunction he can imagine. Nothing, except this marriage, can be worse than such an event. As Hamlet speaks the line we realize he means exactly what he says and will remember it later.

After this outburst there is a pause. He still stands facing Horatio centre stage, but his thought has shifted. His head turns almost imperceptibly. He looks off over Horatio's shoulder into the void of his own grief. Very quietly, in a tender almost brooding tone, he speaks the words that electrify the three who have just seen his father's ghost. Hamlet does not notice their startled looks, nor mark any particular intention in Horatio's question: ' O! where, my lord? ' He turns away from him and walks slowly across the stage to the stool, left, where he had sat at first, and drops down on it. Horatio's astonishing announcement falls on unhearing ears. Hamlet is in another world. There is a pause, then with a little

MARCELLUS.
BERNARDO. } We do, my lord.

HAMLET. Arm'd, say you?

MARCELLUS.
BERNARDO. } Arm'd, my lord.

HAMLET.   From top to toe?

MARCELLUS.
BERNARDO. } My lord, from head to foot.

HAMLET. Then saw you not his face?

HORATIO. O yes! my lord; he wore his beaver up.

HAMLET. What! look'd he frowningly?

HORATIO. A countenance more in sorrow than in anger.

HAMLET. Pale or red?

HORATIO. Nay, very pale.

HAMLET.   And fix'd his eyes upon you?

HORATIO. Most constantly.

HAMLET.   I would I had been there.

HORATIO. It would have much amaz'd you.

HAMLET. Very like, very like. Stay'd it long?

HORATIO. While one with moderate haste might tell a hundred.

MARCELLUS.
BERNARDO. } Longer, longer.

HORATIO. Not when I saw it.

HAMLET.   His beard was grizzled, no?

HORATIO. It was, as I have seen it in his life,
    A sable silver'd.

HAMLET.   I will watch to-night;
    Perchance 'twill walk again.

HORATIO.   I warrant it will.

HAMLET. If it assume my noble father's person,
    I'll speak to it, though hell itself should gape
    And bid me hold my peace. I pray you all,
    If you have hitherto conceal'd this sight,
    Let it be tenable in your silence still;
    And whatsoever else shall hap to-night,
    Give it an understanding, but no tongue:
    I will requite your loves. So, fare you well.
    Upon the platform, 'twixt eleven and twelve,
    I'll visit you.

ALL.   Our duty to your honour.

HAMLET. Your loves, as mine to you. Farewell.   [*Exeunt* HORATIO,
    My father's spirit in arms! all is not well;   MARCELLUS, *and* BERNARDO.
    I doubt some foul play: would the night were come!
    Till then sit still, my soul: foul deeds will rise,
    Though all the earth o'erwhelm them, to men's eyes.

effort, realizing that Horatio has spoken to him, he turns toward him with an almost automatic ' Saw? ' Then as we look at that upturned profile a whole cycle of movement takes place, holding us in breathless suspense. The impossible implication dawns on his mind. He leaps to his feet with a demand, a challenge—' Who? ' In answer to Horatio's words, he cries aloud ' The king, my father! ' and throws himself on Horatio, grasping him by the arms: ' For God's love, let me hear.'

Horatio describes the events on the platform while Hamlet follows his words with burning attention, his face a transparent screen covering his passionate listening. Though he hardly moves, the air seems to vibrate with his accelerated heartbeat. As Horatio speaks of the figure of the dead King walking by the sentries, Hamlet looks off, his imagination building the picture in the air. On ' The apparition comes ' Hamlet drops back a step and Horatio raises his two hands in emphatic gesture. With a swift stride Hamlet steps past him toward the other witnesses who have been standing on the right side of the stage. His impetuous question is to Marcellus, then he swings back to Horatio with urgent appeal: ' Did *you* not speak to it? ' The swift cross and turn, the white swordblade of his face flashing from one to the other as though he would cut to the heart of the mystery, make the invisible pulse of the scene beat faster.

Hamlet moves to the right hand of the table. Horatio is on his left, the two soldiers on his right. There is a pause as he looks out, gathering together the threads of what he has heard, holding the movement suspended as he weighs this portent. ' 'Tis very strange.' At Horatio's quick protests (Horatio remembers that he himself had denied the Ghost) Hamlet begins to return to the immediate issue. The ' Indeed, indeed, sirs, but this troubles me ' is still abstracted. Then he picks up the interrupted inquiry. He is alert, trenchant. Action is visibly taking shape in his mind. He is intent on extracting every detail, catching the witnesses in some contradiction that might weaken their argument.

Each of the questions is keen and practical, yet the words make his father's presence so vivid to him that they are charged with feeling. ' Pale or red? ' There is almost a tremor in the long-drawn ' pale.' It was so that Hamlet last saw him—marble pale in death—the sight still quivers in his voice. His hands lift towards Horatio as the image grows more distinct in his mind. ' And fix'd his eyes upon you? ' The inflection mounts, there is terror in the thought. A silence follows Horatio's answer as Hamlet again is caught by his vision. He stands looking forward. ' I would I had been there ' is an exhalation rather than a spoken word—addressed to no one, husky, without resonance. The ' Very like, very like ' in answer to Horatio's words is automatic. A pause. Then he pulls himself back from the awful, imagined communion.

Turning to the two on his right, he is again authoritative. His voice drives his questions home with increasing firmness. ' I will watch to-night ' rings with the exaltation of a solemn promise. With the words ' If it assume . . .' the terror of this thing which may be ghost or goblin damned is boldly faced. His body straightens. He dedicates himself to that ' noble father ' the thought of whom is always accompanied by a particular vocal tone, a *leit-motif* of admiration and love.

After ' hold my peace ' he stops a moment and then steps forward, drawing the three men to him in a sweeping gesture. He speaks with the command inherent in his position, then turns away, walking toward the doorway, left. His foot is on the step as they make their departing salutation. He turns quickly, reminded by their voices that he has been too absorbed in his own thought to express his appreciation of their devotion. The swift return from the door, his hand out to Horatio, the warm outgiving tone of protests and gratitude in ' Your loves, as mine to you ' is typical of the princely, gracious element in this much-harassed Hamlet which flashes again and again throughout his performance.

Alone on the stage he turns front, the pent-up effect of the revelation breaking out now that he need no longer watch himself in front of others. The menace of the situation has been growing in his mind—the words ' in arms ' are drawn out on a rising note fraught with danger. And ' would the night were come! ' is torn from his throat, harsh, desperate, high-pitched. The last two lines close the scene on a note sinister and full of horror that presages the imminent revelations. He walks slowly left as the lights black out.

Scene 3.—polonius' *house.* laertes *and* ophelia.

laertes. My necessaries are embark'd; farewell:
And, sister, as the winds give benefit
And convoy is assistant, do not sleep,
But let me hear from you.

ophelia.   Do you doubt that?

laertes. For Hamlet, and the trifling of his favour,
Hold it a fashion and a toy in blood,
A violet in the youth of primy nature,
Forward, not permanent, sweet, not lasting,
The perfume and suppliance of a minute;
No more.

ophelia. No more but so?

laertes.   Think it no more:
Perhaps he loves you now, but you must fear,
His greatness weigh'd, his will is not his own,
For he himself is subject to his birth;
He may not, as unvalu'd persons do,
Carve for himself, for on his choice depends
The safety and the health of the whole state;
Then weigh what loss your honour may sustain,
If with too credent ear you list his songs,
Or lose your heart, or your chaste treasure open
To his unmaster'd importunity.
Fear it, Ophelia, fear it, my dear sister;
And keep you in the rear of your affection,
Out of the shot and danger of desire.
[The chariest maid is prodigal enough
If she unmask her beauty to the moon.]

ophelia. I shall the effect of this good lesson keep,
As watchman to my heart. But, good my brother,
Do not, as some ungracious pastors do,
Show me the steep and thorny way to heaven,
Whiles, like a puff'd and reckless libertine,
Himself the primrose path of dalliance treads,
And recks not his own rede.

laertes.   O! fear me not.
I stay too long; but here my father comes.

                    Enter polonius.

(A double blessing is a double grace;
Occasion smiles upon a second leave.)

polonius. Yet here, Laertes! aboard, aboard, for shame!
The wind sits in the shoulder of your sail,

Scene 3: *Polonius' house.*

A room in Polonius' house is suggested by green tapestries cutting off the forestage. There are draped doorways left and right; a chair on the right, and a stool, left. Ophelia sits on the stool, her eyes on her embroidery, listening to her brother's sermonizing. Polonius enters from the right and Laertes meets him, center, dropping on his knee for the requested blessing. Polonius delivers his parting admonitions and sends him on his way with an affectionate salute. As Laertes leaves, picking up his cloak from the back of the chair on the right of the stage, Ophelia follows him to the exit, and then crosses again to her original position. Polonius sits down on the high-backed chair and proceeds to question her ' touching the Lord Hamlet.' Ophelia leaps to her feet in protest, when Polonius insists that the Prince's attentions are not to be taken seriously. ' He hath importun'd me with love in honourable fashion ' she exclaims indignantly and Polonius rises and goes to her with his impatient ' Springes to catch woodcocks.' The scene blacks out as Ophelia with a deep obeisance accepts her father's command to see no more of Hamlet.

And you are stay'd for. There, my blessing with thee!
And these few precepts in thy memory
Look thou character. Give thy thoughts no tongue,
Nor any unproportion'd thought his act.
Be thou familiar, but by no means vulgar;
The friends thou hast, and their adoption tried,
Grapple them to thy soul with hoops of steel;
But do not dull thy palm with entertainment
Of each new-hatch'd, unfledg'd comrade. Beware
Of entrance to a quarrel, but, being in,
Bear 't that th' opposed may beware of thee.
Give every man thine ear, but few thy voice;
Take each man's censure, but reserve thy judgment.
Costly thy habit as thy purse can buy,
But not express'd in fancy; rich, not gaudy;
For the apparel oft proclaims the man;
Neither a borrower, nor a lender be;
For loan oft loses both itself and friend,
And borrowing dulls the edge of husbandry.
This above all: to thine own self be true,
And it must follow, as the night the day,
Thou canst not then be false to any man.
Farewell; my blessing season this in thee!

LAERTES. Most humbly do I take my leave, my lord.

POLONIUS. The time invites you; go, your servants tend.

LAERTES. Farewell, Ophelia; and remember well
What I have said to you.

OPHELIA.   'Tis in my memory lock'd,
And you yourself shall keep the key of it.

LAERTES.   Farewell.   [*Exit.*

POLONIUS. What is 't, Ophelia, he hath said to you?

OPHELIA. So please you, something touching the Lord Hamlet.

POLONIUS. Marry, well bethought:
'Tis told me, he hath very oft of late
Given private time to you; and you yourself
Have of your audience been most free and bounteous.
If it be so,—[as so 'tis put on me,
And that in way of caution,]—I must tell you,
You do not understand yourself so clearly
As it behoves my daughter and your honour.
What is between you? give me up the truth.

OPHELIA. He hath, my lord, of late made many tenders
Of his affection to me.

POLONIUS. Affection! pooh! you speak like a green girl,
Unsifted in such perilous circumstance.

Do you believe his tenders, as you call them?

OPHELIA. I do not know, my lord, what I should think.

POLONIUS. Marry, I'll teach you: think yourself a baby,
That you have ta'en these tenders for true pay,
Which are not sterling. Tender yourself more dearly;
Or,—[not to crack the wind of the poor phrase,
Running it thus,]—you'll tender me a fool.

OPHELIA. My lord, he hath importun'd me with love
In honourable fashion.

POLONIUS. Ay, fashion you may call it: go to, go to.

OPHELIA. And hath given countenance to his speech, my lord,
With almost all the holy vows of heaven.

POLONIUS. Ay, springes to catch woodcocks. I do know,
When the blood burns, how prodigal the soul
Lends the tongue vows: these blazes, daughter,
Giving more light than heat, extinct in both,
(Even in their promise, as it is a-making,)
You must not take for fire. For Lord Hamlet,
Believe so much in him, that he is young,
And with a larger tether may he walk
Than may be given you: in few, Ophelia,
Do not believe his vows. This is for all:
I would not, in plain terms, from this time forth,
Have you so slander any moment's leisure,
As to give words or talk with the Lord Hamlet.
Look to 't, I charge you; come your ways.

OPHELIA. I shall obey, my lord.

SCENE 4.—*The Sentinel's platform before the royal castle.*
HAMLET, HORATIO, *and* MARCELLUS.

HAMLET. The air bites shrewdly; it is very cold.
HORATIO. It is a nipping and an eager air.
HAMLET. What hour now?
HORATIO.   I think it lacks of twelve.
MARCELLUS. No, it is struck.
HORATIO. Indeed? I heard it not: then it draws near the season
  Wherein the spirit held his wont to walk.
  What does this mean, my lord?
HAMLET. The king doth wake to-night and takes his rouse,
  Keeps wassail, and the swaggering up-spring reels;
  And, as he drains his draughts of Rhenish down,
  The kettle-drum and trumpet thus bray out
  The triumph of his pledge.
HORATIO.   Is it a custom?
HAMLET. Ay, marry, is 't:
  But to my mind,—though I am native here
  And to the manner born,—it is a custom
  More honour'd in the breach than the observance.
  This heavy-headed revel east and west
  Makes us traduc'd and tax'd of other nations;
  They clepe us drunkards. . . .
                    Enter Ghost.
HORATIO.   Look, my lord, it comes.
HAMLET. Angels and ministers of grace defend us!
  Be thou a spirit of health or goblin damn'd,
  Bring with thee airs from heaven or blasts from hell,
  Be thy intents wicked or charitable,
  Thou comest in such a questionable shape
  That I will speak to thee: I'll call thee Hamlet,
  King, father; royal Dane, O! answer me:
  Let me not burst in ignorance; but tell
  Why thy canoniz'd bones, hearsed in death,
  Have burst their cerements; why the sepulchre,
  Wherein we saw thee quietly inurn'd,
  Hath op'd his ponderous and marble jaws,
  To cast thee up again. What may this mean,
  That thou, dead corse, again in complete steel
  Revisit'st thus the glimpses of the moon,
  Making night hideous; and we fools of nature
  So horridly to shake our disposition
  With thoughts beyond the reaches of our souls?

Scene 4: *The sentinel's platform before the royal castle.*

Again the brooding night over Elsinore. Hamlet, Horatio and
Marcellus stand on the steps right: Horatio on the lowest, downstage step at the extreme right, Hamlet on the middle landing
nearer the centre, Marcellus half way up the stairs beyond Hamlet.
There is enough light to see Hamlet's strained face above the solid
mass of his long soldier's cloak. His voice is impatient; fear grips
at his throat. He pulls his cloak about him, cold with more than
the nipping air. At the sound of revelry from below and Horatio's
question he finds momentary release in caustic words concerning
his uncle. His voice slashes at Claudius. The accent is high on
' reels ' and Hamlet moves restlessly to and fro on the platform.

With ' Ay, marry, is 't ' he breaks into a swift swinging stride.
He strikes his clenched fist into his palm, warming his numb
hands, swinging the cloak about him—down two steps, up again
and across the landing almost out of sight into the wings, right.
Horatio, standing below and looking upstage watches his impatient
movements. Hamlet's tone is acid, but at the same time absent. He
is not thinking much of what he says, but his speech helps to cover
his inner preoccupation. The quick step and harsh quick words
are the outward sign of all that has been growing in him since he
heard of the Ghost, the tension that rises steadily, notch by notch,
like a tightened violin string till it cracks at the Ghost's departure.
The stage darkens; an ominous wind begins to blow. Hamlet's
pacing brings him opposite Horatio just as the Ghost appears high
on the left, coming down a circular stairway that clings to the
farther side of the left hand turret. Horatio sees it and interrupts
Hamlet's flow of invective. Hamlet is moving forward at the
moment so that his first knowledge of the presence is from Horatio's warning words. The sudden interruption of Hamlet's caged
pacing catches the breath. There is an instant of immobility—
' the rack stands still.'

Then Hamlet turns slowly, slowly, toward the thing at which
Horatio is staring. As the ' eyes of his flesh ' at last see this awful

Say, why is this? wherefore? what should we do?

HORATIO. It beckons you to go away with it,
As if it some impartment did desire
To you alone.

MARCELLUS. Look, with what courteous action
It waves you to a more removed ground:
But do not go with it.

HORATIO.   No, by no means.

HAMLET. It will not speak; then will I follow it.

HORATIO. Do not, my lord.

HAMLET.   Why, what should be the fear?
I do not set my life at a pin's fee;
And for my soul, what can it do to that,
Being a thing immortal as itself?
It waves me forth again; I'll follow it.

HORATIO. What if it tempt you toward the flood, my lord,
Or to the dreadful summit of the cliff
That beetles o'er his base into the sea,
And there assume some other horrible form,
Which might deprive your sovereignty of reason
And draw you into madness?

HAMLET. It waves me still. Go on, I'll follow thee.

MARCELLUS. You shall not go, my lord.

HAMLET.   Hold off your hands!

HORATIO. Be rul'd; you shall not go.

HAMLET.   My fate cries out,
And makes each petty artery in this body
As hardy as the Nemean lion's nerve.
Still am I call'd. Unhand me, gentlemen,
By heaven! I'll make a ghost of him that lets me:
I say, away! Go on, I'll follow thee.   [*Blackout.*

[HORATIO. He waxes desperate with imagination.
Have after. To what issue will this come?

MARCELLUS. Something is rotten in the state of Denmark.

HORATIO. Heaven will direct it.

MARCELLUS.   Nay, let 's follow him.]

HAMLET. Whither wilt thou lead me? speak; I'll go no further.

GHOST. Mark me.

HAMLET.   I will.

GHOST.   My hour is almost come,
When I to sulphurous and tormenting flames
Must render up myself.

HAMLET.   Alas! poor ghost.

GHOST. Pity me not, but lend thy serious hearing
To what I shall unfold.

visitation with which his imagination has been dwelling for so many hours, his overwrought nerves for an instant betray him. He whirls away, hurling himself into Horatio's arms. ' Angels and ministers of grace ' is addressed to the only power that could possibly help in this desperate need. A pause, then slowly he straightens up. His courage, his intention, his will are one. He turns and leaving behind him the comfort and support of human companionship he walks up the stairs toward the vision. With ' I will speak to thee ' he has reached the upper central platform. The Ghost is still on the turret stairs above him as he addresses to it the adjuration ' I'll call thee Hamlet, King, *father* . . . ' sinking to his knee and holding out his hand in appeal.

The upturned face is suspended in mist, the kneeling figure, with outstretched arm, is dark against the dark. Quietly now, the shock relieved by a fronted reality, the deep underlying emotion takes possession of him and moulds the words of this great speech, one of the most beautiful sequences of sound ever invented, into pure harmony. The music swells through the sculptured beauty of those magnificent phrases—' canoniz'd bones,' ' hearsed in death,' ' quietly inurn'd,' ' ponderous and marble jaws,' to a first climax in ' What may this mean,' drops again and reaches a new and different intensity in the ' fools of nature ' line with the subsequent anguished ' wherefore? what should we do? '

The Ghost begins to move, and Hamlet, still kneeling, seems to follow it with his whole being. Horatio speaks and walks up the right hand stairs toward Hamlet. As Marcellus joins him, Hamlet starts toward the Ghost, who has come down the turret stairs and begun to move slowly down the main left flight. Hamlet's first ' then will I follow it ' is spoken in a quiet, hypnotized voice, but when Horatio tries to stop him he comes back to reality,—his tone harsh and impatient. Then as the Ghost moves on he stares after it, scarcely listening to Horatio's protests, again caught up by its mysterious power as the awed tones of ' I'll follow thee ' indicate.

The two men close in on him and the spell is broken. He struggles

HAMLET.   Speak; I am bound to hear.

GHOST. So art thou to revenge, when thou shalt hear.

HAMLET. What?

GHOST. I am thy father's spirit;
    Doom'd for a certain term to walk the night,
    And for the day confin'd to fast in fires,
    Till the foul crimes done in my days of nature
    Are burnt and purg'd away. [But that I am forbid
    To tell the secrets of my prison-house,
    I could a tale unfold whose lightest word
    Would harrow up thy soul, freeze thy young blood,
    Make thy two eyes, like stars, start from their spheres,
    Thy knotted and combined locks to part,
    And each particular hair to stand on end,
    Like quills upon the fretful porpentine:
    But this eternal blazon must not be
    To ears of flesh and blood.] List, list, O list
    If thou didst ever thy dear father love—

HAMLET. O God!

GHOST. Revenge his foul and most unnatural murder.

HAMLET. Murder!

GHOST. Murder most foul, as in the best it is;
    But this most foul, strange, and unnatural.

HAMLET. Haste me to know 't, that I, with wings as swift
    As meditation or the thoughts of love,
    May sweep to my revenge.

GHOST.   I find thee apt;
    [And duller shouldst thou be than the fat weed
    That rots itself in ease on Lethe wharf,
    Wouldst thou not stir in this. Now,] Hamlet, hear:
    'Tis given out that, sleeping in mine orchard,
    A serpent stung me; so the whole ear of Denmark
    Is by a forged process of my death
    Rankly abus'd; but know, thou noble youth,
    The serpent that did sting thy father's life
    Now wears his crown.

HAMLET.   O my prophetic soul!
    My uncle!

GHOST. Ay, that incestuous, that adulterate beast,
    With witchcraft of his wit, with traitorous gifts,—
    [O wicked wit and gifts, that have the power
    So to seduce!]—won to his shameful lust
    The will of my most seeming-virtuous queen.
    [But, soft! methinks I scent the morning air;]
    Brief let me be. Sleeping within mine orchard,

in their hands, his body bent toward the Ghost as though it dragged him by an invisible cord. 'My fate cries out!' is hard and high. The violence of his voice is matched by the swift strength of his gesture as he throws off the two men. A swirl of black folds, the flash of a sword, and Hamlet stands alone on the platform.

'Go on; I'll follow thee.' The voice has changed completely from the bluster of the struggle. The Ghost moves down the steps and Hamlet, his sword held up before him point downward, the cross of the hilt in his hand, walks slowly after him. A complete blackout. Then the spot picks up the Ghost moving toward the right on the main stage.

Hamlet's voice comes from the dark at the foot of the left hand stairs. He is at the end of his endurance. 'Speak; I'll go no further.' He is moving forward toward centre stage when a voice from the void whispers 'Mark me.' Hamlet stops, swaying a little from the impact of that dread sound. 'I will'—breathed out, almost a gasp. The apparition stands motionless, stage right, its back to the audience. It is preternaturally tall. Hamlet must look up to it throughout. The voice comes from space.

As the Ghost speaks its first words, Hamlet's face becomes the focal point of light in an enveloping darkness. Every word the Ghost says is reflected on it. The colloquy seems to be carried on phrase by phrase between the speaker and the listener. Actually Hamlet speaks only five times after the Ghost starts his story, yet the interchange is continuous and mounting in intensity.

Once he has recovered from hearing this 'bodiless creation' actually speak, Hamlet's first movement is of pity. 'Alas! poor ghost.' The tender tone with which the words are uttered brings out another facet of Hamlet's character. He sees the Ghost, now that he is actually face to face with it, not as a menace, a goblin damned, or even as his dead father's troubled spirit—but as a help-less, pitiful thing. The Ghost's stern words galvanize him, and he straightens up to receive the message. 'Speak; I am *bound* to hear.' As the Ghost begins his story, Hamlet's right hand with the sword drops slowly; he leans forward listening with increasing

My custom always in the afternoon,
Upon my secure hour thy uncle stole,
With juice of cursed hebona in a vial,
And in the porches of mine ears did pour
The leperous distilment; whose effect
Holds such an enmity with blood of man
That swift as quicksilver it courses through
The natural gates and alleys of the body,
Thus was I, sleeping, by a brother's hand,
Of life, of crown, of queen, at once dispatch'd;
Cut off even in the blossoms of my sin,
Unhousel'd, disappointed, unanel'd,
No reckoning made, but sent to my account
With all my imperfections on my head:

HAMLET. O, horrible! O, horrible! most horrible!

GHOST. If thou hast nature in thee, bear it not;
Let not the royal bed of Denmark be
A couch for luxury and damned incest.
But, howsoever thou pursuest this act,
Taint not thy mind, nor let thy soul contrive
Against thy mother aught; leave her to heaven,
And to those thorns that in her bosom lodge,
To prick and sting her. Fare thee well at once!
The glow-worm shows the matin to be near,
And 'gins to pale his uneffectual fire;
Adieu, adieu! Hamlet, remember me.   [*Exit.*

HAMLET. O all you host of heaven! O earth! What else?
And shall I couple hell? O fie! Hold, hold, my heart!
And you, my sinews, grow not instant old,
But bear me stiffly up! Remember thee!
Ay, thou poor ghost, while memory holds a seat
In this distracted globe. Remember thee!
Yea, from the table of my memory
I'll wipe away all trivial fond records,
All saws of books, all forms, all pressures past,
That youth and observation copied there;
And thy commandment all alone shall live
Within the book and volume of my brain,
Unmix'd with baser matter: yes, by heaven
O most pernicious woman!
O villain, villain, smiling, damned villain!
My tables,—meet it is I set it down,
That one may smile, and smile, and be a villain;
At least I'm sure it may be so in Denmark:
So, uncle, there you are. Now to my word;

horror to the tale of the Ghost's suffering. His left hand comes up as though warding off the words. The thought of his father ' confin'd to fast in fires ' tortures him. On top of that the adjuration ' If thou didst ever thy dear father love—' is too much. His ' O God! ' is a passionate protest, but it is suspended, short. He does not wish to interrupt the Ghost's tale.

The next line reveals in one word the secret of the menace that broods over Elsinore. ' *Murder!* ' Hamlet listens to it for a palpable moment before his reluctant mind will accept its full significance. He steps back and the sword, no longer held as a cross, but firmly, ready for action, gleams in his right hand. As the Ghost speaks, Hamlet's body vibrates with the fury that the news pours into him. With ' Haste me to know 't ' it breaks into speech and his action, starting at the centre of his being, explodes in dynamic movement on ' *sweep* to my revenge.' But violent as is his gesture, arm up, the whole line from foot to hand a bow drawn taut, his attention remains riveted on the Ghost. As the revelation continues his arm drops. He listens, holding himself in check as best he can so as not to lose a syllable.

A hatred already existing, grounded in a multitude of causes known and others sensed, swells to the fury of ' O my prophetic soul! My uncle! ' as Hamlet hears the tale of the garden and the poisoning. ' Unhousel'd, disappointed, unanel'd—.' Hamlet would indeed burst were he not able to cry out ' O, horrible! O, horrible! most horrible! ' The other, deeper wound that has seared his soul has yet to be touched. The Ghost's next words drive straight to the quick. Hamlet draws back as from the mouth of a pit. The thought of his mother and the murderer together stirs again the depths of his disgust. His left hand rises to choke back the strangled, tearing exclamation that breaks from him on the Ghost's words of ' damned incest.'

The dawn is coming and the Ghost moves slowly toward the right. Hamlet sinks to his knees, his left hand out in supplication. His body bent forward, he strains after the fading figure. The lights black out during a deathly pause. Then as they come on

It is, ' Adieu, adieu! remember me.'
I have sworn 't.

HORATIO. [*Within.*] My lord! my lord!

MARCELLUS. [*Within.*]   Lord Hamlet!

HORATIO. [*Within.*]   Heaven secure him.

HAMLET. So be it!

HORATIO. [*Within.*] Hillo, ho ho, my lord!

HAMLET. Hillo, ho, ho, boy! come, bird, come.

           Enter HORATIO *and* MARCELLUS.

MARCELLUS. How is 't, my noble lord?

HORATIO.   What news, my lord?

HAMLET. O! wonderful.

HORATIO.   Good my lord, tell it.

HAMLET. No; you will reveal it.

HORATIO. Not I, my lord, by heaven!

MARCELLUS.   Nor I, my lord.

HAMLET. How say you, then; would heart of man once think it?
But you'll be secret?

HORATIO.   }
MARCELLUS. }   Ay, by heaven, my lord.

HAMLET. There 's ne'er a villain dwelling in all Denmark,
But he 's an arrant knave.

HORATIO. There needs no ghost, my lord, come from the grave,
To tell us this.

HAMLET.   Why, right; you are i' the right;
And so, without more circumstance at all,
I hold it fit that we shake hands and part;
You, as your business and desire shall point you,—
For every man hath business and desire,
Such as it is,—and, for mine own poor part,
Look you, I'll go pray.

HORATIO. These are but wild and whirling words, my lord.

HAMLET. I am sorry they offend you, heartily;
Yes, faith, heartily.

HORATIO.   There 's no offence, my lord.

HAMLET. Yes, by Saint Patrick, but there is, Horatio,
And much offence, too. Touching this vision here,
It is an honest ghost, that let me tell you;
For your desire to know what is between us,
O'ermaster 't as you may. And now, good friends,
As you are friends, scholars, and soldiers,
Give me one poor request.

HORATIO. What is 't, my lord? we will.

HAMLET. Never make known what you have seen to-night.

again, faintly illuminating the whole scene, Hamlet's cry to heaven rings out and he throws himself on the ground. The taut wire, strung too high, has broken. His body is shaken with sobs, his voice torn and ragged. There is a sort of animal wail of pain in his first exclamation. With ' And shall I couple hell? ' anger begins to galvanize him once again. He turns on himself, self-lacerating, driving unpityingly a body wracked by the impact of the primal emotions of this encounter. The physical paralysis that comes when the immediate cause of an emotion as profound as this is removed shows itself in his labored movements as, little by little, he raises himself on one knee. He is bruised, beaten; only his will remains and forces him up, governing even the ' distracted globe ' which is indeed overburdened to the verge of frenzy.

'Ay, thou poor ghost' brings again the note of tenderness and pity, pity for the dead and for his father in his torment. The second ' Remember thee! ' is an oath. The words that follow come quickly, rising in a swift crescendo of dedication to the final ' yes, by heaven ' which brings him to his feet. A pause, and then the infamy sweeps over him. ' O most pernicious woman! ' His first thought, even before Claudius and murder, is of her. Then his mind turns to Claudius—to the morning scene of flattery and smug smiles, to the laughter and revelry below at this very moment. His voice breaks with anger at such villainy. He moves to the right, almost to the spot where the Ghost had stood. On the tablet from which he has just wiped all ' trivial fond records,' on his brain seared by the Ghost's revelations, he will register this shame. The phrase ends on a high, hard challenge: ' So, uncle, there you are,' as he strikes his forehead with his hand.

Then, deep and very quiet, the oath of consecration, ' Now to my word.' Both hands clasp the sword-hilt. The blade gleams in an arc as he raises it to his lips. He stands straight as a lance, the silver line above his head piercing heavenward in salute. Slowly, with finality, with full and weary prescience, he lowers the sword, ' I have sworn 't.'

The voices of Horatio and Marcellus are heard off left. Hamlet

HORATIO.
MARCELLUS. } My lord, we will not.

HAMLET.   Nay, but swear 't.

HORATIO.   In faith,
My lord, not I.

MARCELLUS.   Nor I, my lord, in faith.

HAMLET. Upon my sword.

MARCELLUS.   We have sworn, my lord, already.

HAMLET. Indeed, upon my sword, indeed.

GHOST. [*Beneath.*] Swear.

HAMLET. Ah, ha, boy! say'st thou so? art thou there, true-penny?
Come on,—you hear this fellow in the cellarage,—
Consent to swear.

HORATIO.   Propose the oath, my lord.

HAMLET. Never to speak of this that you have seen,
Swear by my sword.

GHOST. [*Beneath.*] Swear.

HAMLET. Hic et ubique? then we'll shift our ground.
Come hither, gentlemen,
And lay your hands again upon my sword:
Never to speak of this that you have heard,
Swear by my sword.

GHOST. [*Beneath.*] Swear.

HAMLET. Well said, old mole! canst work i' the earth so fast?
A worthy pioner! once more remove, good friends.

HORATIO. O day and night, but this is wondrous strange!

HAMLET. And therefore as a stranger give it welcome.
There are more things in heaven and earth, Horatio,
Than are dreamt of in your philosophy.
But come;
Here, as before, never, so help you mercy,
How strange or odd soe'er I bear myself,
As I perchance hereafter shall think meet
To put an antic disposition on,
That you, at such times seeing me, never shall,
With arms encumber'd thus, or this head-shake,
Or by pronouncing of some doubtful phrase,
As, ' Well, well, we know,' or, ' We could, an if we would,'
Or, ' If we list to speak,' or, ' There be, an if they might,'
Or such ambiguous giving out, to note
That you know aught of me: this not to do,
So grace and mercy at your most need help you,
Swear.

GHOST. [*Beneath.*] Swear.   [*They swear.*

HAMLET. Rest, rest, perturbed spirit! So, gentlemen,

scarcely hears them. He sways forward over his sword, putting a final period on his secret dedication—' So be it! ' The voices become insistent. With an effort he drags himself back from the pit over which he leans. His shattered nerves are lashed into action. He shouts a falconer's cry in answer to Horatio's halloo and leaps across the stage, throwing himself upon that stalwart friend as he appears, followed by Marcellus, on the middle landing, left. Hamlet, two steps below, his upturned face wild with excitement, his words tumbling out, starts to tell Horatio what has happened. The revelation, so fresh, so convincing as it concerns the hated Claudius, is about to burst from him when he realizes that these things cannot be told. He checks himself with ' But you'll be secret? ' Horatio's protest and his own excitement start him again. ' There's ne'er a villain . . .' rising almost to a shout on ' Denmark.' But Marcellus, hanging on the revelation, moves. Hamlet stops himself in mid-sentence, drops back, his words choked in his throat, his voice falling brokenly as he turns away.

In his effort at control he becomes brusque. He must have some veneer of protection against prying eyes. For the moment he merely denies, tries to escape until he can think again. Horatio's common-sense protest, ' There needs no ghost, my lord,' pricks him to a sharp reply and gives him an excuse to break away from a too dangerous interchange. Swinging toward the two men again he sheathes his sword and starts up the stairs between them, giving his left hand to Horatio, his right to Marcellus.

He is a step or two above Horatio when he stops and looks down at him over his left shoulder: ' For every man hath business and desires . . .' The words are a poignant reminder of Hamlet's own life, blighted in its prime. We are suddenly made to see by the intonation of the voice, by the poised, downward glance of that strained face, all the pathos of youth denied its occupations, the normal fulfillment of its healthy impulses and appetites. Hamlet turns away, his black figure swallowed by darkness as he walks on up the stairs on ' Look you, I'll go pray.'

Horatio, puzzled by the quick alternations of Hamlet's mood,

With all my love I do commend me to you:
And what so poor a man as Hamlet is
May do, to express his love and friending to you,
God willing, shall not lack. Let us go in together;
And still your fingers on your lips, I pray.
The time is out of joint; O cursed spite,
That ever I was born to set it right!
Nay, come, let's go together.

The Sentinel's Platform

SCENE 4

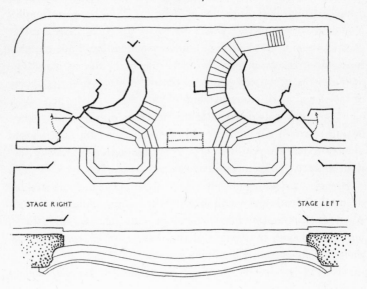

STAGE RIGHT   STAGE LEFT

looks after him, troubled and rebuffed. Nor does Hamlet's cold
' I'm sorry they offend you ' in answer to his protest against ' wild
and whirling words ' reassure him. With Horatio's ' There's no
offence, my lord ' to the retreating figure, Hamlet's hard-won
controls snaps. No offence, indeed! It smells to Heaven. It reeks
in Hamlet's nostrils. He whirls down the stairs, gripping the
astonished Horatio by the arm. Then he realizes that he cannot
leave the situation unexplained. The startled faces of the two men
who have to some extent shared this secret remind him that, somehow, he must silence them. Horatio he will trust—his first impulse
was to tell him—but Marcellus must be both frightened and hood-
winked into secrecy.

He demands the oath at first in the quiet and somewhat peremp-
tory tone of a prince. ' Indeed, upon my sword, indeed.' He
draws his sword and holds it out between them, as they stand all
three on the middle landing, left. As the ominous ' Swear ' comes
from the ' cellarage ' Hamlet's agitation breaks out again, but at the
same time his intention is clear. Marcellus must be deceived. Hamlet
addressed the Ghost this time not as his father's spirit but as a
demon, a familiar. (It is pertinent that throughout the play Hamlet
himself is not sure which it is.) The voice from the air, from the
ground, striking at his overstrained emotions drives him into ex-
travagance. He is caught up, carried along in the whirl of his
own excitement. He sweeps the two men with him into the centre
of the stage, where, back to the audience, he demands the second
oath. As the whispered ' Swear ' is heard again, this time almost
beneath his feet, he turns around on himself, looking down with
a macabre half-laugh. Then he waves them on to the foot of the
right stairway, where once again the oath is proposed.

Horatio's protesting ' O day and night, but this is wondrous
strange! ' halts Hamlet. Standing on the middle landing he looks
down on Horatio, laying his hand on his shoulder, his voice calmer
but charged with the weight of the undreamed-of strangeness of
the secret he is carrying. ' There are more things in heaven and
earth . . .' Then the third oath, and with it the idea which

Horatio himself has given him with his talk of whirling words, the idea latent in the half-intended, half-accidental mystification of Marcellus. On ' How strange . . . soe'er I bear myself ' his left hand goes out, in a movement of wrist and finger outlining an antic gesture. The two men lay their hands once more upon the hilt of his sword while he puts his own on theirs.

As the Ghost's parting admonition fades on the air, Hamlet leans forward over the sword. The four words that follow ' Rest, rest, perturbed spirit! ' are spoken very quietly in a falling cadence of exquisite beauty. All Hamlet's love for his father, his grief for his death and the manner of it, but more than that, the pathos of death itself, the pity of the living for the dead, echo through this single line.

Horatio and Marcellus step back. Hamlet's voice changes to the accent of his usual speech. For the moment he is calm. He steps down from the stairs as he dismisses the two, who move toward the left. Hamlet, still at the right of the stage, stands alone, looking out. His voice is harsh with fatigue. His body sags. ' O cursed spite, that ever I was born to set it right! ' Both hands clasp the sword, holding it awkwardly before him, his knees bend, almost collapsing. He shivers with cold and exhaustion. Horatio, who has stopped centre stage turns and looks at him. Then swinging the russet lined cloak from his own shoulder he wraps it around Hamlet who gropes for the edges, drawing it automatically around him. He lays his drawn sword in the crook of his left arm as he turns, walking head bowed toward the left. He has taken several steps before he realizes that Horatio stands cloakless and silent behind him. Hamlet stops, swings around with a movement that brings him above Horatio. His right arm with the cloak sweeps over Horatio's shoulders in an enveloping gesture of trust and affection. Horatio falls into step beside him and they move off side by side toward the left as the lights black out.

SCENE 5.—POLONIUS' *house.* [POLONIUS *and* REYNALDO.

POLONIUS. Give him this money and these notes, Reynaldo.
REYNALDO. I will, my lord.
POLONIUS. You shall do marvellous wisely, good Reynaldo,
    Before you visit him, to make inquiry
    Of his behaviour.
REYNALDO.   My lord, I did intend it.
POLONIUS. Observe his inclination in yourself,
    And let him ply his music.
REYNALDO.   Well, my lord.
POLONIUS. Farewell!   [*Exit* REYNALDO.
                 Enter OPHELIA.
               How now, Ophelia! what 's the matter?
OPHELIA. Alas! my lord, I have been so affrighted.
POLONIUS. With what, in the name of God?
OPHELIA. My lord, as I was sewing in my closet,
    Lord Hamlet, with his doublet all unbrac'd;
    No hat upon his head; his stockings foul'd,
    Ungarter'd, and down-gyved to his ankle;
    Pale as his shirt; his knees knocking each other;
    And with a look so piteous in purport
    As if he had been loosed out of hell
    To speak of horrors, he comes before me.
POLONIUS. Mad for thy love?
OPHELIA.   My lord, I do not know;
    But truly I do fear it.
POLONIUS.   What said he?
OPHELIA. He took me by the wrist and held me hard,
    Then goes he to the length of all his arm,
    And, with his other hand thus o'er his brow,
    He falls to such perusal of my face
    As he would draw it. Long stay'd he so;
    At last, a little shaking of mine arm,
    And thrice his head thus waving up and down,
    He rais'd a sigh so piteous and profound
    That it did seem to shatter all his bulk
    And end his being. That done, he lets me go,
    And, with his head over his shoulder turn'd,
    He seem'd to find his way without his eyes;
    For out o' doors he went without their help,
    And to the last bended their light on me.
POLONIUS. This is the very ecstasy of love. I am sorry.
    What! have you given him any hard words of late?

SCENE 5. *Polonius' house.*

Ophelia rushes in from the right, terrified. She throws herself on her knees in front of her father, who sits on a chair at the left, and pours out her tale of a Hamlet ' pale as his shirt; his knees knocking each other ' very much as we last saw him on the parapet. The look of one ' loosed out of hell ' is a reminder of the state of mind in which Hamlet has dwelt during the time that has elapsed, almost two months, since the Ghost's as yet unconfirmed revelation. Ophelia's pitiful inadequacy, her inability to understand Hamlet's desperate need, her complete dependence on her father and submission to his will are clearly drawn in this scene. Polonius bustles off to give the King and Queen news of what he considers his great discovery—the secret of Hamlet's ' antic disposition.' The lights black out to come up almost immediately on

OPHELIA. No, my good lord; but, as you did command,
    I did repel his letters and denied
    His access to me.
POLONIUS.   That hath made him mad.
    I am sorry that with better heed and judgment
    I had not quoted him; I fear'd he did but trifle,
    And meant to wrack thee: come, go we to the king:
    This must be known; [which, being kept close, might move
    More grief to hide than hate to utter love.]
    Come.

The Council Chamber
SCENE 6

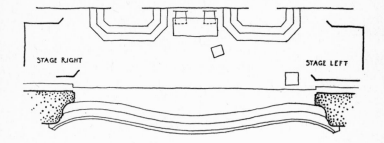

STAGE RIGHT   STAGE LEFT

SCENE 6.—*The council chamber in the castle.* KING, QUEEN, ROSEN-
CRANTZ, GUILDENSTERN, *and Attendants.*

KING. Welcome, dear Rosencrantz and Guildenstern!
Moreover that we much did long to see you,
The need we have to use you did provoke
Our hasty sending. Something have you heard
Of Hamlet's transformation. What it should be
More than his father's death, that thus hath put him
So much from the understanding of himself,
I cannot dream of: I entreat you both,
[That, being of so young days brought up with him,
And since so neighbour'd to his youth and humour,]
That you vouchsafe your rest here in our court
Some little time; so by your companies
To draw him on to pleasures, and to gather,
Whe'r aught to us unknown afflicts him thus,
That, open'd, lies within our remedy.

QUEEN. Good gentlemen, he hath much talk'd of you;
And sure I am two men there are not living
To whom he more adheres. If it will please you
To show us so much gentry and good will
As to expend your time with us awhile,
For the supply and profit of our hope,
Your visitation shall receive such thanks
As fits a king's remembrance.

ROSENCRANTZ.   Both your majesties
Might, by the sovereign power you have of us,
Put your dread pleasures more into command
Than to entreaty.

GUILDENSTERN.   But we both obey,
And here give up ourselves, in the full bent,
To lay our service freely at your feet,
To be commanded.

KING. Thanks, Rosencrantz and gentle Guildenstern.

QUEEN. Thanks, Guildenstern and gentle Rosencrantz;
And I beseech you instantly to visit
My too much changed son. Go, some of you,
And bring these gentlemen where Hamlet is.

GUILDENSTERN. Heavens make our presence, and our practices
Pleasant and helpful to him!

QUEEN.   Ay, amen!
                    [*Exeunt* ROSENCRANTZ, GUILDENSTERN, *and Attendants.*
                        Enter POLONIUS.

SCENE 6. *The council chamber in the castle.*

The King and Queen stand resplendent in the open doorway, left, courtiers and attendants about them; below; on either side, Rosencrantz and Guildenstern listen respectfully to the King's noble phrases about Hamlet's madness and his own deep concern. Claudius' ' What it should be more than his father's death . . . I cannot dream of ' is one of those swift strokes of irony in which the play abounds. The Queen takes up the tale, sweeping down between the two young men, and turning her back to the audience as she addresses them. With their dismissal the King and Queen are left alone to greet Polonius, who enters from the right. He comes to tell of the return of the ambassadors sent to Norway, but principally to impart his news about Hamlet. The Queen sits at the right end of the council table, Polonius on her right, the King opposite and to the left, as Polonius reads the famous letter.

With the words ' How may we try it further? ' Claudius leaves his place and walks thoughtfully away from the table toward the left, Polonius in his wake. The Queen also rises and starts toward them, so that all three are facing left and do not notice the right door swing open and Hamlet, book in hand, start down the step, only to leap back as he sees that the room is occupied. He is closing the door when his ear catches the phrase ' I'll loose my daughter to him ' on the lips of Ophelia's father. He stands a fraction of an instant, transfixed, as the plot against him is outlined in a phrase. Then he draws back, closing the door silently. But the Queen has heard something. With a swift ' Hush ' she moves toward the right. By the time she reaches the door Hamlet is at some distance, dawdling down the lobby stairs.

As he comes through the doorway right, the King and Queen hurry out the opposite exit, leaving Polonius to address the Prince, who by now has entered, closing the door carefully behind him. His antic pretence is in full swing, and the overheard plot has given it an edge of malice. He walks down the steps and across the stage, ignoring Polonius. His right hand is on the top of his head,

POLONIUS. The ambassadors from Norway, my good lord,
   Are joyfully return'd.
KING. Thou still hast been the father of good news.
POLONIUS. Have I, my lord? Assure you, my good liege,
   I hold my duty, as I hold my soul,
   Both to my God and to my gracious king;
   And I do think—[or else this brain of mine
   Hunts not the trail of policy so sure
   As it hath us'd to do] that I have found
   The very cause of Hamlet's lunacy.
KING. O! speak of that; that do I long to hear.
   [He tells me, my sweet queen, that he hath found
   The head and source of all your son's distemper.]
QUEEN. I doubt it is no other but the main;
   His father's death, and our o'erhasty marriage.
POLONIUS. My liege, and madam, to expostulate
   What majesty should be, what duty is,
   Why day is day, night night, and time is time,
   Were nothing but to waste night, day, and time.
   Therefore, since brevity is the soul of wit,
   And tediousness the limbs and outward flourishes,
   I will be brief. Your noble son is mad:
   Mad call I it; for, to define true madness,
   What is 't but to be nothing else but mad?
   But let that go.
QUEEN.   More matter, with less art.
POLONIUS. Madam, I swear I use no art at all.
   That he is mad, 'tis true; 'tis true 'tis pity;
   And pity 'tis 'tis true: a foolish figure;
   But farewell it, for I will use no art.
   I have a daughter, have while she is mine;
   Who, in her duty and obedience, mark,
   Hath given me this: now, gather, and surmise.
   ' To the celestial, and my soul's idol, the most beautified Ophelia.'—
   That 's an ill phrase, a vile phrase; ' beautified ' is a vile phrase; but you
      shall hear. Thus:
   ' In her excellent white bosom, these, &c.'—
QUEEN. Came this from Hamlet to her?
POLONIUS. Good madam, stay awhile; I will be faithful.
                     ' Doubt thou the stars are fire;
                        Doubt that the sun doth move;
                        Doubt truth to be a liar;
                        But never doubt I love.
   ' O dear Ophelia! I am ill at these numbers: I have not art to reckon
   my groans; but that I love thee best, O most best! believe it. Adieu.

his blond hair in disorder, his gait is subtly stagy. The black tunic with its slashed sleeves has been left unbuttoned at the neck, showing a white, ruffled shirt. The ribbons at his knees are untied. His movements are deliberately jerky; stride, gesture and mock absorption in his book throw into contrast Polonius' solemn and slightly alarmed reception of these portents. Hamlet strides past him, eyes glued to the little book he holds in his left hand. Turning on his heel he swings back again with an absent-minded ' Well, God-a-mercy ' only to stop abruptly in mid-career on Polonius' demand for recognition.

Hamlet looks him up and down with a withering glance which would have warned a wiser man to beware, then tosses the barbed ' fishmonger ' phrase at him and resumes his pacing. The word ' honest ' echoed by Polonius brings him up short and he turns toward him, back to the audience, with an expressive gesture of the right arm and hand, picking that one man out of ten thousand, holding him for a moment with voice, thumb and forefinger for the ' honest fishmonger ' to contemplate. Then with a sudden full swing toward Polonius he fixes the startled old man with his glittering eye. 'For if the sun breed maggots ' starts wildly enough but ends with deadly intention. ' Have you a daughter? '

The antic disposition is allowing Hamlet to uncork his animosity and to amuse himself, bitterly enough, at Polonius' expense. Bitterness predominates, since he has just learned that Polonius is as bad as the rest—one with the King and Queen in this sty of corruption which is the court of Denmark. Even Ophelia is perhaps not merely uncomprehending as she seemed in the morning's visitation which she herself has just described; perhaps she also is tainted with the general infection. At any rate he will badger the old fox a bit. With ' Conception is a blessing . . .' he walks slowly around Polonius, stalking him, his head thrust forward, a sardonic solemnity in his warning forefinger. ' Friend, look to 't .' He holds the old man for a moment, eye to eye, as he stands on his left, having completed the circuit, then drops him in disgust and moves on toward the left end of the council table.

' Thine evermore, most dear lady, whilst this machine
is to him,
' HAMLET.'

This in obedience hath my daughter shown me;
And more above, hath his solicitings,
As they fell out by time, by means, and place,
All given to mine ear.

KING.   But how hath she
Receiv'd his love?

POLONIUS.   What do you think of me?

KING. As of a man faithful and honourable.

POLONIUS. I would fain prove so. I went round to work,
And my young mistress thus I did bespeak:
' Lord Hamlet is a prince, out of thy star;
This must not be: ' and then I precepts gave her,
That she should lock herself from his resort,
Admit no messengers, receive no tokens.
Which done, she took the fruits of my advice;
And he, repulsed, [—a short tale to make,—]
Fell [into a sadness, then into a fast,
Thence to a watch, thence into a weakness,
Thence to a lightness; and by this declension]
Into the madness wherein now he raves,
And all we wail for.

KING.   Do you think 'tis this?

QUEEN. It may be, very likely.

POLONIUS. Hath there been such a time,—I'd fain know that,—
That I have positively said, ' 'Tis so,'
When it prov'd otherwise?

KING.   Not that I know.

POLONIUS. Take this from this, if this be otherwise:

KING. How may we try it further?

POLONIUS. You know sometimes he walks four hours together
Here in the lobby.

QUEEN.   So he does indeed.

POLONIUS. At such a time I'll loose my daughter to him; [HAMLET *appears.*
Be you and I behind an arras then;
Mark the encounter; if he love her not,
And be not from his reason fallen thereon,
Let me be no assistant for a state,   [HAMLET *withdraws.*
But keep a farm, and carters.

KING.   We will try it.

QUEEN. But look, where sadly the poor wretch comes reading.

POLONIUS. Away! I do beseech you, both away.
I'll board him presently.   [*Exeunt* KING *and* QUEEN.

While Polonius meditates aloud over this harping on Ophelia, Hamlet walks along the further side of the table, impatiently opening and closing the books that are lying there, moving the pen, ink and sand-box, finally sitting down on the right end of the table, one foot on the stool, his elbow on his knee, his attention once more bent on the book in his hand. But Polonius has not sense enough to leave him alone. The insistent voice interrupts him again: ' What do you read, my lord? ' ' Words,' the answer is instantaneous, mechanical, then a pause, looking out. ' Words, words.' He speaks with sombre emphasis. A quick straightening of the body, the shadow of a gesture indicating futility, unveils the depths of weariness within. ' What is the matter, my lord? ' Hamlet swings around on Polonius with a dangerous, swift movement of his body: ' Between who? ' sharp and hard, a stone thrown into a pool from which the ripples spread in widening circles of implication. What, indeed, is the matter between himself and Ophelia, the Ghost, Claudius, the Queen; what is the matter with Denmark, with the world!

Hamlet returns to the book—his annoyance with Polonius growing. ' Slanders, sir,' he begins, and continues with mounting irony through his malicious description of the old man. His tone is lighter, more sardonic. Once or twice he studies the pages of the book thoughtfully with a glance toward Polonius that seems to check the facts; a pause at ' most weak hams ' during which Polonius is subjected to a thorough scrutiny that measures him from heel to head, then quickly and lightly to the end of the passage, with a gesture over his left shoulder showing the backward march of the crab. He has finished Polonius off and turns his back on him, immersing himself in the book as a refuge against further questioning.

Polonius, however, will not be put off. He begins again with his suggestion about going out of the air. Hamlet's answer, quick, almost flat, is addressed to space: ' Into my grave.' This is the very content of his thought. He drops it without emphasis, a leaden reality, startling after the innuendo, the malice, the double-

Enter HAMLET, *reading.*
O! give me leave.

How does my good Lord Hamlet?

HAMLET. Well, God a-mercy.

POLONIUS. Do you know me, my lord?

HAMLET. Excellent well; you are a fishmonger.

POLONIUS. Not I, my lord.

HAMLET. Then I would you were so honest a man.

POLONIUS. Honest, my lord!

HAMLET. Ay, sir; to be honest, as this world goes, is to be one man picked out of ten thousand.

POLONIUS. That's very true, my lord.

HAMLET. For if the sun breed maggots in a dead dog, being a God kissing carrion,—Have you a daughter?

POLONIUS. I have, my lord.

HAMLET. Let her not walk i' the sun: conception is a blessing; but not as your daughter may conceive. Friend, look to 't.

POLONIUS. [*Aside.*] How say you by that? Still harping on my daughter: yet he knew me not at first; he said I was a fishmonger: he is far gone, far gone: and truly in my youth I suffered much extremity for love; very near this. I'll speak to him again. What do you read, my lord?

HAMLET. Words, words, words.

POLONIUS. What is the matter, my lord?

HAMLET. Between who?

POLONIUS. I mean the matter that you read, my lord.

HAMLET. Slanders, sir: for the satirical rogue says here that old men have grey beards, that their faces are wrinkled, their eyes purging thick amber and plum-tree gum, and that they have a plentiful lack of wit, together with most weak hams: all which, sir, though I most powerfully and potently believe, yet I hold it not honesty to have it thus set down; for you yourself, sir, should be old as I am, if, like a crab, you could go backward.

POLONIUS. [*Aside.*] Though this be madness, yet there is method in 't. Will you walk out of the air, my lord?

HAMLET. Into my grave?

POLONIUS. Indeed, that is out o' the air. [*Aside.*] How pregnant sometimes his replies are! I will leave him, and suddenly contrive the means of meeting between him and my daughter. My honourable lord, I will most humbly take my leave of you.

HAMLET. You cannot, sir, take from me any thing that I will more willingly part withal; except my life, except my life, except my life.

POLONIUS. Fare you well, my lord.   [*Going.*

HAMLET. These tedious old fools!

Enter ROSENCRANTZ *and* GUILDENSTERN.

POLONIUS. You go to seek the Lord Hamlet; there he is.

John Gielgud as Hamlet, New York, 1936

Photograph by Vandamm

edged wit of what has gone before. He speaks as though unconscious of his words—out of his inner thought—and continues
absorbed in his protecting book. As Polonius' leave-taking finally reaches his attention he straightens up with a sigh, turns
toward the old man, bowing slightly as he sits, his tone elaborately
polite as though pronouncing a conventional farewell. The first
' Except my life ' is part of it, then a pause. He looks front; Polonius
is forgotten. He speaks with controlled intensity—but the depths
of his anguish beat against the words, ' except my life, except
my life.' Polonius finally goes out left, as Hamlet swings away
from him, his back hunched, voice and gesture acid with exasperation. ' These tedious old fools! ' snaps from him in a burst of
annoyance. His head bends over his book.

But he is to have no peace. Bland voices greet him from the
doorway by which Polonius has just made his exit. Hamlet jumps
from the end of the table and throws himself on the right-hand
door with an exaggerated imitation of lunatic behaviour. As Rosencrantz and Guildenstern continue to speak, he stops, turns and
seeing who they are comes down the steps toward them. His
voice is pleasant if not warm. ' My excellent good friends! ' As
he comes near the table he drops the book he has been carrying
on it, and with the gesture dismisses, for the moment, the play-
acting with which he has been fooling the meddlesome old man.

With a cordial handshake to one and the other, he stands between them in the centre of the stage. His attitude is relaxed,
his gestures natural. He has at once the ease and authority of a
man of the world. As the banter about fortune proceeds, he leans
a little against the table, looking from one to the other. He can
toss off this sort of thing with the best of them. It is the small
talk of the Renaissance gentleman. His wit, so acrid in his recent
encounter with Polonius, is for the moment light and superficial.
But he notices the forced note in the gaiety of the other two. The
question that he asked Horatio is immediately in his mind.

He takes Guildenstern's arm and walks with him toward the
right. With ' Denmark's a prison ' the underlying torment of

ROSENCRANTZ. [*To* POLONIUS.] God save you, sir!   [*Exit* POLONIUS.

GUILDENSTERN. Mine honoured lord!

ROSENCRANTZ. My most dear lord!

HAMLET. My excellent good friends! How dost thou, Guildenstern? Ah, Rosencrantz! Good lads, how do ye both?

ROSENCRANTZ. As the indifferent children of the earth.

GUILDENSTERN. Happy in that we are not over happy;
On Fortune's cap we are not the very button.

HAMLET. Nor the soles of her shoe?

ROSENCRANTZ. Neither, my lord.

HAMLET. Then you live about her waist, or in the middle of her favours?

GUILDENSTERN. Faith, her privates we.

HAMLET. In the secret parts of Fortune? O! most true; she is a strumpet. What news?

ROSENCRANTZ. None, my lord, but that the world's grown honest.

HAMLET. Then is doomsday near; but your news is not true. Let me question more in particular: what have you, my good friends, deserved at the hands of Fortune, that she sends you to prison hither?

GUILDENSTERN. Prison, my lord!

HAMLET. Denmark 's a prison.

ROSENCRANTZ. Then is the world one.

HAMLET. A goodly one; in which there are many confines, wards, and dungeons, Denmark being one o' the worst.

ROSENCRANTZ. We think not so, my lord.

HAMLET. Why, then, 'tis none to you; for there is nothing either good or bad, but thinking makes it so: to me it is a prison.

ROSENCRANTZ. Why, then your ambition makes it one; 'tis too narrow for your mind.

HAMLET. O God! I could be bounded in a nutshell, and count myself a king of infinite space, were it not that I have bad dreams.

GUILDENSTERN. Which dreams, indeed, are ambition, for the very substance of the ambitious is merely the shadow of a dream.

HAMLET. A dream itself is but a shadow.

ROSENCRANTZ. Truly, and I hold ambition of so airy and light a quality that it is but a shadow's shadow.

HAMLET. Then are our beggars bodies, and our monarchs and outstretched heroes the beggars' shadows. Shall we to the court? for, by my fay, I cannot reason.

ROSENCRANTZ. ⎫
GUILDENSTERN. ⎬ We'll wait upon you.

HAMLET. No such matter; I will not sort you with the rest of my servants, for, to speak to you like an honest man, I am most dreadfully attended. But, in the beaten way of friendship, what make you at Elsinore?

ROSENCRANTZ. To visit you, my lord; no other occasion.

HAMLET. Beggar that I am, I am even poor in thanks; but I thank you: and

his spirit breaks through his surface courtesy. He drops Guildenstern's arm and walks restlessly away, then back past Rosencrantz
whose ' We think not so, my lord ' widens the sense of distance
between them. Hamlet's voice and manner are increasingly serious.
He speaks rather loudly in a firm, external voice, until his own
words ' there is nothing either good or bad . . . ' seem to drive
him momentarily into his own thoughts. He pauses at the end of
his pacing at some distance from the two men, looking away from
them, weariness and suffering in the lines of the drawn face they
cannot see.

Rosencrantz's ' feeler '—the idea that thwarted ambition may
be the source of the trouble—drives him to a momentary betrayal
of his real feeling. The ' O God! ' bursts from him with sudden
violence, his words rush out as though he were about to speak
frankly, but on ' were it not ' he checks himself abruptly. The
tone changes to defensiveness. With an effort he recaptures the
casual manner safest for the occasion and turns back toward the
two with a resumption of the bantering word-play, but without
gaiety, merely an automatic game which quickly wearies him.
With a swift step and gesture he leads them toward the right-hand
doors, sensing that they belong with the court pack, not with him;
with the hunters, not with the hunted. On their word of obsequious attendance he stops abruptly and turns toward them as they
follow him upstage. ' I am most dreadfully attended ' is charged
with indignation. We are reminded that Hamlet is a Prince deprived of his birthright, as well as a man grievously burdened in
mind and spirit and surrounded by prying enemies.

As he speaks the words he suddenly decides to probe once for all
into the meaning of this new menace to his privacy—the presence
of these school-fellows in a situation already so complex. He returns to the question, still unanswered, with which he had greeted
them. This time he addresses himself earnestly to Rosencrantz,
whose answer increases his suspicion and growing indignation.
His ' Beggar that I am ' is sardonically polite. The three men
have returned to the centre of the stage. Hamlet, standing be-

sure, dear friends, my thanks are too dear a halfpenny. Were you not sent for? Is it your own inclining? Is it a free visitation? Come, come, deal justly with me: come, come; nay, speak.

GUILDENSTERN. What should we say, my lord?

HAMLET. Why anything, but to the purpose. You were sent for; and there is a kind of confession in your looks which your modesties have not craft enough to colour: I know the good king and queen have sent for you.

ROSENCRANTZ. To what end, my lord?

HAMLET. That you must teach me. But let me conjure you, by the rights of our fellowship, by the consonancy of our youth, by the obligation of our ever-preserved love, and by what more dear a better proposer could charge you withal, be even and direct with me, whether you were sent for or no!

ROSENCRANTZ. What say you?

HAMLET. Nay, then, I have an eye of you. If you love me, hold not off.

GUILDENSTERN. My lord, we were sent for.

HAMLET. I will tell you why; so shall my anticipation prevent your discovery, and your secrecy to the king and queen moult no feather. I have of late,—but wherefore I know not,—lost all my mirth, forgone all custom of exercises; and indeed it goes so heavily with my disposition this goodly frame, the earth, seems to me a sterile promontory; this most excellent canopy, the air, look you, this brave o'erhanging firmament, this majestical roof fretted with golden fire, why, it appears no other thing to me but a foul and pestilent congregation of vapours. What a piece of work is a man! How noble in reason! how infinite in faculty! in form, in moving, how express and admirable! in action how like an angel! in apprehension how like a god! the beauty of the world! the paragon of animals! And yet, to me, what is this quintessence of dust? man delights not me; no, nor woman neither, though, by your smiling, you seem to say so.

ROSENCRANTZ. My lord, there was no such stuff in my thoughts.

HAMLET. Why did you laugh then, when I said, ' man delights not me '?

ROSENCRANTZ. To think, my lord, if you delight not in man, what lenten entertainment the players shall receive from you: we coted them on the way; and hither are they coming, to offer you service.

HAMLET. He that plays the king shall be welcome; his majesty shall have tribute of me; what players are they?

ROSENCRANTZ. Even those you were wont to take delight in, the tragedians of the city.

HAMLET. How chances it they travel? Do they hold the same estimation they did when I was in the city? Are they so followed?

GUILDENSTERN. No, indeed they are not.

HAMLET. It is not very strange; for my uncle is King of Denmark, and those that would make mows at him while my father lived, give twenty, forty, fifty, a hundred ducats a-piece for his picture in little. 'Sblood, tween the two, turns with deep seriousness from one to the other. His appeal rises to anger. With ' nay, speak ' his voice snaps, he straightens up threateningly: ' Why anything, but to the purpose.' There is a pause and then, with restrained irony, he tells them his opinion. Their ' modesties ' and their majesties the ' good ' King and Queen (with a gesture toward the door by which they departed) are delicately pilloried. But his next words are not ironic. Sincerely, with growing feeling, he makes a last appeal to their decency, addressing himself to Rosencrantz, whose shallow, closed face warns him of the truth. With a weary drop of voice and shoulders he turns away from them toward the table, opening one of the big books lying there as though he had suddenly lost interest in the argument. The two men start to consult each other with a glance and murmured word, but are instantly interrupted by a bang as Hamlet slams the book shut and flashes around on them, intercepting their exchange. Guildenstern hesitates and is lost. ' My lord, we were sent for.'

As Hamlet draws himself up, looking at them with withering contempt, the two men fall away from him, leaving him standing alone in front of the table. A pause and then a startling, humourless laugh followed by a quiet, biting voice, telling them in its tone and in the contemptuous gesture of the left hand on ' moult no feather ' just what he thinks of them. With ' I have of late— ' he moves toward the stool standing in front of the council table, a little toward the left. He shifts its position with his foot as he speaks. He is obviously thinking what he will say to these spies, these false friends, something which will give them food for comment but no information. It is safe enough to describe his all too real melancholy. The secret of it will remain as much a mystery as ever.

He drops down on the stool, his whole body relaxed. His voice is low-pitched, a clear, sorrow-ladened note. As he speaks the phrases grow in power and volume, rising steadily to the magnificent climax of ' fretted with golden fire ' with its beautiful long-drawn vowels, dropping to the sibilant distaste of the ' pestilent congregation of vapours,' rising again through the description of

there is something in this more than natural, if philosophy could find it out.

GUILDENSTERN. There are the players.

HAMLET. Gentlemen, you are welcome to Elsinore. Your hands, come.
You are welcome; but my uncle-father and aunt-mother are deceived.

GUILDENSTERN. In what, my lord?

HAMLET. I am but mad north-north-west: when the wind is southerly I
know a hawk from a handsaw.

Enter POLONIUS.

POLONIUS. Well be with you, gentlemen!

HAMLET. Hark you, Guildenstern; and you too; at each ear a hearer: that
great baby you see there is not yet out of his swaddling-clouts.

ROSENCRANTZ. Happily he 's the second time come to them; for they say
an old man is twice a child.

HAMLET. I will prophesy he comes to tell me of the players; mark it. You
say right, sir; o' Monday morning; 'twas so indeed.

POLONIUS. My lord, I have news to tell you.

HAMLET. My lord, I have news to tell you. When Roscius was an actor
in Rome,—

POLONIUS. The actors are come hither, my lord.

HAMLET. Buzz, buzz!

POLONIUS. Upon my honour,—

HAMLET. Then came each actor on his ass,—

POLONIUS. The best actors in the world, either for tragedy, comedy, history, pastoral, pastoral-comical, historical-pastoral, tragical-historical,
tragical-comical-historical-pastoral, scene individable, or poem unlim-
ited: Seneca cannot be too heavy, nor Plautus too light. For the law of
writ and the liberty, these are the only men.

HAMLET. O Jephthah, judge of Israel, what a treasure hadst thou!

POLONIUS. What a treasure had he, my lord?

HAMLET. Why

        ' One fair daughter and no more,
           The which he loved passing well.'

POLONIUS. [*Aside.*] Still on my daughter.

HAMLET. Am I not i' the right, old Jephthah?

POLONIUS. If you call me Jephthah, my lord, I have a daughter that I love
passing well.

HAMLET. Nay, that follows not.

POLONIUS. What follows, then, my lord?

HAMLET. Why,

        ' As by lot, God wot.'

And then, you know,

        ' It came to pass, as most like it was.'—

look where my abridgment comes.

Enter four or five Players.

You are welcome, masters; welcome, all. I am glad to see thee well:

man with its mounting magnificence of sound and image, to that supreme evocation ' the beauty of the world! the paragon of animals! ' Throughout the speech Hamlet hardly moves, a gesture to Rosencrantz, pointing upward to underline his sardonic explanation of ' this most excellent canopy '; a movement of his right hand outlining the upright carriage of the ' perfect man ' as his words build the vision in the air; for the rest only an upward movement of his body and head as he sits, a subtle enlargement of his whole being as though he were transfigured by the power and beauty his imagination evokes.

A long pause. The light within fades. His head drops forward imperceptibly. ' Quintessence of dust! ' very clearly, very exactly articulated, each consonant and vowel a tiny grain of sand rolled absently between thumb and forefinger. The despair is all the greater to the mind that could conceive such noble images. ' Think'st thou that I who saw the face of God ' Mephistophilis cried in his banishment—and Hamlet, banished from happiness, from the delights of mind, spirit, body, broods: ' Man delights not me.'

Rosencrantz's fatuous grin reminds Hamlet that he has been talking to fools, and worse. Carried away by his own thought he has for a moment uncovered not his secret, but his secret being. With a movement of anger he leaps to his feet and strides across the stage, flinging his words back over his shoulder, exasperated at his own stupidity in talking sense to creatures who could be counted on to laugh at anything sincerely felt. Rosencrantz, alarmed, stumbles into explanations which Hamlet only half hears as he paces across the stage and back. He has reached the left end of the council table when he catches the word ' players.' ' He that plays the king shall be welcome ' he snaps out.

The jibe is at Rosencrantz, but a little also for himself. He turns and sits sidewise on the end of the table, his irritation in hand, but his anger burning. He looks at Rosencrantz who is near him; Guildenstern is at the opposite end of the table. As they talk of the players a more cheerful note comes into Hamlet's

welcome, good friends. O, my old friend! Thy face is valanced since I
saw thee last: comest thou to beard me in Denmark? What! my young
lady and mistress! [By 'r lady, your ladyship is nearer heaven than
when I saw you last, by the altitude of a chopine. Pray God, your
voice, like a piece of uncurrent gold, be not cracked within the ring.]
Masters, you are all welcome. We'll e'en to 't like French falconers, fly
at any thing we see: we'll have a speech straight. Come, give us a taste
of your quality; come, a passionate speech.

FIRST PLAYER. What speech, my good lord?

HAMLET. I heard thee speak me a speech once, but it was never acted; or,
if it was, not above once; for the play, I remember, pleased not the
million; 'twas caviare to the general: but it was—as I received it, an
excellent play, well digested in the scenes, set down with as much
modesty as cunning. One speech in it I chiefly loved; 'twas Æneas' tale
to Dido; and thereabout of it especially, where he speaks of Priam's
slaughter. If it live in your memory, begin at this line: let me see, let
me see:—
' The rugged Pyrrhus, like the Hyrcanian beast,'
'tis not so, it begins with Pyrrhus:—
' The rugged Pyrrhus, he, whose sable arm,
Black as his purpose, did the night resemble
When he lay couched in the ominous horse,
With eyes like carbuncles, the hellish Pyrrhus
Old grandsire Priam seeks.'
So proceed you.

POLONIUS. 'Fore God, my lord, well spoken; with good accent and good
discretion.

FIRST PLAYER.   ' Anon, he finds him
Striking too short at Greeks; his antique sword,
Rebellious to his arm, lies where it falls,
Repugnant to command. Unequal match'd,
Pyrrhus at Priam drives; in rage strikes wide;
But with the whiff and wind of his fell sword
The unnerved father falls.
But, as we often see, against some storm,
A silence in the heavens, the rack stand still,
The bold winds speechless and the orb below
As hush as death, anon the dreadful thunder
Doth rend the region; so, after Pyrrhus' pause,
Aroused vengeance sets him new a-work;
And never did the Cyclops' hammers fall
On Mars's armour, forg'd for proof eterne,
With less remorse than Pyrrhus' bleeding sword
Now falls on Priam.
Out, out, thou strumpet, Fortune! '

voice, but his eyes are fixed on Rosencrantz and he beckons him to come nearer. ' It is not very strange,' he begins quietly enough, then the words come more quickly, more indignantly; with ' 'Sblood, there is something in this more than natural ' his hand shoots out, seizing the miniature that hangs from Rosencrantz's neck and throwing it violently to one side. Rosencrantz leaps back but Hamlet, very suave, passes on—' if philosophy could find it out.'

The trumpets sound, Guildenstern intervenes. With a hearty, sarcastic cordiality Hamlet finishes with these two, putting them once for all in their place. Still sitting on the end of the table he swings his foot forward over the end so that it rests on the stool. His spirits rise now that he knows where he stands with them. Battle is joined, no quarter on either side. A hand to each, a malicious smile on his face, he tells them a secret: ' my uncle-father and aunt-mother are deceived.' Dropping their hands he steps forward over the stool. ' I know a hawk from a handsaw.' His tongue is in his cheek, his finger to his nose as he swings around to greet Polonius who had come in a moment before and with whom he instantly resumes the ' antic ' game.

Hamlet's mood is less violent than in the first encounter with the old man. There is a devil-may-care gaiety about him. The ' Buzz, buzz ' which greets the fulfillment of his prophecy that Polonius would speak of the players is tossed out for the benefit of the two behind him. He watches Polonius with a mocking eye as he counts off the varieties of drama on his fingers, then suddenly with ' O Jephthah, judge of Israel ' he shatters the old man's pleasant preoccupation. As Polonius hesitates, Hamlet walks around him, swinging to his right with the lines about his daughter. Hamlet's grin is not reassuring, but he slips his arm under that of Polonius amicably enough and starts to walk with him across the stage reciting the lines of the Jephthah verse. He is on the left-hand side of the stage when the doors fly open and the players stand in a group at the top of the three steps, right.

Hamlet drops Polonius' arm and turns to them with a cordial

POLONIUS. This is too long.

HAMLET. It shall to the barber's, with your beard. Prithee, say on: he's for a jig or a tale of bawdry, or he sleeps. Say on; come to Hecuba.

FIRST PLAYER. ' But who, O! who had seen the mobled queen '—

HAMLET. ' The mobled queen '?—

POLONIUS. That's good; ' mobled queen ' is good.

FIRST PLAYER. ' Run barefoot up and down, threatening the flames
With bisson rheum; a clout upon that head
Where late the diadem stood; and, for a robe,
About her lank and all o'er-teemed loins,
A blanket, in the alarm of fear caught up;
Who this had seen, with tongue in venom steep'd,
'Gainst Fortune's state would treason have pronounc'd:
[But if the gods themselves did see her then,
When she saw Pyrrhus make malicious sport
In mincing with his sword her husband's limbs,
The instant burst of clamour that she made—
Unless things mortal move them not at all—
Would have made milch the burning eyes of heaven,
And passion in the gods.']

POLONIUS. Look! wh'er he has not turned his colour and has tears in's eyes. Prithee, no more.

HAMLET. 'Tis well; I'll have thee speak out the rest soon. Good my lord, will you see the players well bestowed? Do you hear, let them be well used; for they are the abstracts and brief chronicles of the time: after your death you were better have a bad epitaph than their ill report while you live.

POLONIUS. My lord, I will use them according to their desert.

HAMLET. God's bodikins, man, much better; use every man after his desert, and who should 'scape whipping? Use them after your own honour and dignity: the less they deserve, the more merit is in your bounty. Take them in.

POLONIUS. Come, sirs.

HAMLET. Follow him, friends: we'll hear a play to-morrow. [*Exit* POLONIUS, *with all the Players but the First.*] Dost thou hear me, old friend; can you play the Murder of Gonzago?

FIRST PLAYER. Ay, my lord.

HAMLET. We'll ha't to-morrow night. You could, for a need, study a speech of some dozen or sixteen lines, which I would set down and insert in 't, could you not?

FIRST PLAYER. Ay, my lord.

HAMLET. Very well. Follow that lord; and look you mock him not. [*Exit First Player.*] [*To* ROSENCRANTZ *and* GUILDENSTERN.] My good friends, I'll leave you till night; you are welcome to Elsinore.

ROSENCRANTZ. Good my lord! [*Exeunt* ROSENCRANTZ *and* GUILDENSTERN.

greeting. Gaily, without reservation, he welcomes them to Elsinore. With these people he is at ease. His voice has a happy resonance as he turns from one to the other, drawing them into the room and finally on ' We'll e'en to 't like French falconers ' throwing himself into the chair at the back of the table, right, and motioning the First Player to sit on the stool beside him. With a glance and a gesture he draws Polonius, Rosencrantz and Guildenstern into the circle. The old man sits on the stool at the left end of the table, facing toward Hamlet and the group of actors.

Hamlet talks eagerly to the First Player about the speech he wants, very much the princely patron who loves theatre-talk and has probably a tragedy or two to his credit tucked away in his chest at Wittenberg. The play he wants—' caviare to the general ' —is described with gusto. He starts the line after a moment's hesitation, then breaks off with a smile—and shake of the head. ' 'Tis not so.' Again he starts, groping for the word, then more rapidly with increasing momentum as the lines flood back to his memory. He speaks quickly, emphasizing the rhythm once or twice with his hand, but his delivery is not in the least dramatic. He is merely giving the Player a start. ' So, proceed you.' Polonius' commendation is received with a grimace of impatience at the pompous flattery, and a gesture of dismissal.

Hamlet settles back in his chair to listen, looking up at the Player who stands on the steps of the doorway, right. His attentive face, at first almost happy, clouds slowly as the tale of a king killed, of sack and rapine and disaster unfolds. Polonius' words ' This is too long ' bring him out of his reverie, he turns impatiently on the old man, looking him up and down scornfully. ' He's for a jig or a tale of bawdry, or he sleeps . . . ,' this with emphasis and anger. (It is Shakespeare as well as Hamlet weighting the line.) The players laugh a little, and Hamlet flashes an angry glance at them. There is a long pause as he goes back to the preoccupation the poem had evoked.

From this moment a new tension comes into the scene; again as when Hamlet learned of the Ghost's visitation there is a sense

HAMLET. Ay, so, God be wi' ye! Now I am alone.
O! what a rogue and peasant slave am I:
Is it not monstrous that this player here,
But in a fiction, in a dream of passion,
Could force his soul so to his own conceit
That from her working all his visage wann'd,
Tears in his eyes, distraction in 's aspect,
A broken voice, and his whole function suiting
With forms to his conceit? and all for nothing!
For Hecuba!
What 's Hecuba to him or he to Hecuba
That he should weep for her? What would he do
Had he the motive and the cue for passion
That I have? He would drown the stage with tears,
And cleave the general ear with horrid speech,
Make mad the guilty and appal the free,
Confound the ignorant, and amaze indeed
The very faculties of eyes and ears.
Yet I,
A dull and muddy-mettled rascal, peak,
Like John-a-dreams, unpregnant of my cause,
And can say nothing; no, not for a king,
Upon whose property and most dear life
A damn'd defeat was made. Am I a coward?
Who calls me villain? breaks my pate across?
Plucks off my beard and blows it in my face?
Tweaks me by the nose? gives me the lie i' the throat,
As deep as to the lungs? Who does me this?
Ha!
Swounds, I should take it, for it cannot be
But I am pigeon-liver'd, and lack gall
To make oppression bitter, or ere this
I should have fatted all the region kites
With this slave's offal. Bloody, bawdy villain!
Remorseless, treacherous, lecherous, kindless villain!
O! vengeance!
Why, what an ass am I! This is most brave
That I, the son of a dear father murder'd,
Prompted to my revenge by heaven and hell,
Must, like a whore, unpack my heart with words,
And fall a-cursing, like a very drab,
A scullion!
Fie upon 't! foh! About, my brain! I have heard,
That guilty creatures sitting at a play
Have by the very cunning of the scene

John Gielgud as Hamlet, London, 1934

Photograph by Yvonne Gregory

of a pulse beating with accelerated stroke. He stands for a moment on the brink of disastrous action. Then turning toward the Player with ' Come to Hecuba ' he lets the inevitable train move on. ' The mobled queen ' is spoken in an absorbed distant voice. Polonius' fatuous repetition brings this time a commanding ' Sh ' in rebuke. Hamlet turns impatiently in his chair as though to eliminate an importunate presence. Again he watches the Player, his face intent with thought, flickering with a growing excitement. At the description of Hecuba he gives a sudden, harsh cry, overcome by the picture summoned to his imagination and by the shock of an idea, apprehended vaguely a few moments before but suddenly crystal clear in his mind. His hand covers his face, as though to protect his thought from the prying eyes around him until he has made it his own, hidden it deep within. In a moment he has mastered himself and is listening with all his attention to the Player, sharing his emotion and burning with the mounting fire of his own thought.

Polonius' interruption breaks the spell but Hamlet hardly hears what is said. He rises slowly to his feet, struggling to control the driving force within himself and moves toward the Player, laying a courteous and appreciative hand on his shoulder—' 'Tis well '—there is no use continuing in the presence of such Philistines as Polonius and the other two. Another time will be better. Hamlet looks long at the Player's face and then turns away, striding forward and speaking to Polonius with authority. As he reaches the front he turns around with his back to the audience, commanding the movements of everyone on the stage.

His explosion to Polonius on the subject of treating the players better than they deserve is edged by his effort to control the steadily rising tide that is storming within him. It is one of those outbursts, beside the fact, that relieve tension without revealing its cause, and Polonius hurries out on the impetus of it more than ever convinced that he is dealing with a madman. The players follow him off through the left-hand doors, passing in front of Hamlet, who stops the First Player and draws him down right for the brief, por-

Been struck so to the soul that presently
They have proclaim'd their malefactions;
For murder, though it have no tongue, will speak
With most miraculous organ. I'll have these players
Play something like the murder of my father
Before mine uncle; I'll observe his looks;
I'll tent him to the quick: if he but blench
I know my course. The spirit that I have seen
May be the devil: and the devil hath power
To assume a pleasing shape; yea, and perhaps
Out of my weakness and my melancholy—
As he is very potent with such spirits—
Abuses me to damn me. I'll have grounds
More relative than this: the play 's the thing
Wherein I'll catch the conscience of the king.

tentous interchange about the Gonzago play. The 'dozen or sixteen lines' are forming in his mind; he is intent, agitated, but as the First Player leaves him he remembers his rather cavalier treatment of Polonius in front of the actors. 'Follow that lord; and look you mock him not' is given with a smile of admonition. What Hamlet may permit himself the players are not to ape.

In the meanwhile the two 'good lads' wait on the left-hand side of the stage to pick up their interrupted colloquy with Hamlet. As the First Player leaves him and he moves toward the centre, they come forward to speak to Hamlet, but he is at the end of his endurance. With a swift, repelling gesture, he dismisses them, refusing to accept their hypocritical obeisance. They go out, left, discomfited, and he stands in the middle of the stage, his back to the audience, his hands on the table before him.

'Now I am alone . . .' It is, once again, that desperate cry of nerves too highly strung. His head goes back in a gesture of physical suffering as though the accumulated weight could be thrown off in this moment of release. 'O! what a rogue and peasant slave am I' follows in an explosion of rage and self-scorn. He turns a little toward the spot where the Player had stood, and the burning words pour out. On 'He would drown the stage with tears'— Hamlet swings around facing front, his clenched fist thrust down, his head back, his voice rising in a tornado to the crest of '*amaze indeed* the very faculties of eyes and ears.' Then, suddenly, a drop,— voice, body, carriage all deflated. He moves slowly to the stool at the left end of the table and falls on it, vanquished.

The bitter self-challenge of 'Am I a coward?' rises in swift, staccato exclamations until 'Who does me this?' brings him to his feet with a cry. Again the weary fall, he leans against the table— half sitting—his agitation slowly mounting, this time to a final climax of horror as the hated uncle is excoriated in hissing, virulent words—'treacherous, *lecherous, kindless villain*!' Hamlet is trembling with fury, his body shaking, his voice high. With 'Vengeance!' he snatches his dagger from its sheath and rushes to the doorway right, throwing himself against it as the wave of his futile fury crashes to its height and dies. His raised arm falls, the dagger rolls on the ground, his body sways against the door and he sinks, almost crouching on the top step.

The downward sweep of his self-scorn is as devastating as the upward sweep of his rage. His voice is broken with a sob of humiliation. He sees himself without kindness and judges himself without pity. His courage deserts him, not in the face of danger, physical or supernatural, but in the face of his own incalculable and uncontrollable impulses. ' Fie upon 't! foh! ' The silence that follows is Hamlet's nadir; he is beaten down, almost lost.

Then slowly he moves, raises his head, invokes that bright particular particle that shines even in this black night of his soul. ' About, my brain! ' The idea already seen returns and gives him the needed impulse toward action. He plans the play-trap in a hoarse, whispered voice, rising from the steps, moving a little forward. ' I'll have these players play something like the murder of my father '—the voice is low, the tempo uncertain. It quickens a little with the hope of making his uncle blench. A pause and then very slowly we see in his face that look Ophelia saw, the look of one ' loosed out of hell.' The pathos of his loneliness, of his fear, of his ' weakness and . . . melancholy ' are poignantly revealed in the cadence of his voice, in the line of his figure which seems fragile, helpless, all its informing vigour gone.

He stands for a moment absolutely still, weighing the awful possibility of eternal damnation should he be led by ghost or demon or by his own fevered imagination into committing the very crime he is called upon to avenge. ' I'll have grounds more relative than this ' is a cry of despair and defiance. ' The play's the thing wherein I'll catch the conscience of the king ' is spoken in a frenzy of excitement, reaching this time in one burst the summit of intensity. His body is galvanized, he hurls himself across the intervening space to the chair at the end of the table where he has sat listening to the Player. He pulls the paper toward him, seizes a pen, the light catches his wildly excited face, then blacks out as he bends forward writing frantically.

The Great Hall in the Castle

SCENE 7

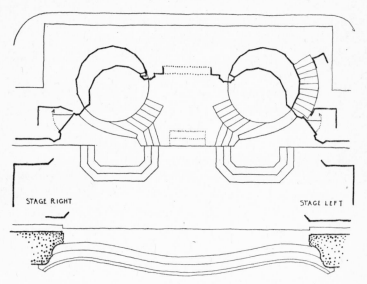

STAGE RIGHT

STAGE LEFT

SCENE 7.—*The great hall in the castle.* KING, QUEEN, POLONIUS, OPHELIA, ROSENCRANTZ, *and* GUILDENSTERN.

KING. And can you, by no drift of circumstance,
Get from him why he puts on this confusion?

ROSENCRANTZ. He does confess he feels himself distracted;
But from what cause he will by no means speak.

GUILDENSTERN. Nor do we find him forward to be sounded,
But, with a crafty madness, keeps aloof,
When we would bring him on to some confession
Of his true state.

QUEEN.   Did he receive you well?

ROSENCRANTZ. Most like a gentleman.

QUEEN.   Did you assay him
To any pastime?

ROSENCRANTZ. Madam, it so fell out that certain players
We o'er-raught on the way; of these we told him,
And there did seem in him a kind of joy
To hear of it: they are about the court,
And, as I think, they have already order
This night to play before him.

POLONIUS.   'Tis most true;
And he beseech'd me to entreat your majesties
To hear and see the matter.

KING. With all my heart; and it doth much content me
To hear him so inclin'd.
Good gentlemen, give him a further edge,
And drive his purpose on to these delights.

ROSENCRANTZ. We shall, my lord.

                    [*Exeunt* ROSENCRANTZ *and* GUILDENSTERN.

KING.   Sweet Gertrude, leave us too;
For we have closely sent for Hamlet hither,
That he, as 'twere by accident, may here
Affront Ophelia.
Her father and myself, lawful espials,
Will so bestow ourselves, that, seeing, unseen,
We may of their encounter frankly judge,
And gather by him, as he is behav'd,
If 't be the affliction of his love or no
That thus he suffers for.

QUEEN.   I shall obey you.
And for your part, Ophelia, I do wish
That your good beauties be the happy cause
Of Hamlet's wildness; so shall I hope your virtues

'*The Great Hall in the Castle*'

Designed by Jo Mielziner for the New York production of Hamlet

SCENE 7. *The great hall in the castle.*

The full stage is revealed in bright light. Flights of stairs sweep up left and right to an upper platform behind which a high arched doorway opens on a tapestry-hung corridor. There are entrances left and right to the landings that break the sweep of the stairs about three steps up from the stage level. In the middle a low archway opens beneath the upper platform. Semi-circular walls rise towering on either side, enclosing the huge room.

The King and Queen, with Polonius and Ophelia stand on the central platform, Rosencrantz and Guildenstern on the stairway, left. Hamlet's state of mind, the arrival of the players, the plan for an entertainment that evening are discussed. After the two young men have been dismissed, Ophelia is given her instructions, and Polonius and the King withdraw through the central arch as Hamlet's step is heard approaching.

He comes in, blown on the wind of his excitement. He has been sent for, probably for no good purpose. He looks around, questioning, defiant. Then, seeing no one, drops into his own brooding thoughts. ' To be, or not to be,' very quiet, unemphatic; a dark, profound, inward note. He walks slowly down the three steps and forward. The lights suspend his thinking face in a timeless abstraction. A deep line cuts his forehead. Each successive idea seems to take form before our eyes as Hamlet pauses, weighs, and then moves on to its expression. He makes visible the movement of his mind, so that the concept seems to shine through the transparent mask before the word gives it substance. The longing for annihilation, the impulse toward the void, which underlies the speech is made visible in that still black figure, audible in the exhausted tone, the grey timbre of ' To die: to sleep; *no more* ' and again ' To die, to sleep; to sleep.' The word echoes in his ear. He stops, checked by his intelligence on the brink of longed-for nothingness. ' Ay, there's the rub.' He speaks more quickly, the mystic contemplation fading as he enumerates the burdens, general rather than particular, which men endure. An occasional very slight gesture marks the

Will bring him to his wonted way again,
To both your honours.

OPHELIA.   Madam, I wish it may.   [*Exit* QUEEN.

POLONIUS. Ophelia, walk you here. Gracious, so please you,
We will bestow ourselves. [*To* OPHELIA.] Read on this book;
That show of such an exercise may colour
Your loneliness. I hear him coming; let 's withdraw, my lord.

[*Exeunt* KING *and* POLONIUS.

Enter HAMLET.

HAMLET. To be, or not to be: that is the question:
Whether 'tis nobler in the mind to suffer
The slings and arrows of outrageous fortune,
Or to take arms against a sea of troubles,
And by opposing end them? To die: to sleep;
No more; and, by a sleep to say we end
The heart-ache and the thousand natural shocks
That flesh is heir to, 'tis a consummation
Devoutly to be wish'd. To die, to sleep;
To sleep: perchance to dream: ay, there 's the rub;
For in that sleep of death what dreams may come
When we have shuffled off this mortal coil,
Must give us pause. There 's the respect
That makes calamity of so long life;
For who would bear the whips and scorns of time,
The oppressor's wrong, the proud man's contumely,
The pangs of dispriz'd love, the law's delay,
The insolence of office, and the spurns
That patient merit of the unworthy takes,
When he himself might his quietus make
With a bare bodkin? who would fardels bear,
To grunt and sweat under a weary life,
But that the dread of something after death,
The undiscover'd country from whose bourn
No traveller returns, puzzles the will,
And makes us rather bear those ills we have
Than fly to others that we know not of?
Thus conscience does make cowards of us all;
And thus the native hue of resolution
Is sicklied o'er with the pale cast of thought,
And enterprises of great pith and moment
With this regard their currents turn awry,
And lose the name of action. Soft you now!

thought. The 'bare bodkin' is merely suggested by a movement of the left hand, as though a dagger lay point inward in his palm. Then his hand drops to his side and he pauses again looking into that future after death in which he believes, but which he understands as little as any of us. 'The undiscover'd country from whose bourn no traveller returns.' There is a pause while he seems to see in his mind's eye the vision on the parapet—ghost or goblin damned —or merely as it appears now in the cold light of reason a figment of his own too active mind. With 'puzzles the will' his tone becomes anxious, a note of bafflement creeps into his voice and he begins pacing restlessly across the stage, left to right and back again as the exasperation of his own inaction, his sense of frustration and block grows upon him.

He is downstage left when he sees Ophelia coming in through the high arched opening of the upper stage. She walks down the left flight, her eyes on her book, and Hamlet, remembering suddenly both the plot and the fact that he was 'sent for,' glances again around the lobby and then makes a dash for the opposite door. Halfway across the stage he thinks better of it. He stops and turns, facing Ophelia who has now reached the middle platform and stands a few steps above him.

His first words are formal, yet there is a suppressed eagerness in the question which her conventional rejoinder instantly chills. On 'Well, well, well,' he again turns to go but her words stop him. 'I never gave you aught' is spoken with biting emphasis. It is after all Ophelia who has disprized his love and he repudiates his former affection for her in a time-honoured formula. As she speaks her little set piece about the gifts and holds a string of pearls out to him, he breaks into an ironic laugh, his anger roused by her obviously dictated behaviour.

Turning suddenly on her he seizes her by both arms as though determined to startle her with his 'are you honest?' into speaking from her own heart and not from her father's lips. Ophelia, alarmed and as ever inadequate, again answers with a set phrase. Hamlet, holding her in a compelling grip, drags her a few steps forward

The fair Ophelia! Nymph, in thy orisons
Be all my sins remember'd.

OPHELIA.   Good my lord,
How does your honour for this many a day?

HAMLET. I humbly thank you; well, well, well.

OPHELIA. My lord, I have remembrances of yours,
That I have longed long to re-deliver;
I pray you, now receive them.

HAMLET.   No, not I;
I never gave you aught.

OPHELIA. My honour'd lord, you know right well you did;
And, with them, words of so sweet breath compos'd
As made the things more rich: their perfume lost,
Take these again; for to the noble mind
Rich gifts wax poor when givers prove unkind.
There, my lord.

HAMLET. Ha, ha! are you honest?

OPHELIA. My lord!

HAMLET. Are you fair?

OPHELIA. What means your lordship?

HAMLET. That if you be honest and fair, your honesty should admit no discourse to your beauty.

OPHELIA. Could beauty, my lord, have better commerce than with honesty?

HAMLET. Ay, truly; for the power of beauty will sooner transform honesty from what it is to a bawd than the force of honesty can translate beauty into his likeness: this was sometime a paradox, but now the time gives it proof. I did love thee once.

OPHELIA. Indeed, my lord, you made me believe so.

HAMLET. You should not have believed me; for virtue cannot so inoculate our old stock but we shall relish of it; I loved you not.

OPHELIA. I was the more deceived.

HAMLET. Get thee to a nunnery: why wouldst thou be a breeder of sinners? I am myself indifferent honest; but yet I could accuse me of such things that it were better my mother had not borne me. I am very proud, revengeful, ambitious; with more offences at my beck than I have thoughts to put them in, imagination to give them shape, or time to act them in. What should such fellows as I do crawling between heaven and earth? We are arrant knaves, all; believe none of us. Go thy ways to a nunnery. Where 's your father?

OPHELIA. At home, my lord.

HAMLET. Let the doors be shut upon him, that he may play the fool no where but in 's own house. Farewell.

OPHELIA. O! help him, you sweet heavens!

HAMLET. If thou dost marry, I'll give thee this plague for thy dowry: be thou as chaste as ice, as pure as snow, thou shalt not escape calumny.

and tries again to make her speak frankly, but without success. He drops her arms and steps back. ' I did love thee once.' The words are sincere but they ring with the finality of a thing past. At her eager answer he moves away from her. He is almost at the stair, right, when he whirls on her with ' You should not have believed me.'

Ophelia turns away heart-broken and tearful and starts up the stairs on the left. The catch in her voice, the forlorn droop of her head, move him. He leaps across the stage after her. She stops and he stands for a moment at her back, his arms raised as though to gather her to him, then they sink slowly. He speaks the first ' Get thee to a nunnery ' in a whisper almost tenderly, then walks up the stairs beside her, standing on the middle landing, looking down into her upturned face. He seems to be arguing with her, pleading with her. By admitting his own faults, he would draw her to him in mutual confidence: ' I am very proud, revengeful, ambitious.' Ophelia's proximity, the pathetic tear-stained face turned up to him, draw him. ' We are arrant knaves, all.' The words are harsh but his tone is tender. He is not thinking of what they mean— not thinking at all. Their bodies sway toward each other—for a moment it seems as though their natural affection would break the nightmare spell, but ' Go thy ways to a nunnery ' cuts Ophelia to the quick and she walks away. In a flash Hamlet is after her down the steps, half across the stage—a final hope, a final test. He takes her arm and jerks her around, facing him. Eye to eye, he asks the fatal question: ' Where's your father? ' There is a breathless moment of suspense as Hamlet grips her tight, driving her to the truth. Then the lie: ' At home, my lord.'

With a violent gesture he throws her from him, hurling the chain of pearls at her feet and breaking into a storm of fury. Slashing his words at her and at Polonius behind the arras, he turns and rushes off left only to come back across the middle landing for the marriage ' plague.' Again he turns away, and again returns, each successive outburst more violent than the last, and each weighted with double and treble significance for the invisible listeners.

Get thee to a nunnery, go; farewell. Or, if thou wilt needs marry, marry a fool; for wise men know well enough what monsters you make of them. To a nunnery, go; and quickly too. Farewell.

OPHELIA. O heavenly powers, restore him!

HAMLET. I have heard of your paintings too, well enough; God hath given you one face, and you make yourselves another: you jig, you amble, and you lisp, and nickname God's creatures, and make your wantonness your ignorance. Go to, I'll no more on 't; it hath made me mad. I say, we will have no more marriages; those that are married already, all but one, shall live; the rest shall keep as they are. To a nunnery, go.

[*Exit.*

OPHELIA. O! what a noble mind is here o'erthrown:
The courtier's, soldier's, scholar's, eye, tongue, sword;
The expectancy and rose of the fair state,
The glass of fashion and the mould of form,
The observ'd of all observers, quite, quite down!
And I, of ladies most deject and wretched,
That suck'd the honey of his music vows,
Now see that noble and most sovereign reason,
Like sweet bells jangled, out of tune and harsh;
That unmatch'd form and feature of blown youth
Blasted with ecstasy: O! woe is me,
To have seen what I have seen, see what I see!

Re-enter KING *and* POLONIUS.

KING. Love! his affections do not that way tend;
Nor what he spake, though it lack'd form a little,
Was not like madness. There 's something in his soul
O'er which his melancholy sits on brood;
[And, I do doubt, the hatch and the disclose
Will be some danger;]
He shall with speed to England,
For the demand of our neglected tribute:
[Haply the seas and countries different
With variable objects shall expel
This something-settled matter in his heart,
Whereon his brains still beating puts him thus
From fashion of himself.] What think you on 't?

POLONIUS. It shall do well: but yet do I believe
The origin and commencement of his grief
Sprung from neglected love. How now, Ophelia!
You need not tell us what Lord Hamlet said;
We heard it all. My lord, do as you please;
But, if you hold it fit, after the play,
Let his queen mother all alone entreat him
To show his griefs: let her be round with him;

Hamlet has reached by now a pitch of excitement beyond his own control. His indignation, spurred by Ophelia's betrayal and the closing in of the net of his uncle's treachery, put him beside himself. He is indeed in a ' towering passion ' as he will describe a similar outburst later, and at the height of the whirlwind he shouts ' It hath made me mad '—loud enough for everyone to hear. With a quick glance around to see, if possible, where the ' lawful espials ' are hidden, the threatening ' all but one, shall live ' is thrown against the listening walls. Suddenly, he is exhausted. He looks down at Ophelia's terror-stricken face that swims up to him from the depths of his fatigue . . . His two hands go up—palms out, as though pushing the vision away—denying the last faint shadow of hope that lies in that once loved face. ' To a nunnery, go ' is broken, spent. He turns and goes slowly, haltingly out, his head down, an outstretched hand feeling blindly for support as he makes his way through the low doorway.

Ophelia is left alone to lament what she takes to be madness, and the King enters on the upper platform with his caustic comment—denying both the love and the insanity, and full of his resolution to get rid of a dangerous adversary as quickly as possible. Polonius, indifferent to the harrowing experience his daughter has just been through and undaunted by the rising menace of Hamlet's increasing determination, plans the next espials which are to have such fatal consequences.

And I'll be plac'd, so please you, in the ear
Of all their conference. If she find him not,
To England send him, or confine him where
Your wisdom best shall think.

KING.   It shall be so:
Madness in great ones must not unwatch'd go.

ACT II.

HAMLET. Speak the speech, I pray you, as I pronounced it to you, trippingly on the tongue; but if you mouth it, as many of your players do, I had as lief the town-crier spoke my lines. Nor do not saw the air too much with your hand, thus; but use all gently: for in the very torrent, tempest, and—as I may say—whirlwind of passion, you must acquire and beget a temperance, that may give it smoothness. O! it offends me to the soul to hear a robustious periwig-pated fellow tear a passion to tatters, to very rags, to split the ears of the groundlings, I would have such a fellow whipped for o'er-doing Termagant; it out-herods Herod: pray you, avoid it.

FIRST PLAYER. I warrant your honour.

HAMLET. Be not too tame neither, but let your own discretion be your tutor: suit the action to the word, the word to the action; with this special observance, that you o'erstep not the modesty of nature; for anything so overdone is from the purpose of playing, whose end, both at the first and now, was and is, to hold, as 'twere, the mirror up to nature; to show virtue her own feature, scorn her own image, and the very age and body of the time his form and pressure. Now, this overdone, or come tardy off, though it make the unskilful laugh, cannot but make the judicious grieve; the censure of which one must in your allowance o'erweigh a whole theatre of others. O! there be players that I have seen play, and heard others praise, and that highly, not to speak it profanely, that, neither having the accent of Christians nor the gait of Christian, pagan, nor man, have so strutted and bellowed that I have thought some of nature's journeymen had made men and not made them well, they imitated humanity so abominably.

FIRST PLAYER. I hope we have reformed that indifferently with us.

HAMLET. O! reform it altogether. And let those that play your clowns speak no more than is set down for them; for there be of them that will themselves laugh, to set on some quantity of barren spectators to laugh too, though in the mean time some necessary question of the play be then to be considered; that 's villainous, and shows a most pitiful ambition in the fool that uses it. Go, make you ready. [*Exeunt Players.*

Enter POLONIUS, ROSENCRANTZ, *and* GUILDENSTERN.

How now, my lord! will the king hear this piece of work?

POLONIUS. And the queen too, and that presently.

HAMLET. Bid the players make haste.   [*Exit* POLONIUS.

Will you two help to hasten them?

ACT II

SCENE 8. *The great hall in the castle.*

As the curtain goes up on the second act, the stage is in darkness, except for a pool of light at the front where the players are silently rehearsing. The First Player, in the costume of the Player King, stands a little to the right, the Second, with the black cloak of Lucianus, the script in his left hand, practices a sweeping gesture with his other arm—right to left and downward, as though pouring imaginary poison in the ear of an imaginary sleeping king.

Hamlet, standing in the dark on the middle landing, left, watches them for a moment, then swings down and forward, taking the two pages of parchment—the dozen or sixteen lines he has written —from the Player's hand. ' Speak the speech, I pray you ' is both a command and an admonition. It is spoken firmly but with a certain lift—authoritative, interested. There is again the note of gaiety, of pleasure in things of the intellect expressed in his warm welcome of the actor troupe. From time to time his eyes drop to the script in his hand as he speaks. It is important that this should be done right—' Be not too tame neither '—the King must get the point. As he tries to make clear to them the purpose of playing, he pauses a moment, his left hand comes up, he gropes in his mind for the simplest, clearest simile, and then, with an expressive gesture, finds it in the mirror which he seems to hold for a moment in space. With ' O! there be players . . .' he turns to the Third Player who has strolled over during the previous lines and now stands at his left, addressing him with quiet humour, neither portentous nor over-emphatic. As the First Player answers, Hamlet is reading his script. There is a brief silence before he comes out of his abstraction with a smiling, delicately ironic ' O! reform it altogether.'

The reproof to the clown, again to the Player on his left, is more emphatic. The ' villanous ' very strong—then with a sweep of his arm he sends them off through the arched doorway, centre, to prepare for the play: ' Go, make you ready.' As they leave he

ROSENCRANTZ. ⎫
GUILDENSTERN. ⎬ We will, my lord.
                      [Exeunt ROSENCRANTZ *and* GUILDENSTERN

HAMLET. What, ho! Horatio!

HORATIO. Here, sweet lord, at your service.

HAMLET. Horatio, thou art e'en as just a man
  As e'er my conversation cop'd withal.

HORATIO. O! my dear lord,—

HAMLET.   Nay, do not think I flatter;
  [For what advancement may I hope from thee,
  That no revenue hast but thy good spirits
  To feed and clothe thee? Why should the poor be flatter'd?
  No; let the candied tongue lick absurd pomp,
  And crook the pregnant hinges of the knee
  Where thrift may follow fawning. Dost thou hear?]
  Since my dear soul was mistress of her choice
  And could of men distinguish, her election
  Hath seal'd thee for herself; for thou hast been
  As one, in suffering all, that suffers nothing,
  A man that fortune's buffets and rewards
  Hast ta'en with equal thanks; and bless'd are those
  Whose blood and judgment are so well co-mingled
  That they are not a pipe for fortune's finger
  To sound what stop she please. Give me that man
  That is not passion's slave, and I will wear him
  In my heart's core, ay, in my heart of heart,
  As I do thee. Something too much of this.
  There is a play to-night before the king;
  One scene of it comes near the circumstance
  Which I have told thee of my father's death:
  I prithee, when thou seest that act afoot,
  Even with the very comment of thy soul
  Observe mine uncle; if his occulted guilt
  Do not itself unkennel in one speech,
  It is a damned ghost that we have seen,
  And my imaginations are as foul
  As Vulcan's stithy. Give him heedful note;
  For I mine eyes will rivet to his face,
  And after we will both our judgments join
  In censure of his seeming.

HORATIO.   Well, my lord:
  If he steal aught the whilst this play is playing,
  And 'scape detecting, I will pay the theft.

HAMLET. They are coming to the play; I must be idle:
  Get you a place.

greets Polonius who comes hurrying in from the right. Rosencrantz and Guildenstern, following in Polonius' wake, are quickly
despatched in the direction of the players, and Hamlet, turning,
sees Horatio coming down the stairway, left. With a quick, impetuous movement he crosses to him. Horatio stands on the middle
landing, Hamlet below him looking up.

The words of friendship, spoken with intense feeling, are
accented by the gravity of his upturned face. Horatio is the one
stable point in this shifting, treacherous vortex. Hamlet's hand
is on his arm. His words describe not only what Horatio is, but
what he himself is not. The self-criticism is profound, but not
bitter—too deeply weighted for bitterness. The words come slowly.
' Give me that man that is not *passion's slave*.' He seems to hold
the image of his own passion-driven life before us as he pauses
after the evocative words. ' Heart's core,' ' heart of heart '—organ
notes, rounded, vibrant, pulsing with force and profound feeling.
He stands for a moment, holding Horatio's arm, then breaks away
with a quick change of mood, leading Horatio forward. His anxiety,
his doubts, his driving obsession are with him again. He tells the
plan. His face is again harassed, his voice lacerated with that haunting dread of being ' damned,' whether by devils of his own ' foul
imagination ' matters little.

The lights go up revealing the full stage as the courtiers begin
to arrive, some entering through the central arch and taking their
places right and left on the upper platforms, others coming on either
side of the lower stage and mounting the stairs. As soon as he hears
voices approaching, Hamlet draws away from Horatio, leaps up
the left stairway and takes his stand near the throne-like chairs
that have been placed in the centre of the upper platform overlooking the main stage where the play is to be performed. Hamlet's
manner is once more in the antic mood, slightly exaggerated, more
mocking than mad; his ruffled hair looks wind-blown, he moves
with swift, graceful energy. As the King leads Gertrude in through
the right lower entrance and starts up the stairs, Hamlet comes
down toward them. His excitement lends edge to the barbed re-

Enter KING, QUEEN, POLONIUS, OPHELIA, ROSENCRANTZ, GUILDENSTERN, *and Others.*

KING. How fares our cousin Hamlet?

HAMLET. Excellent, i' faith; of the chameleon's dish: I eat the air, promise-crammed; you cannot feed capons so.

KING. I have nothing with this answer, Hamlet; these words are not mine.

HAMLET. No, nor mine now. [*To* POLONIUS.] My lord, you played once i' the university, you say?

POLONIUS. That did I, my lord, and was accounted a good actor.

HAMLET. And what did you enact?

POLONIUS. I did enact Julius Cæsar: I was killed i' the Capitol; Brutus killed me.

HAMLET. It was a brute part of him to kill so capital a calf there. Be the players ready?

ROSENCRANTZ. Ay, my lord; they stay upon your patience.

QUEEN. Come hither, my good Hamlet, sit by me.

HAMLET. No, good mother, here 's metal more attractive.

POLONIUS. [*To the* KING.] O ho! do you mark that?

HAMLET. Lady, shall I lie in your lap?

OPHELIA. No, my lord.

HAMLET. I mean, my head upon your lap?

OPHELIA. Ay, my lord.

HAMLET. Do you think I meant country matters?

OPHELIA. You are merry, my lord.

HAMLET. Who, I?

OPHELIA. Ay, my lord.

HAMLET. O God, your only jig-maker. What should a man do but be merry? for, look you, how cheerfully my mother looks, and my father died within 's two hours.

OPHELIA. Nay, 'tis twice two months, my lord.

HAMLET. So long? Nay, then, let the devil wear black, for I'll have a suit of sables. O heavens! die two months ago, and not forgotten yet? Then there 's hope a great man's memory may outlive his life half a year; [but, by 'r lady, he must build churches then].

Enter PROLOGUE.

OPHELIA. What means this, my lord?

HAMLET. Marry, this is miching mallecho; it means mischief. We shall know by this fellow: the players cannot keep counsel; they'll tell all.

PROLOGUE. For us and for our tragedy,
Here stooping to your clemency,
We beg your hearing patiently.

HAMLET. Is this a prologue, or the posy of a ring?

OPHELIA. 'Tis brief, my lord.

torts, delivered with elaborate courtesy, with which he answers the King's greeting. As the royal pair and their train pass him, he drops to the main stage and with a gesture halts Polonius for the swift, light interchange, with its tragically ironic reference to the killing of this ' capital calf.'

The pace quickens. The King and Queen, blazing with jewels, gorgeous and complacent, take their places, surrounded by the court which glitters in its brightest colours. Ophelia on the right-hand side of the upper platform finds herself the uncomfortable target of Hamlet's two-edged wit. He sits beside her at the top of the stairs, a little to the right and behind the Queen, and slashes first at one and then at the other under the cover of his antic liberty. But it is the Queen with whom he is chiefly concerned— Ophelia has been left behind in the perilous adventure. His mother and the King are, from now on, the centre of his burning attention. Wherever he moves on the stage he seems to hold them at the focal point of an intense watchfulness.

As the Prologue speaks the opening verse, Hamlet gets to his feet and starts slowly down the stairs, stopping long enough at his mother's side to drop the withering ' as woman's love ' as though casually into her ear. At the middle landing he halts and drops down on the top of the third step from whence he can look up into the faces of the King and Queen and yet be near the players. His right hand holds the two pages of manuscript in a grip so tight the edges curl. In his crouching immobility he seems to radiate force. He drives the players on with his pulsing excitement. Once or twice his hand beats the rhythm of the galloping lines. Hamlet this time is the hunter, not the hunted. Wary, alert, strung taut in every fibre of his mind and body, he is closing in on his quarry.

For the moment it is the Queen's turn. Watching her as she sits handsome, sensual, obtuse, he cannot resist comment. The ' Wormwood, wormwood ' is mocking, given with a laugh that is edged with gall. As the Player Queen protests her faithfulness, Hamlet gets to his feet, his eyes fixed on his mother. With a courtly

HAMLET. As woman's love.

Enter two PLAYERS, KING *and* QUEEN

PLAYER KING. Full thirty times hath Phœbus' car gone round
Neptune's salt wash and Tellus' orbed ground,
Since love our hearts and Hymen did our hands
Unite commutual in most sacred bands.

PLAYER QUEEN. So many journeys may the sun and moon
Make us again count o'er ere love be done!
But, woe is me! you are so sick of late,
So far from cheer and from your former state,
That I distrust you. Yet, though I distrust,
Discomfort you, my lord, it nothing must.

PLAYER KING. Faith, I must leave thee, love, and shortly too;
My operant powers their functions leave to do:
And thou shalt live in this fair world behind,
Honour'd, belov'd; and haply one as kind
For husband shalt thou—

PLAYER QUEEN.   O! confound the rest;
Such love must needs be treason in my breast:
In second husband let me be accurst;
None wed the second but who kill'd the first.

HAMLET. Wormwood, wormwood.

PLAYER QUEEN. The instances that second marriage move,
Are base respects of thrift, but none of love;
A second time I kill my husband dead,
When second husband kisses me in bed.

PLAYER KING. I do believe you think what now you speak;
But what we do determine oft we break
What to ourselves in passion we propose,
The passion ending, doth the purpose lose.
So think thou wilt no second husband wed;
But die thy thoughts when thy first lord is dead.

PLAYER QUEEN. Nor earth to me give food, nor heaven light!
Sport and repose lock from me day and night!
Both here and hence pursue me lasting strife,
If, once a widow, ever I be wife!

HAMLET. If she should break it now!

PLAYER KING. 'Tis deeply sworn. Sweet, leave me here awhile;
My spirits grow dull, and fain I would beguile
The tedious day with sleep.

PLAYER QUEEN.   Sleep rock thy brain;
And never come mischance between us twain!   [*Exit.*

HAMLET. Madam, how like you this play?

QUEEN. The lady doth protest too much, methinks.

HAMLET. O! but she'll keep her word.

flourish of his right hand he seems to present the situation for her inspection. ' If she should break it now! ' What absurd sentimentalities, his mocking tone implies. What old-fashioned nonsense! He walks slowly up the stairs to his mother's side. ' Madam, how like you this play? ' He is standing beside her, looking down, holding her with his cool, conventional question. His mother answers quietly and he moves on. ' O! but she'll keep her word ' is accompanied by another mocking laugh.

He walks on behind the throne, pausing between the King and Queen to answer the former's question. He leans forward, his head almost on a level with the King's, ' they do but jest ' very suave. Then, quickly, coming around to the King's left hand, the word ' poison ' falls with ominous significance straight into the King's ear. Before the King has had time to move, Hamlet is walking on down the left-hand stairs with a blandly cheerful ' No offence i' the world.' He is half-way down when the King's question, ' What do you call the play? ' stops him. ' The Mousetrap ' is tossed out with a quick, negligent gesture of the hand, dropped with a lack of emphasis more effective than a dozen underscorings.

Half-way down the stairs he turns toward the King; the battle is on now, the points unbated with a vengeance. Hamlet's voice rises. ' You shall see anon; 'tis a *knavish* piece of work ' is accentuated by a blow of his hand on the script, a sharp tearing sound that makes the King start. Then very smooth and dangerous, ' your majesty and we that have *free souls* '—he bows a little as though in compliment.

With the entrance of Lucianus the pace accelerates sharply. Hamlet makes no more effort to hide his mounting excitement. He is on the middle platform, left, exactly opposite the place from whence he had watched his mother during the first part of the play. Now his piercing intentness is fixed on Claudius. ' This is one Lucianus, *nephew* to the king.' He introduces murder with a flourish. Then he turns on the Player. ' Begin.' The whole stage throbs with Hamlet's driving excitement. He crouches on the

KING. Have you heard the argument? Is there no offence in 't?

HAMLET. No, no, they do but jest, poison in jest; no offence i' the world.

KING. What do you call the play?

HAMLET. The Mouse-trap. Marry, how? Tropically. This play is the image of a murder done in Vienna: Gonzago is the duke's name; his wife, Baptista. You shall see anon; 'tis a knavish piece of work: but what of that? your majesty and we that have free souls, it touches us not: let the galled jade wince, our withers are unwrung.

Enter Player as LUCIANUS.

This is one Lucianus, nephew to the king.

OPHELIA. You are a good chorus, my lord.

HAMLET. Begin, murderer; pox, leave thy damnable faces, and begin. Come; the croaking raven doth bellow for revenge.

LUCIANUS. Thoughts black, hands apt, drugs fit, and time agreeing;

Confederate season, else no creature seeing;

Thou mixture rank, of midnight weeds collected,

With Hecate's ban thrice blasted, thrice infected,

Thy natural magic and dire property,

On wholesome life usurp immediately.

HAMLET. He poisons him i' the garden for 's estate. His name 's Gonzago; the story is extant, and writ in very choice Italian. You shall see anon how the murderer gets the love of Gonzago's wife.

OPHELIA. The king rises.

HAMLET. What! frighted with false fire?

QUEEN. How fares my lord?

POLONIUS. Give o'er the play.

KING. Give me some light: away!

ALL. Lights, lights, lights!   [*Exeunt all except* HAMLET *and* HORATIO.

HAMLET.   Why, let the stricken deer go weep,

The hart ungalled play;

For some must watch, while some must sleep:

So runs the world away.

O good Horatio! I'll take the ghost's word for a thousand pound. Didst perceive?

HORATIO. Very well, my lord.

HAMLET. Upon the talk of the poisoning?

HORATIO. I did very well note him.

HAMLET. Ah, ha! Come, some music! come, the recorders!

For if the king like not the comedy,

Why then, belike, he likes it not, perdy.

Come, some music!

Re-enter ROSENCRANTZ *and* GUILDENSTERN.

GUILDENSTERN. Good my lord, vouchsafe me a word with you.

HAMLET. Sir, a whole history.

GUILDENSTERN. The king, sir,—

stairs, his hand, again, beating the measure of Lucianus' lines as though he would whip them forward to their desperate goal.

As the King loses his self-control, Hamlet snatches the words from the Player: ' He poisons him i' the garden . . . You shall see anon how the murderer gets the love of Gonzago's wife.' The words are a bomb that blows the King to his feet. Like a coiled spring released, Hamlet is up the stairs, shouting above the hubbub. ' What! frighted with *false fire*? ' He stands in the King's path, a threatening black flame. The court rushes out left and right, melting before the impact of a battle it cannot understand. Hamlet leaps onto the throne waving the pages of the script above his head and shouting his triumphant jingle. The Ghost's words have been confirmed a hundredfold! The guilty creature has indeed been un-kenneled and the strain of months and days has suddenly snapped. In an explosion of released tension, Hamlet tears the ' dozen or sixteen lines ' into a thousand pieces and scatters them abroad. Horatio is sent off to fetch music, and Hamlet throws himself back on the throne, shaken, his breath coming in gasps, his whole body quivering.

At the same moment Rosencrantz and Guildenstern enter hastily from the right with their demands and messages. He takes no trouble to cover his hatred of the two men and his bitter wit mocks their sycophancy with rapier blows. When Guildenstern mentions the King, Hamlet leans eagerly toward him, hoping for the worst, but the answer is merely a threat and Hamlet leans back again on the throne, mocking and slashing at the two men as they stand below him on the stairway. ' I am tame, sir; pronounce ' he exclaims, in a voice and manner wildly opposite. His outflung left arm grasps the back of the throne, his right hand grips the chair arm with a force that threatens to break it: ' My wit's diseased! ' It is the climax of his outburst.

With a visible effort he concentrates more closely on the words of the two messengers. ' O wonderful son, that can so astonish a mother! ' is given its full ironic effect. Hamlet is calmer now but more menacing. His withering rejoinders are scarcely veiled in-sults, intended to infuriate these tools of the King. When Rosen-

HAMLET. Ay, sir, what of him?

GUILDENSTERN. Is in his retirement marvellous distempered.

HAMLET. With drink, sir?

GUILDENSTERN. Good my lord, put your discourse into some frame.

HAMLET. I am tame, sir; pronounce.

GUILDENSTERN. The queen, your mother, in most great affliction of spirit, hath sent me to you.

HAMLET. You are welcome.

GUILDENSTERN. Nay, good my lord, this courtesy is not of the right breed. If it shall please you to make me a wholesome answer, I will do your mother's commandment.

HAMLET. Sir, I cannot.

GUILDENSTERN. What, my lord?

HAMLET. Make you a wholesome answer; my wit's diseased; but, sir, such answer as I can make, you shall command; or, rather, as you say, my mother: therefore no more, but to the matter: my mother, you say,—

ROSENCRANTZ. Then, thus she says: your behaviour hath struck her into amazement and admiration.

HAMLET. O wonderful son, that can so astonish a mother! But is there no sequel at the heels of this mother's admiration? Impart.

ROSENCRANTZ. She desires to speak with you in her closet ere you go to bed.

HAMLET. We shall obey, were she ten times our mother. Have you any further trade with us?

ROSENCRANTZ. My lord, you once did love me.

HAMLET. So I do still, by these pickers and stealers.

ROSENCRANTZ. Good my lord, what is your cause of distemper? [you do surely bar the door upon your own liberty; if] you deny your griefs to your friend.

HAMLET. Sir, I lack advancement.

ROSENCRANTZ. How can that be when you have the voice of the king himself for your succession in Denmark?

HAMLET. Ay, sir, but ' While the grass grows, '—the proverb is something musty.

Enter Players, with recorders.

O! the recorders: let me see one. To withdraw with you: why do you go about to recover the wind of me, as if you would drive me into a toil?

GUILDENSTERN. O! my lord, if my duty be too bold, my love is too unmannerly.

HAMLET. I do not well understand that. Will you play upon this pipe?

GUILDENSTERN. My lord, I cannot.

HAMLET. I pray you.

GUILDENSTERN. Believe me, I cannot.

HAMLET. I do beseech you.

GUILDENSTERN. I know no touch of it, my lord.

HAMLET. 'Tis as easy as lying; govern these ventages with your finger and

crantz finally challenges him with his smug ' you once did love me,'
Hamlet indicates by a quick gesture of strong fingers a cheerful
willingness to strangle the ' good lad.' Rosencrantz's answer, with
its veiled threat, unlooses the lightning. Hamlet comes to his feet
with a snap. Standing on the extreme edge of the platform he towers
wrathfully above the two men. ' I lack advancement ' is not merely
a statement, but a proclamation of his thwarted right to power. He
leaps in one bound down to the middle landing where Rosencrantz
is standing and drives him backward with his ' Ay, sir, but " While
the grass grows." ' Rosencrantz is saved from annihilation by the
sudden appearance of one of the players through the low archway.
The recorder which he brings diverts Hamlet's attention and gives
Guildenstern time to come down the steps and around to Hamlet's
left, closing in on him on the side opposite Rosencrantz. With a
movement of annoyance, Hamlet becomes conscious of Guildenstern's presence. He turns on him roughly, taking him by the arm
and leading him down and forward to the centre of the stage with a
swift impatient swing and a sharp challenge: ' why do you go about
to recover the wind of me . . . ? '

Hamlet is aware that the chase is on again—and he once more
the hunted. The recorder gleams in his hand. Rosencrantz comes
down the three steps and stands on his right. Swiftly, phrase on
phrase, he builds the satiric simile, the first lines almost gently,
smilingly—' as easy as lying '—and then in a rising storm to the
furious ' 'Sblood, do you think I am easier to be played on than a
pipe? ' He stands between the two men, erect, vibrant, suddenly
tall and masterful. ' Though you can *fret* me, you cannot play
upon me.' Before they have collected their wits he has stepped
away from them. ' God bless you, sir! ' addressed to Polonius, is
spoken in the same breath, as Hamlet swings forward and to the
right to meet the old man who has just hurried in with further
messages from the Queen. Polonius is caught up on the rising tide
of Hamlet's indignation. ' Do you see yonder cloud . . . ? ' The
imaginary cloud floats over the audience. Polonius looks up and out,
obedient and startled. Hamlet looks at him and then very thought-

thumb, give it breath with your mouth, and it will discourse most eloquent music. Look you, these are the stops.

GUILDENSTERN. But these cannot I command to any utterance of harmony; I have not the skill.

HAMLET. Why, look you now, how unworthy a thing you make of me. You would play upon me; you would seem to know my stops; you would pluck out the heart of my mystery; you would sound me from my lowest note to the top of my compass; and there is much music, excellent voice, in this little organ, yet cannot you make it speak. 'Sblood, do you think I am easier to be played on than a pipe? Call me what instrument you will, though you can fret me, you cannot play upon me.

Enter POLONIUS.

God bless you, sir!

POLONIUS. My lord, the queen would speak with you, and presently.

HAMLET. Do you see yonder cloud that's almost in shape of a camel?

POLONIUS. By the mass, and 'tis like a camel, indeed.

HAMLET. Methinks it is like a weasel.

POLONIUS. It is backed like a weasel.

HAMLET. Or like a whale?

POLONIUS. Very like a whale.

HAMLET. Then I will come to my mother by and by. [*Aside.*] They fool me to the top of my bent. [*Aloud.*] I will come by and by.

POLONIUS. I will say so.   [*Exit.*

HAMLET. By and by is easily said. Leave me, friends.

fully squints through the recorder. ' Methinks it is like a weasel.'

Polonius' continued assent adds a last fillip to Hamlet's exasperation. He walks past the old man flinging out his bitter aside and rounding on him with ' By and by is easily said.' Then in two strides he is up the step to the middle landing, right, completing the zigzag swirl of movement that started when he leaped down from the upper platform. As Rosencrantz and Guildenstern move forward to follow him, he turns on them with the crack of a whip. A flash of upraised hands holding the recorder between them. A downward stroke and a sharp report as the recorder breaks in two across his knee. Then with a flourish he hands a piece to each of the King's hounds. ' Leave me, friends! ' high and hard. The spiral snaps off at its apex. The lights black out.

SCENE 9.—*The* KING'S *dressing room.* KING, ROSENCRANTZ, *and* GUILDEN-
STERN.

KING. I like him not, nor stands it safe with us
To let his madness range. Therefore prepare you;
I your commission will forthwith dispatch,
And he to England shall along with you.
(The terms of our estate may not endure
Hazard so dangerous as doth hourly grow
Out of his lunacies.)
Arm you, I pray you, to this speedy voyage.

ROSENCRANTZ. ⎱
GUILDENSTERN. ⎰   We will haste us.

[*Exeunt* ROSENCRANTZ *and* GUILDENSTERN
Enter POLONIUS.

POLONIUS. My lord, he 's going to his mother's closet:
Behind the arras I'll convey myself
To hear the process; I'll warrant she'll tax him home;
I'll call upon you ere you go to bed
And tell you what I know.

KING.   Thanks, dear my lord.   [*Exit* POLONIUS.
O! my offence is rank, it smells to heaven;
It hath the primal eldest curse upon 't;
A brother's murder! Pray can I not,
Though inclination be as sharp as will:
My stronger guilt defeats my strong intent;
[And, like a man to double business bound,
I stand in pause where I shall first begin,
And both neglect.] What if this cursed hand
Were thicker than itself with brother's blood,
Is there not rain enough in the sweet heavens
To wash it white as snow?
                              But, O! what form of prayer
Can serve my turn? ' Forgive me my foul murder '?
That cannot be; since I am still possess'd
Of those effects for which I did the murder,
My crown, mine own ambition, and my queen.
May one be pardon'd and retain the offence?
[In the corrupted currents of this world
Offence's gilded hand may shove by justice,
And oft 'tis seen the wicked prize itself
Buys out the law; but 'tis not so above;
There is no shuffling, there the action lies
In his true nature, and we ourselves compell'd
Even to the teeth and forehead of our faults

SCENE 9. *The king's dressing room.*

A green curtain with a draped doorway, right, a prie-dieu left, a chair opposite, suggest the King's closet. The King, ' marvelous distempered,' talks with Rosencrantz and Guildenstern and informs them that they are to conduct Hamlet to England immediately. As he dismisses them, Polonius, much ruffled from his encounter with Hamlet, comes in from the right on his way to the Queen. Finally the King is left alone with his evil conscience. He turns toward the prie-dieu and is about to kneel when he thinks he hears a noise behind the arras. Drawing his sword he moves swiftly and stealthily to the draped doorway, right, swings back the hanging and finds—nothing. Before he again attempts his devotions he lays his sword on the chair near the doorway, then moves left for his tormented meditation on his sins. As he finally sinks to his knees and buries his head in his hands, the arras over the doorway behind him is shaken and Hamlet appears on the wind of his tempestuous passage to his mother's room. It brings him as far as the chair before he sees the King. At the sight he stops abruptly, grasping the back of the chair to break the impetus of his forward movement. As he does so his eye falls on the unsheathed sword. ' Now might I do it pat.' His voice is a harsh whisper, his hand reaches down for the sword as his eyes burn into the King's back. ' And now I'll do 't '—up straight, his sword arm back—the recoil of a piston ready to drive home. Then—nothing.

Thought, in Hamlet as swift as action, blocks the current, and one of his haunting thoughts is this of heaven and hell. His father in hell, his dearest foe in heaven. The intolerable image flashes before him, stopping his hand. His arm, his body, sinks. His voice, feverish, agitated, paints the picture in detail; with ' Up, sword ' he swings the gleaming steel into the cradle of his left arm. Crouching forward he pours out the venomous words. Then with a swift, stealthy swing he is at the doorway again. One last glance, a flash, and he is gone. The King starts up, his eyes fall on the empty chair. He moves forward with a gesture of alarm as Hamlet's voice is heard off-stage calling ' Mother! '

To give in evidence. What then? what rests?]
Try what repentance can: what can it not?
Yet what can it, when one can not repent?
O wretched state! (O bosom black as death!
O limed soul, that struggling to be free
Art more engaged!) Help, angels! make assay;
Bow, stubborn knees; and heart with strings of steel
Be soft as sinews of the new-born babe.
All may be well.   [*Kneels.*

Enter HAMLET.

HAMLET. Now might I do it pat, now he is praying;
And now I'll do 't; and so he goes to heaven;
And so am I reveng'd. That would be scann'd:
A villain kills my father; and for that,
I, his sole son, do this same villain send
To heaven.
Why, this is hire and salary, not revenge.
He took my father grossly, full of bread,
With all his crimes broad blown, as flush as May;
            And am I then reveng'd,
To take him in the purging of his soul,
When he is fit and season'd for his passage?
No.
Up, sword, and know thou a more horrid hent;
When he is drunk asleep, or in his rage,
Or in the incestuous pleasure of his bed,
At gaming, swearing, or about some act
That has no relish of salvation in 't;
Then trip him, that his heels may kick at heaven,
And that his soul may be as damn'd and black
As hell, whereto it goes. My mother stays:
(This physic but prolongs thy sickly days.)   [*Exit.*
KING. My words fly up, my thoughts remain below:
Words without thoughts never to heaven go.

The Queens Private Apartment

SCENE 10

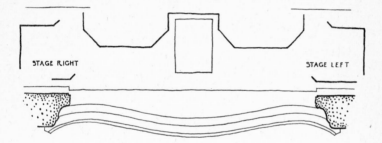

STAGE RIGHT   STAGE LEFT

SCENE 10.—*The* QUEEN's *private apartment.* QUEEN *and* POLONIUS.

POLONIUS. He will come straight. Look you lay home to him;
 Tell him his pranks have been too broad to bear with,
 And that your Grace hath screen'd and stood between
 Much heat and him. I'll silence me e'en here.
 Pray you, be round with him.
HAMLET. [*Within.*] Mother, mother, mother!
QUEEN.   I'll warrant you;
 Fear me not. Withdraw, I hear him coming. [POLONIUS *hides.*

Enter HAMLET.

HAMLET. Now, mother, what 's the matter?
QUEEN. Hamlet, thou hast thy father much offended.
HAMLET. Mother, you have my father much offended.
QUEEN. Come, come, you answer with an idle tongue.
HAMLET. Go, go, you question with a wicked tongue.
QUEEN. Why, how now, Hamlet!
HAMLET.   What 's the matter now?
QUEEN. Have you forgot me?
HAMLET.   No, by the rood, not so:
 You are the queen, your husband's brother's wife;
 And,—would it were not so!—you are my mother.
QUEEN. Nay then, I'll set those to you that can speak.
HAMLET. Come, come, and sit you down; you shall not budge;
 You go not, till I set you up a glass
 Where you may see the inmost part of you.
QUEEN. What wilt thou do? thou wilt not murder me?
 Help, help, ho!
POLONIUS. [*Behind.*] What, ho! help! help! help!
HAMLET. How now! a rat? Dead, for a ducat, dead!
POLONIUS. [*Behind.*] O! I am slain.
QUEEN. O me! what hast thou done?
HAMLET. Nay, I know not: is it the king?
QUEEN. O! what a rash and bloody deed is this!
HAMLET. A bloody deed! almost as bad, good mother,
 As kill a king, and marry with his brother.
QUEEN. As kill a king!
HAMLET.   Ay, lady, 'twas my word.
 Thou wretched, rash, intruding fool, farewell!
 I took thee for thy better; [take thy fortune;]
 Leave wringing of your hands: peace! sit you down,
 And let me wring your heart; for so I shall,
 If it be made of penetrable stuff,
 If damned custom have not brass'd it so
 That it is proof and bulwark against sense.

'The Queen's Private Apartment'

Designed by Jo Mielziner for the New York production of Hamlet

SCENE 10. *The queen's private apartment.*

A couch in the centre without head or foot board, above it an ornate gold canopy from which hang long draped curtains, grey and orange predominating. The walls are hung with tapestries. There is a covered doorway, right. The Queen, greatly disturbed, walks to and fro talking to Polonius. At the sound of Hamlet's voice off-stage Polonius hides behind the hangings at the head of the bed. Hamlet comes in with a rush. The storm that has been rising since the beginning of the play scene sweeps him into his mother's presence. The first clash between them is swift and sharp, lightning-flashes of will against will. But Hamlet's drive is the greater. His words are charged with the demoniac energy of the thought that had festered in his mind for months. The unsheathed sword gleams on his arm. His mother is terrified and cries out. Polonius answers from behind the curtain. For one terrible moment Hamlet stands transfixed, staring at the spot behind ' the royal bed of Denmark ' where only his father's betrayer and murderer could be.

With a tearing cry he leaps across the stage onto the bed and drives his sword through and through the curtain. ' Dead, for a ducat, dead! ' At last, at last! He turns, sword flashing above his head, a towering figure of revenge and atonement on the couch, which the terrified and moaning woman below him has defiled. ' O! what a rash and bloody deed is this! ' she cries, and he in a frenzy shouts his answer: ' Almost as bad, good mother, as kill a king, and marry with his brother.' The horror within horror, the fear within the fear, is spoken. ' As kill a king! ' Gertrude straightens up, stands rooted, stiff with astonishment, staring at her son. Her surprise breaks across Hamlet's exaltation, checking it. He sways a little, his arm drops, his voice sinks with ' Ay, lady, 'twas my word.' His uncertainty once more floods over him. He steps down from the bed and lifts a corner of the hanging.

A deathly, motionless pause. Hamlet leans forward looking at

QUEEN. What have I done that thou dar'st wag thy tongue
  In noise so rude against me?
HAMLET.   Such an act
  That blurs the grace and blush of modesty,
  Calls virtue hypocrite, takes off the rose
  From the fair forehead of an innocent love
  And sets a blister there, makes marriage vows
  As false as dicers' oaths; heaven's face doth glow,
  Yea, this solidity and compound mass,
  With tristful visage, as against the doom,
  Is thought-sick at the act.
QUEEN.   Ay me! what act,
  That roars so loud and thunders in the index?
HAMLET. Look here, upon this picture, and on this;
  The counterfeit presentment of two brothers.
  See, what a grace was seated on this brow;
  Hyperion's curls, the front of Jove himself,
  An eye like Mars, to threaten and command,
  A station like the herald Mercury
  New-lighted on a heaven-kissing hill,
  A combination and a form indeed,
  Where every god did seem to set his seal,
  To give the world assurance of a man.
  This was your husband: look you now, what follows.
  Here is your husband; like a mildew'd ear,
  Blasting his wholesome brother. Have you eyes?
  Could you on this fair mountain leave to feed,
  And batten on this moor? Ha! have you eyes?
  You cannot call it love, for at your age
  The hey-day in the blood is tame, it 's humble,
  And waits upon the judgment; and what judgment
  Would step from this to this?
  O shame! where is thy blush? Rebellious hell,
  If thou canst mutine in a matron's bones,
  To flaming youth let virtue be as wax,
  And melt in her own fire.
QUEEN.   O Hamlet! speak no more;
  Thou turn'st mine eyes into my very soul;
  And there I see such black and grained spots
  As will not leave their tint.
HAMLET.   Nay, but to live
  In the rank sweat of an enseamed bed,
  Stew'd in corruption, honeying and making love
  Over the nasty sty,—

Polonius' body, then slowly, slowly, infinitely weary, he straightens up. The bloodstained sword gleams in his hand as he swings it down on the bed in front of him. 'Thou wretched, rash, intruding fool . . . !'—the voice rasps with scorn. He sinks on the bed, his head down. 'I took thee for thy better.' As the Queen moans and wrings her hands at this admission of murderous intent, Hamlet rouses himself. He had come to tell his mother what he thought of her. His telling now is charged with 'superfluous death.'

He takes her roughly by the arm and pushes her down on the end of the bed. Standing over her he pours out the excoriating words he has held too long in check. Now at last this 'most pernicious woman' who has so profoundly betrayed not only his father but himself, this mother whom he loves and hates, will be brought to a reckoning. His voice is a storm of pent passion. Daggers, indeed! The words are whips and cudgels, stinging in the sibilance of 'sets a blister there' and 'as false as dicers' oaths' (a swift gesture of the left hand throwing dice and decency aside), shattering in the thud of the heavy vowels of 'solidity and compound mass' of 'tristful visage as against the doom' until finally with 'thought-sick at the *act*' he stands upright, towering above the Queen.

Her challenging 'Ay me! what act . . . ?' brings him down on the couch beside her. He *will* make her see what he sees. His left hand outstretched seems to summon the beloved figure of his father before their eyes. His voice vibrates with the tender note of love and admiration which always accompanies the thought of him. The noble words are a carpet for a majestic presence. The tone is quiet, full, rich. It is a moment of healing calm at the heart of the storm. The image his words evoke is there 'to give the world assurance of a man.' Deeply moved, Gertrude turns to Hamlet as though she would throw herself into his arms, but his hands fly up pushing her off, repudiating her. His left hand swings out, downward, backward. 'Look you now, what follows.' There, on the ground, in the pit, he paints the picture of the 'mildew'd ear' which is his uncle.

Scorching phrase on phrase he throws into her face as Gertrude

QUEEN.   O! speak to me no more;
  These words like daggers enter in mine ears;
  No more, sweet Hamlet!
HAMLET.   A murderer, and a villain;
  A slave that is not twentieth part the tithe
  Of your precedent lord; a vice of kings;
  A cutpurse of the empire and the rule,
  That from a shelf the precious diadem stole,
  And put it in his pocket!
QUEEN.   No more!
HAMLET. A king of shreds and patches,—
                    Enter Ghost.

  Save me, and hover o'er me with your wings,
  You heavenly guards! What would your gracious figure?
QUEEN. Alas! he 's mad!
HAMLET. Do you not come your tardy son to chide,
  That, laps'd in time and passion, lets go by
  The important acting of your dread command?
  O! say.
GHOST. Do not forget: this visitation
  Is but to whet thy almost blunted purpose.
  But, look! amazement on thy mother sits;
  O! step between her and her fighting soul;
  Speak to her, Hamlet.
HAMLET.   How is it with you, lady?
QUEEN. Alas! how is 't with you,
  That you do bend your eye on vacancy
  And with the incorporal air do hold discourse?
                  O gentle son!
  Upon the heat and flame of thy distemper
  Sprinkle cool patience. Whereon do you look?
HAMLET. On him, on him! Look you, how pale he glares!
  His form and cause conjoin'd, preaching to stones,
  Would make them capable. Do not look upon me;
  Lest with this piteous action you convert
  My stern effects: then what I have to do
  Will want true colour; tears perchance for blood.
QUEEN. To whom do you speak this?
HAMLET.   Do you see nothing there?
QUEEN. Nothing at all; yet all that is I see.
HAMLET. Nor did you nothing hear?
QUEEN.   No, nothing but ourselves.
HAMLET. Why, look you there! look, how it steals away;
  My father, in his habit as he liv'd;
  Look! where he goes, even now, out at the portal.   [*Exit Ghost.*

draws back and away from him. The tempo quickens, again the beating of a demoniac pulse. Hamlet is on his feet, his tongue unleashed. ' Nay, but to live in the rank sweat of an enseamed bed.' The words lance the cankering sore to the quick. Beside himself, oblivious to his mother's horrified protests, to her pleas for mercy, her upraised hands warding off his searing words, he storms on— ' A murderer, and a villain . . . a vice of kings '—with mounting force until again erect, menacing, he seems to grow tall, his voice thunders. ' A king of shreds and patches—'

The rending cry is halted in mid-air. He stands absolutely motionless, his hand above his head. The lights have dimmed out, leaving a single shaft that falls on Hamlet's upturned face, on the ghostly figure near the wall at the extreme left. There is a moment of suspense, then Hamlet's awed whisper: ' Save me, and hover o'er me with your wings, you heavenly guards! ' His hand drops, he turns, very slowly. He has forgotten his mother. Completely bewildered, she stares at him as he drops to his knees, his back to her, his hand held out toward the Ghost. His voice has changed. The hard, virulent note is gone. Deep, tender, heartsick, the slow tragic words move with the falling cadence of a funeral march: ' Do you not come your tardy son to chide . . . ? '

Hamlet's drawn face expresses the exhaustion of his torn spirit ' laps'd in time and passion.' He listens to his father's words and at his bidding the hand which was stretched toward the ghostly visitant gropes backward toward his mother, sitting behind him on the couch. ' How is it with you, lady? ' He speaks in a detached voice—a somnambulist's voice. He does not look at her. She bends over him, distracted: ' Whereon do you look? ' Hamlet does not move. ' On him, on him! ' His eyes are fixed on the Ghost, his hand goes out again to the vision. The Ghost moves, and Hamlet turns to his mother, urgent—' Do you see nothing there? '—and then desperately: ' look, how it steals away! ' The Ghost moves swiftly to the right—past the seeing and the unseeing alike. The lights black out as Hamlet springs across the stage in its wake and stops, with a moan, at the portal through which it has dis-

QUEEN. This is the very coinage of your brain:
　This bodiless creation ecstasy
　Is very cunning in.
HAMLET. Ecstasy!
　My pulse, as yours, doth temperately keep time,
　And makes as healthful music. It is not madness
　That I have utter'd: bring me to the test,
　And I the matter will re-word, which madness
　Would gambol from. Mother, for love of grace,
　Lay not that flattering unction to your soul,
　That not your trespass but my madness speaks;
　It will but skin and film the ulcerous place,
　Whiles rank corruption, mining all within,
　Infects unseen. Confess yourself to heaven;
　Repent what 's past; avoid what is to come;
　And do not spread the compost on the weeds
　To make them ranker. Forgive me this my virtue;
　For in the fatness of these pursy times
　Virtue itself of vice must pardon beg,
　Yea, curb and woo for leave to do him good.
QUEEN. O Hamlet! thou hast cleft my heart in twain.
HAMLET. O! throw away the worser part of it,
　And live the purer with the other half.
　Good-night; but go not to mine uncle's bed;
　Assume a virtue, if you have it not.
　　　　　　　Refrain to-night;
　And that shall lend a kind of easiness
　To the next abstinence: Once more, good-night:
　And when you are desirous to be bless'd,
　I'll blessing beg of you. For this same lord,
　I do repent: [but heaven hath pleas'd it so,
　To punish me with this, and this with me,
　That I must be their scourge and minister.]
　I will bestow him, and will answer well
　The death I gave him. So, again, good-night.
　I must be cruel only to be kind:
　Thus bad begins and worse remains behind.
　One word more, good lady.
QUEEN.　　　　　　　　What shall I do?
HAMLET. Not this, by no means, that I bid you do:
　Let the bloat king tempt you again to bed;
　Pinch wanton on your cheek; call you his mouse;
　And let him, for a pair of reechy kisses,
　Or paddling in your neck with his damn'd fingers,
　Make you to ravel all this matter out,

appeared. He leans against the doorway until his mother's voice recalls him.

The room is once more suffused with its normal light as he walks toward his mother, roused to a new effort in his battle for her conscience. His first outburst is over; his voice is strong, insistent. He will not let her off. ' Lay not that flattering unction to your soul.' The imagery of corruption is still in his mind but he is no longer ridden by it. His appeal is burningly intense but less murky. At ' Confess yourself to heaven ' he falls on his knees, his arms about her, as though he would hold her bodily from evil. He pleads now not only with his own need but with something of his father's nobility. She bends over him weeping. ' O Hamlet! thou hast cleft my heart in twain.'

She sinks on the end of the couch, and he, his arms still around her, bids her a tender good-night. For a long moment his head rests on her breast and then slowly, with a kind of despair, he makes his final request: ' go not to mine uncle's bed.' ' Refrain to-night.' He holds her close. Then, straightening up, he looks into her face with deep tenderness and pleading, with humility, with the pathos of his young, proud spirit, thus curbed and wooing: ' And when you are desirous to be bless'd . . . ' His head bowed over the hands he holds between his own he sits for a long moment motionless. Then he rises slowly and walks around her as she remains seated on the end of the couch.

His step drags. The burden of the new calamity involved in Polonius' death is upon him. His voice hardens and then once more very tenderly he turns back to his mother. Kneeling on the couch behind her, his arms about her, he kisses her shoulder as the ominous words ' and worse remains behind ' seem to close their interview.

The Queen gets to her feet and starts toward the door, but Hamlet is not through. Her movement in the direction of the King, the sight of Polonius' dead body, brings back with a rush all the complexities of his predicament. He can trust no one—above all not his mother, who like Ophelia—and far worse—had

That I essentially am not in madness,
But mad in craft.

QUEEN. Be thou assur'd, if words be made of breath,
And breath of life, I have no life to breathe
What thou hast said to me.

HAMLET. I must to England; you know that?

                                              Alack!
QUEEN.
I had forgot: 'tis so concluded on.

HAMLET. There's letters seal'd; and my two school-fellows,
Whom I will trust as I will adders fang'd,
They bear the mandate; they must sweep my way,
And marshal me to knavery. Let it work;
For 'tis the sport to have the enginer
Hoist with his own petar: and it shall go hard
But I will delve one yard below their mines,
And blow them at the moon. O! 'tis most sweet,
When in one line two crafts directly meet.
This man shall set me packing;
I'll lug the guts into the neighbour room.
Mother, good-night. Indeed this counsellor
Is now most still, most secret, and most grave,
Who was in life a foolish prating knave.
Come, sir, to draw toward an end with you.
Good-night, mother.

permitted herself to be used as a tool for his enemy, had tolerated a spy at the most intimate and private of colloquies between mother and son. His anger rises in a sudden tide, stirring once more the dregs of his deep-rooted loathing. His words, again, sting and slash. The bloat king is not to be told Hamlet is sane. Gertrude protests, in tears, sitting on the bed, leaning toward him pleadingly.

Hamlet drops on his knee opposite her. The talk is of England and knavery, swift, ironic. The mine which he will delve is described almost with relish, the gesture that blows them all to the moon brings him to his feet with a swagger. It is in a mood of defiance that he leans down toward the body of the ' foolish prating knave ' and shouts his final good-night to his mother, who has turned and fled from the room. As she disappears through the doorway his braggadoccio drops from him like the false mask that it is. He sways against the wall, his head and shoulders sink. For a moment he looks after her and then, with repressed anguish, the one word ' Mother '—the cry of a child left in the dark—the hopeless, lost cry of a creature torn from its one safe anchorage.

(SCENE 11.—*The* KING's *dressing room.* KING, QUEEN, ROSENCRANTZ, *and* GUILDENSTERN.

KING. There's matter in these sighs. Where is your son?

QUEEN. [*To* ROSENCRANTZ *and* GUILDENSTERN.] Bestow this place on us a
 little while.   [*Exeunt* ROSENCRANTZ *and* GUILDENSTERN
 Ah! my good lord, what have I seen to-night.

KING. What, Gertrude? How does Hamlet?

QUEEN. Mad as the sea and wind, when both contend
 Which is the mightier. In his lawless fit,
 Behind the arras hearing something stir,
 Whips out his rapier, cries, 'A rat! a rat!'
 And, in his brainish apprehension, kills
 The unseen good old man.

KING. It had been so with us had we been there.
 His liberty is full of threats to all;
 To you yourself, to us, to every one.
 Where is he gone?

QUEEN. To draw apart the body he hath kill'd;
 O'er whom his very madness, like some ore
 Among a mineral of metals base,
 Shows itself pure: he weeps for what is done.

KING.   This vile deed
 We must, with all our majesty and skill,
 Both countenance and excuse. Ho! Guildenstern!
     Re-enter ROSENCRANTZ *and* GUILDENSTERN.
 Hamlet in madness hath Polonius slain,
 And from his mother's closet hath he dragg'd him:
 Go seek him out; speak fair, and bring the body
 Into the chapel. I pray you, haste in this.)

Scene 11. *The King's dressing room.*

The Queen hurries in, breathless with the terror of the scenes she has just lived through. She finds the King in conversation with Rosencrantz and Guildenstern, who are quickly dismissed, while she tells the story of Hamlet's latest ' dangerous lunacy.' Claudius' terrified ' It had been so with us had we been there ' startles her into an ever clearer realization of the enmity existing between the two—but she is quick to speak of Hamlet as ' mad ' and therefore unaccountable. The King calls in Guildenstern and sends him in pursuit of Hamlet.

(SCENE 12.—*The great hall in the castle.* HAMLET *alone.*

HAMLET. Safely stowed.

ROSENCRANTZ. ⎫
GUILDENSTERN. ⎭ [*Within.*] Hamlet! Lord Hamlet!

HAMLET. What noise? who calls on Hamlet?
　　O! here they come.
　　　　　　　　　Enter ROSENCRANTZ *and* GUILDENSTERN.

ROSENCRANTZ. What have you done, my lord, with the dead body?

HAMLET. Compounded it with dust, whereto 'tis kin.

ROSENCRANTZ. Tell us where 'tis, that we may take it thence
　　And bear it to the chapel.

HAMLET. Do not believe it.

ROSENCRANTZ. Believe what?

HAMLET. That I can keep your counsel and not mine own. Besides, to be
　　demanded of a sponge! what replication should be made by the son of a
　　king?

ROSENCRANTZ. Take you me for a sponge, my lord?

HAMLET. Ay, sir, that soaks up the king's countenance, his rewards, his
　　authorities. But such officers do the king best service in the end: when
　　he needs what you have gleaned, it is but squeezing you, and, sponge,
　　you shall be dry again.

ROSENCRANTZ. I understand you not, my lord.

HAMLET. I am glad of it: a knavish speech sleeps in a foolish ear.
　　　　　　　　　　　Enter KING.

KING. How now! what hath befall'n?

ROSENCRANTZ. Where the dead body is bestow'd, my lord,
　　We cannot get from him.

KING. Now, Hamlet, where's Polonius?

HAMLET. At supper.

KING. At supper! Where?

HAMLET. Not where he eats, but where he is eaten: a certain convocation
　　of politic worms are e'en at him. Your worm is your only emperor for
　　diet: we fat all creatures else to fat us, and we fat ourselves for maggots:
　　your fat king and your lean beggar is but variable service; two dishes,
　　but to one table: that's the end.

KING. Where is Polonius?

HAMLET. In heaven; send thither to see: if your messenger find him not
　　there, seek him i' the other place yourself. But, indeed, if you find him
　　not within this month, you shall nose him as you go up the stairs into
　　the lobby.

KING. [*To some Attendants.*] Go seek him there.

HAMLET. He will stay till you come.　　　　　　[*Exeunt Attendants.*

KING. Hamlet, this deed, for thine especial safety,
　　Which we do tender, as we dearly grieve

John Gielgud as Hamlet, New York, 1936

Photograph by Vandamm

SCENE 12. *The great hall in the castle.*

The hall is empty, except for Hamlet who is leaning down near the low archway, centre. He straightens up and comes forward, in his hand the green scarf Polonius had been wearing. He hears his name called and looks about startled; then as he sees his uncle's brace of spies appear at the upper entrance in hot pursuit, he shrugs his shoulders with contemptuous acceptance ' O! here they come.' He is in a dangerous humour, the dance of death, with macabre accompaniments, is on. He joins battle with Rosencrantz at once— ' Do not believe it . . . That I can keep your counsel and not mine own.' He strikes up the point of every one of Rosencrantz's questions, and runs his own lightning-quick jibes under his opponent's guard.

Rosencrantz stands on the middle landing, fuming with rage and helpless in the hands of this King's son who is no longer melancholy or hysterical, but alert, ruthless, scathing. In Hamlet's hands Polonius' green scarf becomes the sponge that the King makes of his servants, to be squeezed and thrown aside as Hamlet throws it behind him on the floor. One foot on the lower stair, he looks up at the two ' good lads ' with a taunting smile, then sharply, lightly, with a double-edged malice that spares himself as little as it spares his opponents, he turns from them and moves away, tossing a proverb at them as a parting gift: ' A knavish speech sleeps in a foolish ear.' But the King has come in and is half-way down the right stairway. Before Hamlet can get away he stops him with his demand for Polonius' body.

Hamlet drops back against the side of the low centre archway, looking from the King on his right to the King's men on his left. The chase is closing in but the danger only stirs his blood and sharpens his tongue. A few more bandarillos for the bull-neck of the King. He throws his darts with malicious joy: first, ' your fat king '—a gesture to the right; and ' your lean beggar,' left, to the two young men; then again the talk of heaven and hell. Hamlet

For that which thou hast done, must send thee hence
With fiery quickness: therefore prepare thyself;
The bark is ready, and the wind at help,
The associates tend, and every thing is bent
For England.

HAMLET.   For England!

KING.   Ay, Hamlet.

HAMLET.   Good.

KING. So is it, if thou knew'st our purposes.

HAMLET. I see a cherub that sees them. But, come; for England! Farewell,
dear mother.

KING. Thy loving father, Hamlet.

HAMLET. My mother: father and mother is man and wife, man and wife
is one flesh, and so, my mother. Come, for England!   [*Exit.*

KING. Follow him at foot; tempt him with speed aboard:
Delay it not, I'll have him hence to-night.
Away! for every thing is seal'd and done
That else leans on the affair: pray you, make haste.

                    [*Exeunt* ROSENCRANTZ *and* GUILDENSTERN.

And, England, if my love thou hold'st at aught,—
                    Thou mayst not coldly set
Our sovereign process, which imports at full,
The present death of Hamlet. Do it, England.)

walks over to the King and stands below him, twisting the point around—' seek him i' the other place yourself.'

Standing with his arms crossed, his foot on the lowest step, Hamlet looks appraisingly up at the King. On Claudius' remark as to how dearly he tenders his nephew's safety Hamlet's hand goes to his face in mock shame for such crass hypocrisy. ' The associates tend ' shifts Hamlet's attention across to the other two. Then back to the King on the ominous word, England. ' Good.' Hamlet's answer is an acceptance of a challenge. He will not allow the King to gloze over their shared knowledge of the battle drawn. Though Hamlet does not know of the death warrant in the pocket of his one-time friends, he knows the King's intention as the King knows his—' I see a cherub that sees them.' Lightly, playing with fire and death, he points up at the heavens above Claudius' head.

' But, come; for England! ' He swings away from the King and toward the ' associates.' Halfway across to the left exit he stops and turns, his back to the audience. ' Farewell, dear mother ' is flung full in the King's face, both hands blowing a mocking kiss. The King, helpless and furious, thunders at him, but Hamlet, irrepressible, slashes once more at that ' bed of Denmark ' which so obsesses him. His tone, however, is less virulent than usual. He can already jest at what is no longer a festering wound but is becoming a scar.

Before the King can answer, he is on his way. Three strides bring him opposite Rosencrantz. He slaps him on the shoulder with a comradely blow that nearly knocks him down, and sweeps out, once more leading the chase. Guildenstern is given his orders and the King left alone vents his rage and consoles himself in the thought of the instant death to which Hamlet goes so blithely.

Scene 13.—*A plain in Denmark.* FORTINBRAS, *a Captain, and Soldiers.*

FORTINBRAS. Go, captain, from me greet the Danish king;
 Tell him that, by his licence, Fortinbras
 Claims the conveyance of a promis'd march
 Over his kingdom. You know the rendezvous.
 If that his majesty would aught with us,
 We shall express our duty in his eye,
 And let him know so.
CAPTAIN.   I will do 't, my lord.
FORTINBRAS. Go softly on.   [*Exeunt* FORTINBRAS *and Soldiers.*
          Enter HAMLET, ROSENCRANTZ, GUILDENSTERN, *&c.*

HAMLET. Good sir, whose powers are these?
CAPTAIN. They are of Norway, sir.
HAMLET. How purpos'd, sir, I pray you?
CAPTAIN. Against some part of Poland.
HAMLET. Who commands them, sir?
CAPTAIN. The nephew to old Norway, Fortinbras.
HAMLET. Goes it against the main of Poland, sir,
 Or for some frontier?
CAPTAIN. Truly to speak, and with no addition,
 We go to gain a little patch of ground
 That hath in it no profit but the name.
HAMLET. Why, then the Polack never will defend it.
CAPTAIN. Yes, 'tis already garrison'd.
HAMLET. Two thousand souls and twenty thousand ducats
 Will not debate the question of this straw:
 [This is the imposthume of much wealth and peace,
 That inward breaks, and shows no cause without
 Why the man dies.] I humbly thank you, sir.
CAPTAIN. God be wi' you, sir.   [*Exit.*
ROSENCRANTZ.   Will 't please you go, my lord?
HAMLET. I'll be with you straight. Go a little before.
                              [*Exeunt all except* HAMLET.

 How all occasions do inform against me,
 And spur my dull revenge! What is a man,
 If his chief good and market of his time
 Be but to sleep and feed? a beast, no more.
 Sure he that made us with such large discourse,
 Looking before and after, gave us not
 That capability and god-like reason
 To fust in us unus'd. Now, whe'r it be
 Bestial oblivion, or some craven scruple
 Of thinking too precisely on the event,

Scene 13. *A plain in Denmark.*

A back drop suggests a barren stretch of plain with gnarled trees breaking the grey expanse. Fortinbras talks with one of his captains and there is a sound of martial music in the distance. As the two soldiers are leaving, right, Hamlet comes in from the opposite side with Rosencrantz, Guildenstern and an attendant. He recalls the captain for a moment's colloquy on the subject of Fortinbras' expedition against Poland. The spectacle of this army of men ready to do battle, to die, for a ' straw ' arrests his attention. Shading his eyes with his hand he looks out toward the distant encampment. For a long moment he stands lost in thought and then dismisses the soldier. A word from Rosencrantz reminds him of the presence of his associates—and he sends them on ahead remaining alone in contemplation of his obsessing problem; thought and action in eternal conflict.

' How all occasions do inform against *me.*' Very quietly the noble music of the lines reflect the new stage in Hamlet's progress. Though he is concerned with his delays, self-accusatory, warring still with his own shortcomings and weaknesses, his tone is firm, the timbre of his voice strong and resonant, his few gestures clear cut, decisive. He is as merciless as ever in his judgment of himself, yet he can think of his shortcomings without the hysterical despair of his Hecuba musings. He speaks with scorn in his voice of that ' thought, which, quarter'd, hath but one part wisdom and ever three parts coward,' but without the devastating bitterness of the moment when he saw all his actions ' sicklied o'er with the pale cast of thought.' Though he exhorts himself as ever to action, recalling unmercifully those excitements of his reason and his blood which he lets sleep, his growing resolution has, this time, an inner assurance.

The movement of the speech is steadily up and on, rising in power and passion. It is not broken by the sudden outburst, the flashes and reversals that marked his usual thought. Taking the

A thought, which, quarter'd, hath but one part wisdom,
And ever three parts coward, I do not know
Why yet I live to say ' This thing 's to do ';
Sith I have cause and will and strength and means
To do 't. Examples gross as earth exhort me:
Witness this army of such mass and charge
Led by a delicate and tender prince,
Whose spirit with divine ambition puff'd
Makes mouths at the invisible event,
Exposing what is mortal and unsure
To all that fortune, death and danger dare,
Even for an egg-shell. Rightly to be great
Is not to stir without great argument,
But greatly to find quarrel in a straw
When honour 's at the stake. How stand I then,
That have a father kill'd, a mother stain'd,
Excitements of my reason and my blood,
And let all sleep, while, to my shame, I see
The imminent death of twenty thousand men,
That, for a fantasy and trick of fame,
Go to their graves like beds, fight for a plot
Whereon the numbers cannot try the cause,
Which is not tomb enough and continent
To hide the slain? O! from this time forth,
My thoughts be bloody, or be nothing worth!

theme of the soldiers, ready to die for a futile cause, as before he took the players' mimic passion by which to measure of his own failing, he builds a nobler mansion for his self-accusation. He moves into a world greater than his own—and evokes through his illuminated face, his burning eyes, his awed and vibrant voice, the vision of the countless multitudes who, for an idea, an abstraction, have gone 'to their graves like beds.' Borne on the flood of this mighty tide Hamlet dedicates himself anew to his own mission. His hands strike downward, holding the edge of his cloak, his head is up and back, his whole movement vigorous. ' From this time forth, my thoughts be bloody, or be nothing worth! ' The words ring out with finality as the lights black out.

Scene 14.—*The great hall in the castle.* QUEEN *and* HORATIO.

QUEEN. I will not speak with her.

HORATIO. She is importunate, indeed distract:
Her mood will needs be pitied.

QUEEN.   What would she have?

HORATIO. [She speaks much of her father; says she hears
There's tricks i' the world; and hems, and beats her heart;
Spurns enviously at straws; speaks things in doubt,
That carry but half sense:]
'Twere good she were spoken with, for she may strew
Dangerous conjectures in ill-breeding minds.

QUEEN. Let her come in.   [*Exit* HORATIO.
To my sick soul, as sin's true nature is,
Each toy seems prologue to some great amiss:
           Re-enter HORATIO *with* OPHELIA.

OPHELIA. Where is the beauteous majesty of Denmark?

QUEEN. How now, Ophelia!

OPHELIA.   How should I your true love know
              From another one?
          By his cockle hat and staff,
              And his sandal shoon.

QUEEN. Alas! sweet lady, what imports this song?

OPHELIA. Say you? nay, pray you, mark.
          He is dead and gone, lady,
              He is dead and gone;
          At his head a grass-green turf;
              At his heels a stone.

   O, ho!

QUEEN. Nay, but, Ophelia,—

OPHELIA. Pray you, mark.
         White his shroud as the mountain snow,—
             Enter KING.

QUEEN. Alas! look here, my lord.

OPHELIA.   Larded with sweet flowers;
          Which bewept to the grave did go
             With true-love showers.

KING. How do you, pretty lady?

OPHELIA. Well, God 'ild you! They say the owl was a baker's daughter.
Lord! we know what we are, but know not what we may be. God be
at your table!

KING. Conceit upon her father.

OPHELIA. Pray you, let's have no words of this; but when they ask you
what it means, say you this:

Scene 14. *The great hall in the castle.*

The Queen comes down the right stairway in deep perturbation. Ophelia demands admittance, and Horatio advises her to see the unfortunate girl who since the death of her father is ' distract ' and in a most pitiable state. Reluctantly the Queen consents and in a moment Ophelia appears. Her hair is about her shoulders, her dress, a flowing yellow gown touched with orange, is in disorder. She has drawn an orange stocking, as though it were a glove, over her left hand and arm. Her round eyes roll, her gestures are uncontrolled. She addresses the Queen in a bold, challenging tone, and then with a meaningful yet childish intentness she sings the snatches of song that run through her head.

The King comes in and Ophelia wanders on through her pathetic, bawdy songs while the three observers watch her helplessly. Suddenly the thought of her brother galvanizes her into violence. She dashes across the stage, up the left-hand stairway and out through the central arch shouting a wild ' Good-night, sweet ladies; good-night, good-night! ' Horatio follows her, but Claudius and Gertrude have only a moment's respite. A courtier rushes in, right, to announce that Laertes is back, the rabble at his heels. The doors crash and there is a struggle at the upper entrance while the King and Queen, standing alone on the main stage, watch indignantly. Laertes breaks away and runs down the right-hand stairs, to be stopped by the Queen before he reaches the bottom. The interchange between wronged son and suave monarch is swift and effective.

The King has almost calmed Laertes when again Ophelia's voice is heard. She comes in by the upper central arch, through the crowd assembled there. She is strewing grasses as she comes, oblivious to the presence of that brother whose name she had just invoked. She wanders down the left stairway where Laertes meets her, but she passes him unheeding. On the middle landing she stops to pick her imaginary herbs, and then, again, on the main stage

> To-morrow is Saint Valentine's day,
>> All in the morning betime,
> And I a maid at your window,
>> To be your Valentine:
> Then up he rose, and donn'd his clothes,
>> And dupp'd the chamber-door;
> Let in the maid, that out a maid
>> Never departed more.

KING. Pretty Ophelia!

OPHELIA. Indeed, la! without an oath, I'll make an end on 't:
>> By Gis and by Saint Charity,
>> Alack, and fie for shame!
> Young men will do 't, if they come to 't;
>> By Cock they are to blame.
> Quoth she, before you tumbled me,
>> You promis'd me to wed:
> So would I ha' done, by yonder sun,
>> An thou hadst not come to my bed.

KING. How long hath she been thus?

OPHELIA. I hope all will be well. We must be patient: but I cannot choose but weep, to think they should lay him i' the cold ground. My brother shall know of it: and so I thank you for your good counsel. Come, my coach! Good-night, ladies; good-night, sweet ladies; good-night, good-night. [*Exit.*

KING. Follow her close; give her good watch, I pray you. [*Exit* HORATIO.
[O! this is the poison of deep grief; it springs
All from her father's death.] O Gertrude, Gertrude!
When sorrows come, they come not single spies,
But in battalions. First, her father slain;
Next, your son gone; (the people muddied,
Thick and unwholesome in their thoughts and whispers,
Last, and as much containing as all these,
Her brother is in secret come from France,
Feeds on his wonder, keeps himself in clouds,
And wants not buzzers to infect his ear
With pestilent speeches of his father's death;
O my dear Gertrude! this gives me superfluous death.) [*A noise within.*

QUEEN.   Alack! what noise is this?

Enter a Gentleman.

KING. Where are my Switzers? Let them guard the door.
What is the matter?

GENTLEMAN.   Save yourself, my lord;
The young Laertes, in a riotous head,
O'erbears your officers. The rabble call him lord;
They cry, ' Choose we; Laertes shall be king! '

she leans down for the rosemary and columbine, the fennel and the rue that she and the Queen are to wear so differently. Finally she wanders out through the low central archway, the Queen following her. Claudius intercepts Laertes as he too would go in pursuit and leads him off to a secret conference as the lights black out.

> Caps, hands, and tongues, applaud it to the clouds,
> ' Laertes shall be king, Laertes king!'

QUEEN. How cheerfully on the false trail they cry!
> O! this is counter, you false Danish dogs!

KING. The doors are broke.   [*Noise within.*

Enter LAERTES, *armed; Danes following.*

LAERTES. Where is the king? Sirs, stand you all without.

DANES. No, let's come in.

LAERTES.   I pray you, give me leave.

DANES. We will, we will.

LAERTES. I thank you: keep the door. O thou vile king!
> Give me my father.

QUEEN.   Calmly, good Laertes.

LAERTES. That drop of blood that's calm proclaims me bastard,
> [*Cries cuckold to my father.*]

KING.   What is the cause, Laertes,
> That thy rebellion looks so giant-like?
> Let him go, Gertrude; do not fear our person:
> There's such divinity doth hedge a king,
> That treason can but peep to what it would,
> Acts little of his will. Tell me, Laertes,
> Why thou art thus incens'd. Let him go, Gertrude.
> Speak, man.

LAERTES.   Where is my father?

KING.   Dead.

QUEEN.   But not by him.

KING. Let him demand his fill.

LAERTES. How came he dead? I'll not be juggled with.
> To hell, allegiance! vows, to the blackest devil!
> Let come what comes; only I'll be reveng'd
> Most throughly for my father.

KING.   Who shall stay you?

LAERTES. My will, not all the world:

KING.   Good Laertes,
> That I am guiltless of your father's death,
> And am most sensibly in grief for it,
> It shall as level to your judgment pierce
> As day does to your eye.

DANES. [*Within.*]   Let her come in.

Re-enter OPHELIA.

> [O rose of May!]

> Dear maid, kind sister, sweet Ophelia!
> O heavens! is't possible a young maid's wits
> Should be as mortal as an old man's life?

OPHELIA.   They bore him barefac'd on the bier;

> Hey non nonny, nonny, hey nonny;
> And in his grave rain'd many a tear;—
Fare you well, my dove!

LAERTES. Hadst thou thy wits, and didst persuade revenge,
It could not move thus.

OPHELIA.   You must sing, a-down a-down,
                And you call him a-down-a.
O how the wheel becomes it! It is the false steward that stole his master's
daughter.

LAERTES. This nothing's more than matter.

OPHELIA. There's rosemary, that's for remembrance; pray, love, remember: and there is pansies, that's for thoughts.

LAERTES. A document in madness, thoughts and remembrance fitted.

OPHELIA. There's fennel for you, and columbines; there's rue for you!
and here's some for me; we may call it herb of grace o' Sundays. O;
you must wear your rue with a difference. There's a daisy; I would
give you some violets, but they withered all when my father died.
They say he made a good end,—
                For bonny sweet Robin is all my joy.

LAERTES. Thought and affliction, passion, hell itself,
She turns to favour and to prettiness.

OPHELIA.   And will he not come again?
                And will he not come again?
                    No, no, he is dead;
                    Go to thy death-bed,
                He never will come again.
                His beard was as white as snow
                All flaxen was his poll,
                    He is gone, he is gone,
                    And we cast away moan:
                God ha' mercy on his soul!
And of all Christian souls! I pray God. God be wi' ye!

LAERTES. Do you see this, O God?

KING. Laertes, I must commune with your grief,
Or you deny me right.
Be you content to lend your patience to us,
And we shall jointly labour with your soul
To give it due content.

LAERTES.   Let this be so:
His means of death, his obscure burial,
Cry to be heard, as 'twere from heaven to earth,
That I must call 't in question.

KING.   So you shall;
And where the offence is let the great axe fall.
I pray you go with me.

SCENE 15.—HORATIO's *house. Enter* HORATIO *and a Sailor.*

(SAILOR. There's a letter for you, sir;—it comes from the ambassador
that was bound for England;—if your name be Horatio, as I am let
to know it is.)

HORATIO. ' Horatio, when thou shalt have overlooked this, give these
fellows some means to the king: they have letters for him. Ere we were
two days old at sea, a pirate of very warlike appointment gave us chase.
Finding ourselves too slow of sail, we put on a compelled valour; in the
grapple I boarded them: on the instant they got clear of our ship, so I
alone became their prisoner. They have dealt with me like thieves of
mercy, but they knew what they did; I am to do a good turn for them.
Let the king have the letters I have sent; and repair thou to me with as
much haste as thou wouldst fly death. These good fellows will bring
thee where I am. Rosencrantz and Guildenstern hold their course for
England: of them I have much to tell thee. Farewell.

> ' He that thou knowest thine,
>> ' HAMLET.'

(Come, I will give you way for these your letters;
And do't the speedier, that you may direct me
To him from whom you brought them.)

Scene 15. *Horatio's house.*

It is dark. By the faint light of a lantern the cloaked figures of Horatio and a sailor who has brought him a letter from Hamlet can be seen. Horatio reads the letter which announces Hamlet's unexpected return to Denmark. A ransom is to be paid to the pirates who had captured Hamlet; the bearer of the letter is to be given admittance to the King; and Horatio is to join Hamlet at once. Horatio takes the lantern from the sailor and leads him off to attend to these commissions.

Scene 16.—*The council chamber in the castle.* KING *and* LAERTES.

KING.　Now must your conscience my acquittance seal,
　　And you must put me in your heart for friend,
　　Sith you have heard, and with a knowing ear,
　　That he which hath your noble father slain
　　Pursu'd my life.
(LAERTES.　　　　　　It well appears: but tell me
　　Why you proceeded not against these feats,
KING.　Why to a public count I might not go,
　　Is the great love the general gender bear him;
　　Who, dipping all his faults in their affection,
　　Convert his gyves to graces.)
LAERTES.　And so have I a noble father lost;
　　A sister driven into desperate terms,
　　Whose worth, if praises may go back again,
　　Stood challenger on mount of all the age
　　For her perfections. But my revenge will come.
KING.　Break not your sleeps for that;
　　　　　　　　　　　Enter a Messenger.
　　How now! what news?
MESSENGER.　　　　　　Letters, my lord, from Hamlet:
　　[This to your majesty; this to the queen.]
KING.　Leave us.　　　　　　　　　　[*Exit Messenger.*
　　' High and mighty, you shall know I am set naked on your kingdom.
　　To-morrow shall I beg leave to see your kingly eyes; when I shall, first
　　asking your pardon thereunto, recount the occasions of my sudden and
　　more strange return.　　　　　　　　　　　　HAMLET.'
　　What should this mean? Are all the rest come back?
　　Or is it some abuse and no such thing?
LAERTES.　Know you the hand?
KING.　　　　　　　　　　'Tis Hamlet's character.
LAERTES.　　　　　　　　　　　　　Well let him come:
　　It warms the very sickness in my heart,
　　That I shall live and tell him to his teeth,
　　' Thus diddest thou.'
KING.　　　　　　　If it be so, Laertes,
　　Will you be rul'd by me?
LAERTES.　　　　　　　　Ay, my lord;
　　So you will not o'errule me to a peace.
KING.　To thine own peace. [If he be now return'd,
　　As checking at his voyage, and that he means
　　No more to undertake it, I will work him

SCENE 16. *The council chamber in the castle.*

In the meanwhile the King has been closeted with Laertes and has the impetuous young man well in hand. He has persuaded him of his own innocence in the matter of Polonius' death and also of Hamlet's 'dangerous lunacies.' Laertes, from the leader of a revolt, has become a tool of the King. At this moment Hamlet's letter is delivered and the King realizes that he has instant use for this newly acquired instrument of his will. In a few flattering phrases, interlarded with reminders that spur revenge, the King has persuaded Laertes to take part in the plot which will rid Claudius of Hamlet without involving his own good name. The duel with the unbated, envenomed rapier in Laertes' hand, the poisoned cup for extra measure are swiftly planned and accepted. The plotting is interrupted by the Queen who comes in with the news of Ophelia's drowning. Laertes is overcome. He throws himself down by the council table while the Queen bends over him telling him the tragic details of Ophelia's end. As she finishes he leaps to his feet and rushes out by the right doorway as the lights black out.

To an exploit, now ripe in my device,
Under the which he shall not choose but fall;
And for his death no wind of blame shall breathe,
But even his mother shall uncharge the practice
And call it accident.

LAERTES.   My lord, I will be rul'd:
The rather, if you could devise it so
That I might be the organ.]

KING.   It falls right.
You have been talk'd of since your travel much,
And that in Hamlet's hearing, for a quality
Wherein, they say, you shine; your sum of parts
Did not together pluck such envy from him
As did that one.

LAERTES.   What part is that, my lord?

KING. [A very riband in the cap of youth,]
Here was a gentleman of Normandy:
He made confession of you,
And gave you such a masterly report
For art and exercise in your defence,
And for your rapier most especially,
That he cried out, 'twould be a sight indeed
If one could match you: this report of his
Did Hamlet so envenom with his envy
That he could nothing do but wish and beg
Your sudden coming o'er, to play with him.
Now, out of this,—

LAERTES.   What out of this, my lord?

KING. Laertes, was your father dear to you?
Or are you like the painting of a sorrow,
A face without a heart?

LAERTES.   Why ask you this?

KING. (Not that I think you did not love your father,)
                    But, to the quick o' the ulcer;
Hamlet comes back; what would you undertake
To show yourself your father's son indeed
More than in words?

LAERTES.   To cut his throat i' the church.

KING. [No place, indeed, should murder sanctuarize;
Revenge should have no bounds. But, good Laertes,]
Will you do this, keep close within your chamber.
Hamlet return'd shall know you are come home;
We'll put on those shall praise your excellence,
And set a double varnish on the fame
The Frenchman gave you, bring you, in fine, together,

And wager on your heads: he, being remiss,
Most generous and free from all contriving,
Will not peruse the foils; so that, with ease
Or with a little shuffling, you may choose
A sword unbated, and, in a pass of practice
Requite him for your father.

LAERTES.   I will do 't;
And, for that purpose, I'll anoint my sword.
I bought an unction of a mountebank,
So mortal that, but dip a knife in it,
Where it draws blood no cataplasm so rare,
Collected from all simples that have virtue
Under the moon, can save the thing from death
That is but scratch'd withal; I'll touch my point
With this contagion, that, if I gall him slightly,
It may be death.

KING.   Let 's further think of this;
We'll make a solemn wager on your cunnings:
I ha 't:
When in your motion you are hot and dry,—
As make your bouts more violent to that end,—
And that he calls for drink, I'll have prepar'd him
A chalice for the nonce, whereon but sipping,
If he by chance escape your venom'd stuck,
Our purpose may hold there. But stay! what noise?
                    Enter QUEEN.
[How now, sweet queen!]

QUEEN. One woe doth tread upon another's heel,
So fast they follow: your sister 's drown'd, Laertes.

LAERTES. Drown'd! [O, where?]

QUEEN. There is a willow grows aslant a brook,
That shows his hoar leaves in the glassy stream;
There with fantastic garlands did she come,
Of crow-flowers, nettles, daisies, and long purples,
[That liberal shepherds give a grosser name,
But our cold maids do dead men's fingers call them:]
There, on the pendent boughs her coronet weeds
Clambering to hang, an envious sliver broke,
When down her weedy trophies and herself
Fell in the weeping brook. Her clothes spread wide,
And, mermaid-like, awhile they bore her up;
Which time she chanted snatches of old tunes,
As one incapable of her own distress,
Or like a creature native and indu'd
Unto that element; but long it could not be

Till that her garments, heavy with their drink,
Pull'd the poor wretch from her melodious lay
To muddy death.

[LAERTES.   Alas! then, she is drown'd!

QUEEN. Drown'd, drown'd.

LAERTES. Too much of water hast thou, poor Ophelia,
And therefore] I forbid my tears; but yet
It is our trick, nature her custom holds,
Let shame say what it will; [when these are gone
The woman will be out.] Adieu, my lord!
I have a speech of fire, that fain would blaze,
But that this folly douts it.

A Churchyard

SCENE 17

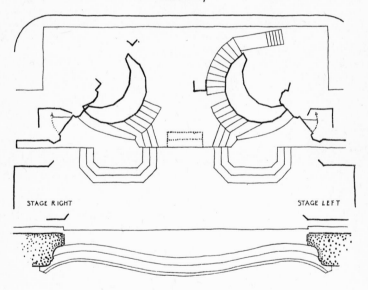

STAGE RIGHT   STAGE LEFT

Scene 17.—*A churchyard. Two gravediggers.*

FIRST GRAVEDIGGER. Is she to be buried in Christian burial that wilfully seeks her own salvation?

SECOND GRAVEDIGGER. I tell thee she is; and therefore make her grave straight: the crowner hath sat on her, and finds it Christian burial.

FIRST GRAVEDIGGER. How can that be, unless she drowned herself in her own defence?

SECOND GRAVEDIGGER. Why, 'tis found so.

[FIRST GRAVEDIGGER. It must be ' se offendendo '; it cannot be else. For here lies the point: if I drown myself wittingly it argues an act; and an act hath three branches; it is, to act, to do, and to perform: argal, she drowned herself wittingly.

SECOND GRAVEDIGGER. Nay, but hear you, goodman delver,—

FIRST GRAVEDIGGER. Give me leave. Here lies the water; good: here stands the man; good: if the man go to this water, and drown himself, it is, will he, nill he, he goes; mark you that? but if the water come to him, and drown him, he drowns not himself: argal, he that is not guilty of his own death shortens not his own life.

SECOND GRAVEDIGGER. But is this law?

FIRST GRAVEDIGGER. Ay, marry, is 't; crowner's quest law.]

SECOND GRAVEDIGGER. Will you ha' the truth on 't? If this had not been a gentlewoman she should have been buried out o' Christian burial.

FIRST GRAVEDIGGER. Why, there thou sayest; and the more pity that great folk should have countenance in this world to drown or hang themselves more than their even Christian. Come, my spade. There is no ancient gentlemen but gardeners, ditchers, and grave-makers; they hold up Adam's profession.

SECOND GRAVEDIGGER. Was he a gentleman?

FIRST GRAVEDIGGER. A' was the first that ever bore arms.

SECOND GRAVEDIGGER. Why, he had none.

FIRST GRAVEDIGGER. What! art a heathen? How dost thou understand the Scripture? The Scripture says, Adam digged; could he dig without arms? I'll put another question to thee; if thou answerest me not to the purpose, confess thyself—

SECOND GRAVEDIGGER. Go to.

FIRST GRAVEDIGGER. What is he that builds stronger than either the mason, the shipwright, or the carpenter?

SECOND GRAVEDIGGER. Who builds stronger than a mason, a shipwright, or a carpenter?

FIRST GRAVEDIGGER. Cudgel thy brains no more about it, for your dull ass will not mend his pace with beating; and, when you are asked this question next, say, ' a grave-maker: ' the houses that he makes last till doomsday. Go, get thee to Yaughan; fetch me a stoup of liquor.

[*Exit Second Gravedigger.*

SCENE 17. *A churchyard.*

The full stage has taken on the grey dimness of a graveyard. At the left, on the upper level, the corner of a church looms darkly; an archway gives access to a flight of steps that disappears behind the rounded tower. In the centre, front, an open sepulchre shows its black mouth. A low wall surrounds it on three sides and stairways lead up right and left to the upper platform that dominates the grave. Two gravediggers are sitting on either side of the wall surrounding the sepulchre discussing the burial of the person whose grave they are preparing. As they talk the older of the two climbs into the grave and starts digging, finally sending off his fellow to fetch him a much needed ' stoup of liquor.' The old fellow digs and sings, not noticing the advent of two young men, who, wrapped in long travelling cloaks, make their way down the winding stair back of the church. They walk to the edge of the upper platform and look down at the gravedigger. ' Has this fellow no feeling of his business, that he sings at grave-making? ' Hamlet's voice is quiet, speculative, unhurried. He watches for a moment and then turns and walks slowly down the left stair, stopping part way down to lean against the top of the archway that dominates the grave. Horatio continues down the stair and seats himself on the lower landing.

There is an unhurried crepuscular calm about Hamlet's mood. He moves and speaks with assurance. His voice has a deep underlying sadness, but the acrid taste has left it. He can smile and exchange grim jests with the gravedigger with a humour untinged by the brutal undertow that swept through his macabre banter over Polonius' body. He bends over the open grave and questions the gravedigger with a detached, almost impersonal interest— ' Whose grave 's this . . . ? '

' How absolute the knave is! ' Hamlet turns from his futile questioning and walks on down the stairway to the main stage. His hat is off and his still face reflects an inner, fatalistic calm. He

Enter HAMLET *and* HORATIO.

FIRST GRAVEDIGGER.
> In youth, when I did love, did love,
> Methought it was very sweet,
> To contract, O! the time for-a my behove,
> O! methought there was nothing meet.

HAMLET. Has this fellow no feeling of his business, that he sings at grave-making?

[HORATIO. Custom hath made it in him a property of easiness.

HAMLET. 'Tis e'en so; the hand of little employment hath the daintier sense.]

FIRST GRAVEDIGGER.
> But age, with his stealing steps,
> Hath claw'd me in his clutch,
> And hath shipped me intil the land,
> As if I had never been such.   [*Throws up a skull.*

HAMLET. That skull had a tongue in it, and could sing once; how the knave jowls it to the ground, as if it were Cain's jaw-bone, that did the first murder!

FIRST GRAVEDIGGER.
> A pick-axe, and a spade, a spade,
> For and a shrouding sheet;
> O! a pit of clay for to be made
> For such a guest is meet.

HAMLET. I will speak to this fellow. Whose grave 's this, sir?

FIRST GRAVEDIGGER. Mine, sir.
> O! a pit of clay for to be made
> For such a guest is meet.

HAMLET. I think it be thine, indeed; for thou liest in 't.

FIRST GRAVEDIGGER. You lie out on 't, sir, and therefore it is not yours; for my part, I do not lie in 't, and yet it is mine.

HAMLET. Thou dost lie in 't, to be in 't and say it is thine: 'tis for the dead, not for the quick; therefore thou liest.

FIRST GRAVEDIGGER. 'Tis a quick lie, sir; 'twill away again, from me to you.

HAMLET. What man dost thou dig it for?

FIRST GRAVEDIGGER. For no man, sir.

HAMLET. What woman, then?

FIRST GRAVEDIGGER. For none, neither.

HAMLET. Who is to be buried in 't?

FIRST GRAVEDIGGER. One that was a woman, sir; but, rest her soul, she 's dead.

HAMLET. How absolute the knave is! we must speak by the card, or equivocation will undo us. How long hast thou been a grave-maker?

' The Churchyard '

Designed by Jo Mielziner for the New York production of Hamlet

smiles with Horatio over the gravedigger's quips and resumes the conversation which turns on Prince Hamlet and the madness for which he was sent to England. As he talks he sits down on the edge of the sepulchre wall, taking a silver box from his sleeve and refreshing himself with a pinch of snuff. He holds the box out to the gravedigger and smiles again over the old fellow's explanation of the reason for Hamlet's losing his wits.

The conversation dies away as Hamlet sits lost in thought gazing down into the grave with its skulls and scattered bones. Then with a deeper note in his voice, he touches the thought which comes inevitably to his too vivid imagination: ' How long will a man lie i' the earth ere he *rot*? ' The last word falls on the ear with hollow resonance. The gravedigger explains at length, illustrating his point with the skull which he had placed on the edge of the wall some time before. ' Whose do you think it was? ' Hamlet protests his ignorance with a laugh. The gravedigger's answer comes like a bolt—' this . . . was Yorick's skull.'

' This? ' Hamlet's shock is caught and impaled on the word. He stares at the skull incredulously. Talk of death and decay is one thing; the presence of a friend in this disguise another. There is a long pause. The gravedigger turns and is about to throw the skull away when Hamlet stops him. ' Let me see.' He takes it in his hand. Still turned toward the gravedigger he stares down at the skull and then up at the man. ' Alas! poor Yorick,' is almost a question—tossed out quickly, unemphatically in a tone of wonder. Then Hamlet turns to Horatio who has risen and stands on his left, the questioning note still in his voice: ' I knew him, Horatio; a fellow of infinite jest . . . ' Hamlet is on his feet, the skull in his right hand, at arm's length before him. ' He hath borne me on his back a thousand times . . . ' A gesture of his left hand evokes the picture of the princeling on the jester's shoulder—' and now how abhorred in my imagination . . . ' the word is heavy with the charnel-house atmosphere of the thought, but Hamlet keeps his imagination within bounds. The death's head on my lady's dressing table is restrained—for Hamlet.

FIRST GRAVEDIGGER. Of all the days i' the year, I came to 't that day that our last King Hamlet overcame Fortinbras.

HAMLET. How long is that since?

FIRST GRAVEDIGGER. Cannot you tell that? every fool can tell that; it was the very day that young Hamlet was born; he that is mad, and sent into England.

HAMLET. Ay, marry; why was he sent into England?

FIRST GRAVEDIGGER. Why, because he was mad: he shall recover his wits there; or, if he do not, 'tis no great matter there.

HAMLET. Why?

FIRST GRAVEDIGGER. 'Twill not be seen in him there; there the men are as mad as he.

HAMLET. How came he mad?

FIRST GRAVEDIGGER. Very strangely, they say.

HAMLET. How strangely?

FIRST GRAVEDIGGER. Faith, e'en with losing his wits.

HAMLET. Upon what ground?

FIRST GRAVEDIGGER. Why, here in Denmark; I have been sexton here, man and boy, thirty years.

HAMLET. How long will a man lie i' the earth ere he rot?

FIRST GRAVEDIGGER. Faith, if he be not rotten before he die,—he will last you some eight year or nine year; a tanner will last you nine year.

HAMLET. Why he more than another?

FIRST GRAVEDIGGER. Why, sir, his hide is so tanned with his trade that he will keep out water a great while, and your water is a sore decayer of your whoreson dead body. Here's a skull now; this skull hath lain you i' the earth three-and-twenty years.

HAMLET. Whose was it?

FIRST GRAVEDIGGER. A whoreson mad fellow's it was: whose do you think it was?

HAMLET. Nay, I know not.

FIRST GRAVEDIGGER. A pestilence on him for a mad rogue! a' poured a flagon of Rhenish on my head once. This same skull, sir, was Yorick's skull, the king's jester.

HAMLET. This!

FIRST GRAVEDIGGER. E'en that.

HAMLET. Let me see.—[*Takes the skull.*]—Alas! poor Yorick. I knew him, Horatio; a fellow of infinite jest, of most excellent fancy; he hath borne me on his back a thousand times; and now, how abhorred in my imagination it is! my gorge rises at it. Here hung those lips that I have kissed I know not how oft. Where be your gibes now? your gambols? your songs? your flashes of merriment, that were wont to set the table on a roar? Not one now, to mock your own grinning? quite chapfallen? Now get you to my lady's chamber, and tell her, let her paint an inch thick, to this favour she must come; make her laugh at that. Prithee,

' Dost thou think Alexander looked o' this fashion i' the earth? ' He holds the skull up for Horatio's inspection: ' And smelt so? ' With a very slight grimace he tosses the skull to the waiting gravedigger and, watching him as he drops it into the earth, the fingers of his right hand rub against each other, brushing off the taint of corruption. ' To what base uses we may return, Horatio! ' His tone continues its speculative, quiet commentary as he traces the ultimate end of even the mightiest actors of great deeds upon the stage of life.

Suddenly Hamlet catches sight of the funeral procession approaching. He steps down from the landing and across the stage toward the right, describing the approaching group in quick phrases. With a swing of enveloping cloaks the two men withdraw to the shadow of the church on the extreme left as the priest, Laertes, the King and Queen and a handful of mourners follow Ophelia's shrouded body in from the right. The priest mounts to the centre of the middle platform overlooking the grave. Laertes, between the King and Queen, stands facing him on the main stage, their backs to the audience. Ophelia's body is lowered into the grave in silence and the two bearers carry the empty bier away. Laertes speaks and Hamlet moves forward listening intently to Laertes' words. As he realizes what has happened, his voice, hushed but startled, murmurs her name. During Laertes' tirade Hamlet walks unnoticed up the steps, from whence he can look down on the grave into which Laertes has leapt. Suddenly his control breaks. He speaks, strides down the stairs and stops on the landing. The heavy folds of the travelling cloak whirl about him and fall to the ground: ' This is I, Hamlet the Dane.' The force of his voice is like the blow of steel on flint. He dominates them all for a moment. Then Laertes is out of the grave and at his throat in a bound. They struggle on the lowest steps of the stair and are finally parted; Hamlet with Horatio beside him is in the centre of the stage in front of Ophelia's grave, Laertes to the left, the King next to him. Gertrude stands between the two, trying to calm Hamlet and placate Laertes. Hamlet is gasping for breath. His

Horatio, tell me one thing.

HORATIO. What 's that, my lord?

HAMLET. Dost thou think Alexander looked o' this fashion i' the earth?

HORATIO. E'en so.

HAMLET. And smelt so? pah!

HORATIO. E'en so, my lord.

HAMLET. To what base uses we may return, Horatio! Why may not
imagination trace the noble dust of Alexander, till he find it stopping a
bung-hole?

> Imperious Cæsar, dead and turn'd to clay,
> Might stop a hole to keep the wind away:
> O! that that earth, which kept the world in awe,
> Should patch a wall to expel the winter's flaw.

But soft! but soft! aside: here comes the king.
The queen, the courtiers: who is that they follow?
And with such maimed rites? [This doth betoken
The corse they follow did with desperate hand
Fordo its own life; 'twas of some estate.]
Couch we awhile, and mark.   [*Retiring with* HORATIO.

Enter Priest: the Corpse of OPHELIA, LAERTES, KING, QUEEN, *their Trains.*

LAERTES. What ceremony else?

HAMLET.   That is Laertes,
A very noble youth: mark.

LAERTES. What ceremony else?

FIRST PRIEST. Her obsequies have been as far enlarg'd
As we have warrantise: her death was doubtful,
And, but that great command o'ersways the order,
She should in ground unsanctified have lodg'd
Till the last trumpet.

LAERTES. Must there no more be done?

FIRST PRIEST.   No more be done:
We should profane the service of the dead,
To sing a requiem, and such rest to her
As to peace-parted souls.

LAERTES.   Lay her i' the earth;
And from her fair and unpolluted flesh
May violets spring! I tell thee, churlish priest,
A ministering angel shall my sister be,
When thou liest howling. ———————

HAMLET.   What! the fair Ophelia?

QUEEN. Sweets to the sweet: farewell!
I hop'd thou shouldst have been my Hamlet's wife;
I thought thy bride-bed to have deck'd, sweet maid,
And not have strewed thy grave.

mother's question is like fire to dynamite. ' I lov'd Ophelia! ' It is a passionate protest— not merely of thwarted love but of a thwarted life. The accumulated rage and despair that had gathered during these months burst their bonds. For a moment he is in revolt against the fate laid upon him—against the sacrifice he has been forced to make of all that was happy, gay, living, in order to expiate the sins of the fathers. His youth, his love, his will to live, rise in rebellion. He breaks from the restraining hands as with wild words he storms ' the burning zone.'

Then suddenly he stops. He buries his face in his hands; his body shakes with sobs. ' Nay, an thou'lt mouth, I'll rant as well as thou.' While his mother quiets Laertes, Hamlet masters himself. His passion subsides. He straightens up, his hands drop and he speaks to Laertes with moving dignity. ' What is the reason that you use me thus? I loved you ever.' There is a pause and then he turns slowly and wearily away from them all, walking upstage toward the head of Ophelia's grave. Again he stops and turns, looks down into it for a long moment, and then very slowly up at the King and Laertes who stand forward and to the left. ' But it is no matter.' The couplet is a final fling at the curs who snarl at his heels. Again he turns away and walks, a solitary figure, up the steps and into the darkness.

LAERTES.   O! treble woe
  Fall ten times treble on that cursed head
  Whose wicked deed thy most ingenious sense
  Depriv'd thee of. Hold off the earth awhile,
  Till I have caught her once more in mine arms. [*Leaps into the grave*.
  Now pile your dust upon the quick and dead,
  Till of this flat a mountain you have made,
  To o'ertop old Pelion or the skyish head
  Of blue Olympus.

HAMLET. [*Advancing*.] What is he whose grief
  Bears such an emphasis? whose phrase of sorrow
  Conjures the wandering stars, and makes them stand
  Like wonder-wounded hearers? this is I,
  Hamlet the Dane.

LAERTES.   The devil take thy soul!

HAMLET. Thou pray'st not well.
  I prithee, take thy fingers from my throat;
  For though I am not splenetive and rash
  Yet have I in me something dangerous,
  Which let thy wisdom fear. Away thy hand!

KING. Pluck them asunder.

QUEEN.   Hamlet! Hamlet!

ALL. Gentlemen,—

HORATIO.   Good my lord, be quiet.

HAMLET. Why, I will fight with him upon this theme
  Until my eyelids will no longer wag.

QUEEN. O my son! what theme?

HAMLET. I lov'd Ophelia: forty thousand brothers
  Could not, with all their quantity of love,
  Make up my sum. What wilt thou do for her?

KING. O! he is mad, Laertes.

QUEEN. For love of God, forbear him.

HAMLET. 'Swounds, show me what thou'lt do:
  Woo 't weep? woo 't fight? woo 't fast? woo 't tear thyself?
  Woo 't drink up eisel? eat a crocodile?
  I'll do 't. Dost thou come here to whine?
  To outface me with leaping in her grave?
  Be buried quick with her, and so will I:
  And, if thou prate of mountains, let them throw
  Millions of acres on us, till our ground,
  Singeing his pate against the burning zone,
  Make Ossa like a wart! Nay, an thou'lt mouth,
  I'll rant as well as thou.

QUEEN.   This is mere madness:
  And thus a while the fit will work on him;
  Anon, as patient as the female dove,
  When that her golden couplets are disclos'd,
  His silence will sit drooping.
HAMLET.   Hear you, sir;
  What is the reason that you use me thus?
  I lov'd you ever: but it is no matter;
  Let Hercules himself do what he may,
  The cat will mew and dog will have his day.

SCENE 18.—*A corridor in the castle.* HAMLET *and* HORATIO.

HAMLET.   Rashly,—
    And prais'd be rashness for it, let us know,
    Our indiscretion sometimes serves us well
    When our deep plots do pall; and that should teach us
    There 's a divinity that shapes our ends,
    Rough-hew them how we will.
HORATIO. So Guildenstern and Rosencrantz go to 't.
HAMLET. Why, man, they did make love to this employment;
    They are not near my conscience;
    ['Tis dangerous when the baser nature comes
    Between the pass and fell-incensed points
    Of mighty opposites.]
HORATIO.   Why, what a king is this!
HAMLET. Does it not, think'st thee, stand me now upon—
    He that hath kill'd my king and whor'd my mother,
    Popp'd in between the election and my hopes,
    Thrown out his angle for my proper life,
    And with such cozenage—is 't not perfect conscience
    To quit him with this arm? and is 't not to be damn'd
    To let this canker of our nature come
    In further evil?
HORATIO. It must be shortly known to him from England
    What is the issue of the business there.
HAMLET. It will be short: the interim is mine;
    And a man's life 's no more than to say ' One.'
    But I am very sorry, good Horatio,
    That to Laertes I forgot myself;
    For, by the image of my cause, I see
    The portraiture of his: I'll count his favours:
    But, sure, the bravery of his grief did put me
    Into a towering passion.
HORATIO.   Peace! who comes here?
                    Enter OSRIC.
OSRIC. Your lordship is right welcome back to Denmark.
HAMLET. I humbly thank you, sir. Dost know this water-fly?
HORATIO. No, my good lord.
HAMLET. Thy state is the more gracious.
OSRIC. Sweet lord, if your lordship were at leisure, I should impart a thing
    to you from his majesty.
HAMLET. I will receive it, sir, with all diligence of spirit. Your bonnet to
    his right use; 'tis for the head.
OSRIC. I thank your lordship, 'tis very hot.

SCENE 18. *A corridor in the castle.*

Hamlet and Horatio enter from the left, deep in conversation. Hamlet is once more restored to the quiet, integrated mood which marked his return from the sea. As he stands talking to Horatio, his left hand hooked on his dagger-belt, his slender figure, alert yet relaxed, seems to radiate power. He moves with his usual freedom and grace but with an increased poise. He speaks of the King, even of his mother, without the anguish that has torn his spirit before. The conflict is resolved and he waits with calm acceptance the inevitable end. No man is master of his fate, but Hamlet is at last master of his soul. His words concerning Laertes' ' cause,' so similar and so profoundly different from his own, are spoken with sympathy and understanding.

The conversation is interrupted by the appearance of Osric, befeathered and beruffled and full of mincing words. Hamlet is amused by this ' water-fly ' and turns willingly from more serious matters to make mild sport of him. The wit that he has used so often as a searing two-edged dagger is now the lightest of verbal rapiers—very carefully bated to do no serious hurt to the victim. The by-play with the hat is lightly given and taken. But the diversion is short. The King's wager, Laertes' challenge, are freighted with doom. Hamlet glances at Horatio who moves toward him as though to protest. But Hamlet stops him before he speaks. There is a long pause while Hamlet looks with prescient vision into the future. Then with a gesture of acceptance he turns to Osric. ' Sir, I will walk here in the hall.' Another pause as Hamlet turns the words and their strange significance over in his mind—' I will win for him, an I can.'

Osric accepts the answer enthusiastically, deaf to the thundering undercurrent of battle and death. Hamlet has a smile for him, even while he hears the ominous sound. His suggestion that Osric should use such ' flourish ' his nature wills in his answer to the King is accompanied by a light gesture of the mind rather than of the hand, and a quick, disarming smile. Osric pauses near the exit,

HAMLET. No, believe me, 'tis very cold; the wind is northerly.

OSRIC. It is indifferent cold, my lord, indeed.

HAMLET. But yet methinks it is very sultry and hot for my complexion.

OSRIC. Exceedingly, my lord; it is very sultry, as 'twere, I cannot tell how. But, my lord, his majesty bade me signify to you that he has laid a great wager on your head. Sir, this is the matter,—

HAMLET. I beseech you, remember—

OSRIC. Nay, good my lord; for mine ease, in good faith. Sir, here is newly come to court Laertes; believe me, an absolute gentlemen, full of most excellent differences, of very soft society and great showing.

HAMLET. What imports the nomination of this gentleman?

OSRIC. Of Laertes?

HAMLET. Of him, sir.

OSRIC. I know you are not ignorant of what excellence Laertes is—I mean, sir, for his weapon.

HAMLET. What 's his weapon?

OSRIC. Rapier and dagger.

HAMLET. That 's two of his weapons; but, well.

OSRIC. The king, sir, hath wagered that in a dozen passes between yourself and him, he shall not exceed you three hits; he hath laid on twelve for nine, and it would come to immediate trial, if your lordship would vouchsafe the answer.

HAMLET. Sir, I will walk here in the hall; if it please his majesty, 'tis the breathing time of day with me; let the foils be brought, the gentleman willing, and the king hold his purpose, I will win for him an I can.

OSRIC. Shall I re-deliver you so?

HAMLET. To this effect, sir; after what flourish your nature will.

OSRIC. The queen desires you to use some gentle entertainment to Laertes before you fall to play.

HAMLET. She well instructs me.

OSRIC. I commend my duty to your lordship.

HAMLET. Yours, yours.   [*Exit* OSRIC.

HORATIO. You will lose this wager, my lord.

HAMLET. I do not think so; since he went into France, I have been in continual practice; I shall win at the odds. But thou wouldst not think how ill all 's here about my heart; but it is no matter.

HORATIO. Nay, good my lord,—

HAMLET. It is but foolery; but it is such a kind of gain-giving as would perhaps trouble a woman.

HORATIO. If your mind dislike any thing, obey it; I will forestal their repair hither, and say you are not fit.

HAMLET. Not a whit, we defy augury; there 's a special providence in the fall of a sparrow. If it be now, 'tis not to come; if it be not to come, it will be now; if it be not now, yet it will come: the readiness is all. Since no man has aught of what he leaves, what is 't to leave betimes? Let be.

right. He has a final message, this one from the Queen, and Hamlet walks over to him to receive it. His mother's words echo what he has just said to Horatio, and he turns toward the latter as he answers Osric with quiet gravity,—'She well instructs me'—and then dismisses the incongruous messenger of death.

Horatio is deeply concerned. He moves toward Hamlet, this time speaking his protest, but Hamlet reassures him as far as the actual fencing is concerned. He is in practice. He is also deeply conscious of his inner strength. But . . . there is a long pause as he stands very quietly in the centre of the stage looking out. His sentences are short, with pauses between, as with clear eyes, a clear unhurried voice, deep, bell-like, limpid, he weighs within himself the time that is and is to be. He does not move at all, nor is there any rise in inflection or any marked emphasis on a particular word or phrase, yet each pause marks an increase of power which flows into him and emanates from him as though he were charged with a mysterious invisible current of energy. He seems most poignantly alive as with complete prevision he accepts death. The slow, inward words are an act of renunciation. Very quietly he turns toward Horatio, his hand on his arm. His pale face seems already suspended in eternity. Two words only mark the poignant moment: 'Let be.'

Scene 19.—*The great hall in the castle.* KING, QUEEN, HAMLET, HORATIO, LAERTES, *Lords,* OSRIC, *and Attendants.*

KING. Come, Hamlet, come, and take this hand from me.
HAMLET. Give me your pardon, sir; I've done you wrong;
  But pardon 't, as you are a gentleman.
  This presence knows,
  And you must needs have heard, how I am punish'd
  With sore distraction. Sir, in this audience,
  Let my disclaiming from a purpos'd evil
  Free me so far in your most generous thoughts,
  That I have shot mine arrow o'er the house,
  And hurt my brother.
[LAERTES.   I am satisfied in nature,
  Whose motive, in this case, should stir me most
  To my revenge; but in my terms of honour
  I stand aloof, and will no reconcilement,
  Till by some elder masters, of known honour,
  I have a voice and precedent of peace,
  To keep my name ungor'd. But till that time,
  I do receive your offer'd love like love,
  And will not wrong it.
HAMLET.   I embrace it freely;
  And will this brother's wager frankly play.]
  Give us the foils. Come on.
LAERTES.   Come, one for me.
HAMLET. I'll be your foil, Laertes; in mine ignorance
  Your skill shall, like a star i' the darkest night,
  Stick fiery off indeed.
LAERTES.   You mock me, sir.
HAMLET. No, by this hand.
KING. Give them the foils, young Osric. Cousin Hamlet,
  You know the wager?
HAMLET.   Very well, my lord;
  Your Grace hath laid the odds o' the weaker side.
KING. I do not fear it; I have seen you both;
  But since he is better'd, we have therefore odds.
LAERTES. This is too heavy; let me see another.
HAMLET. This likes me well. These foils have all a length?
OSRIC. Ay, my good lord.
KING. Set me the stoups of wine upon that table.
  If Hamlet give the first or second hit,
  [Or quit in answer of the third exchange,
  Let all the battlements their ordnance fire;]

SCENE 19. *The great hall in the castle.*

The court has assembled for the fencing match. The Queen and her attendants are on the middle landing to the right, the King with Laertes forward toward the left. At some distance behind the Queen, who is seated on a high-backed chair, is a table with the wine and cups. Osric holds foils across his arm and daggers in his hand, for the match is to be played with rapier and dagger, in which sport Laertes excels. Hamlet and Horatio enter from the left and salute the Queen, and Hamlet turns at the King's bidding to take Laertes' hand. In a warm voice, candid, generous, he asks Laertes' pardon for the sins he has so inadvertently committed against him. Obviously he cannot tell him in this company—or elsewhere—that he killed Polonius thinking to kill the King, nor explain the cause of his ' sore distraction, ' but he can tell Laertes with deep sincerity that he and Laertes both are but the victims of a greater evil.

With a warm handclasp he leaves Laertes and comes forward to the right of the stage, where, aided by Horatio, he slips off his coat and prepares for the bout. Osric approaches with the foils and Laertes takes one; then at a signal from the King exchanges it for another. Hamlet has been standing with his back to the King during this manœuvre, but now he is ready and turns to Osric who presents him with the foils and dagger. He takes the first foil that comes to his hand and tries it against the ground to test its flexibility. As the King drinks to his health he and Laertes stand at salute on either side of the stage, ready for the match.

They fall to with vigour. Hamlet is gay, alert, quick on his feet, stimulated as always by the tonic of activity. To him this is a ' brother's wager ' and he plays it with frank enjoyment. His prescience of disaster was not connected with Laertes and is already forgotten.

The first bout ends in Hamlet's favour. The combatants have changed places and he is on the left of the stage, facing the King who has approached the table, and now puts the treacherous

> The king shall drink to Hamlet's better breath;
> And in the cup an union shall he throw,
> Richer than that which four successive kings
> In Denmark's crown have worn. Give me the cups;
> [And let the kettle to the trumpet speak,
> The trumpet to the cannoneer without,
> The cannons to the heavens, the heavens to earth,]
> ' Now the king drinks to Hamlet! ' Come, begin;
> And you, the judges, bear a wary eye.

HAMLET. Come on, sir.

LAERTES. 　　　　　　Come, my lord. 　　　　　　　　　[*They play.*

HAMLET. 　　　　　　　　　　　　One.

LAERTES. 　　　　　　　　　　　　　　No.

HAMLET. 　　　　　　　　　　　　　　　　Judgment.

OSRIC. A hit, a very palpable hit.

LAERTES. 　　　　　　　　　Well; again.

KING. Stay; give me drink. Hamlet, this pearl is thine;
> Here's to thy health. Give him the cup.

HAMLET. I'll play this bout first; set it by awhile.
> Come.—[*They play.*] Another hit; what say you?

LAERTES. A touch, a touch, I do confess.

KING. Our son shall win.

QUEEN. 　　　　　　　　He's faint, and scant of breath.
> Here, Hamlet, take my napkin, rub thy brows;
> The queen carouses to thy fortune, Hamlet.

HAMLET. Good madam!

KING. 　　　　　　　　　Gertrude, do not drink.

QUEEN. I will, my lord; I pray you, pardon me.

KING. It is the poison'd cup: it is too late.

HAMLET. I dare not drink yet, madam; by and by.

QUEEN. Come, let me wipe thy face.

LAERTES. My lord, I'll hit him now.

KING. 　　　　　　　　　　I do not think 't.

LAERTES. And yet 'tis almost 'gainst my conscience.

HAMLET. Come, for the third, Laertes. You but dally;
> I pray you, pass with your best violence.
> I am afeard you make a wanton of me.

LAERTES. Say you so? come on. 　　　　　　　　　[*They play.*

OSRIC. Nothing, neither way.

LAERTES. Have at you now.

KING. 　　　　　　　Part them! they are incens'd.

HAMLET. Nay, come, again.

OSRIC. 　　　　　　Look to the queen there, ho!

HORATIO. They bleed on both sides. How is it, my lord?

' union ' in the cup—offering it to Hamlet in token of his victory. Hamlet refuses, and they fight again, this time with increasing energy, circling around the stage until Hamlet finds himself near the Queen when the second hit is called.

He is a little breathless, but youthfully happy with his success. He turns to his mother, who, standing on the step above him, wipes his face with her kerchief, and kisses him before she picks up the poisoned cup to toast his victory. His hearty, enthusiastic ' Good madam! ' answers her as she drinks a deep draught of death to his success. The King's horrified protest comes too late. The Queen drinks again and holds the cup out to Hamlet—who again refuses it and turns back to Laertes with a gay challenge.

They fight a bout without result; then Laertes lunges quickly before Hamlet expects him. The point touches Hamlet's right arm and he realizes instantly the full murderous intent of this friendly wager. He claps his hand over the wound, dropping the dagger. A sharp, sibilant exclamation breaks from his lips. His face, a moment before laughing, animated, has become steely with rage. He closes with Laertes, who has also thrown down his dagger and is ready for him. But Hamlet is quicker. He strikes up Laertes' sword, comes in under his guard and as he passes seizes the unbated weapon with his left hand. They whirl and face each other, Laertes disarmed. Hamlet with the two rapiers in his hands looks down at the weapon he has taken from Laertes, then up at the murderous ' friend ' with an expression of anger and profound contempt. With a deft movement of his right hand he tosses his own blunt foil to Laertes, transferring the unbated weapon to his right hand and challenging Laertes once more as the King tries to part them: ' Nay, come, again.' Hamlet will not stop now.

Swift as lightning he is upon Laertes, who falls mortally wounded. The Queen rises from her throne in agony. Hamlet leaps to her side and holds her in his arms as she cries out the horror of her discovery. ' The drink, the drink,—O my dear Hamlet! The drink . . . ! ' With a terrible cry of rage Hamlet lets her go and

OSRIC. How is it, Laertes?

LAERTES. Why, as a woodcock to mine own springe, Osric;
I am justly kill'd with mine own treachery.

HAMLET. How does the queen?

KING.   She swounds to see them bleed.

QUEEN. No, no, the drink, the drink,—O my dear Hamlet!
The drink, the drink; I am poison'd.

HAMLET. O villainy! Ho! let the door be lock'd:
Treachery! seek it out.

LAERTES. It is here, Hamlet. Hamlet, thou art slain;
No medicine in the world can do thee good;
In thee there is not half an hour of life;
The treacherous instrument is in thy hand,
Unbated and envenom'd. The foul practice
Hath turn'd itself on me; [lo! here I lie,
Never to rise again.] Thy mother's poison'd.
I can no more. The king, the king's to blame.

HAMLET. The point envenom'd too!—
Then, venom, to thy work.   [*Stabs the* KING.

ALL. Treason! treason!

KING. O! yet defend me, friends; I am but hurt.

HAMLET. Here, thou incestuous, murderous, damned Dane,
Drink off this potion;—is thy union here?
Follow my mother.   [KING *dies.*

LAERTES.   He is justly serv'd;
It is a poison temper'd by himself.
Exchange forgiveness with me, noble Hamlet:
Mine and my father's death come not upon thee,
Nor thine on me!   [*Dies.*

HAMLET. Heaven made thee free of it! I follow thee.
I am dead, Horatio. Wretched queen, adieu!
You that look pale and tremble at this chance,
That are but mutes or audience to this act,
Had I but time,—as this fell sergeant, death,
Is strict in his arrest,—O! I could tell you—
But let it be. Horatio, I am dead;
Thou livest; report me and my cause aright
To the unsatisfied.

HORATIO.   Never believe it;
I am more an antique Roman than a Dane:
Here's yet some liquor left.

HAMLET.   As thou'rt a man,
Give me the cup: let go; by heaven, I'll have 't.
O God! Horatio, what a wounded name,

leaps up the stairs to close the doors, but Laertes' voice stops him. He turns as Laertes speaks, the full treachery of the ghastly plot dawning on his outraged mind. As the King moves, sword in hand, to stop Laertes' revelation, Hamlet leaps down upon him, knocking the sword from his hand and running him through with the fatal weapon which has already done so much deadly work. The King struggles to his feet calling for help and manages to stagger up the stairs, left, as Hamlet, discarding the sword, picks up the poisoned cup which has been standing near his mother and leaps up the right-hand stairway to meet the King.

A quick struggle on the upper platform, a last bitter quibble on Hamlet's part, and the King is doubly served with his own murderous weapons. Hamlet, the cup still in his hand, comes slowly down the left stairs to where Laertes lies in his last agony. The forgiveness which this time Laertes asks is given by Hamlet without reservation as he takes the dying man's hand in a last clasp. ' Heaven make thee free of it.' ' Hamlet stands a moment looking down. ' I follow thee.' Then he raises his head and moves forward. ' I am dead, Horatio.'

Again, as in the graveyard scene, a note of wonder, almost of surprise, colours his tone. He has thought and talked and lived with death, he has longed for it and revolted against it, but its presence is an astonishment. He moves with difficulty across the stage and up the two steps to the Queen, kissing her forehead in farewell. His right arm is already becoming numb. He stands for a moment on the platform beside his mother's chair and speaks to the courtiers. But he cannot finish—the poison is working in him. ' Horatio, I am dead! ' Horatio goes up to him and he leans against him, his strength ebbing. He seems almost spent but when Horatio seizes the poisonous draught from him and starts to drink it, he is galvanized into sudden life. With a swift violence that takes the other man by surprise he seizes the cup and throws it on the ground; then, his left hand on Horatio's shoulder, his wounded right held awkwardly against his side, he makes his immortal plea: ' If thou didst ever hold me in thy heart, absent thee from felicity awhile.'

Things standing thus unknown, shall live behind me.
If thou didst ever hold me in thy heart,
Absent thee from felicity awhile,
And in this harsh world draw thy breath in pain,
To tell my story. What warlike noise is this?

OSRIC. Young Fortinbras, with conquest come from Poland,
To the ambassadors of England gives
This warlike volley.

HAMLET.   O! I die, Horatio;
The potent poison quite o'er-crows my spirit:
I cannot live to hear the news from England,
But I do prophesy the election lights
On Fortinbras: he has my dying voice;
So tell him, with the occurrents, more and less,
Which have solicited—The rest is silence.   [*Dies.*

HORATIO. Now cracks a noble heart. Good-night, sweet prince,
And flights of angels sing thee to thy rest!
Why does the drum come hither?

        Enter FORTINBRAS, *the English Ambassadors, and Others.*

FORTINBRAS. Where is this sight?

HORATIO.   What is it ye would see?
If aught of woe or wonder, cease your search.

FORTINBRAS. This quarry cries on havoc. O proud death!
What feast is toward in thine eternal cell,
[That thou so many princes at a shot
So bloodily hast struck?]

HORATIO. Give order that these bodies
High on a stage be placed to the view;
And let me speak to the yet unknowing world
How these things came about.

[FORTINBRAS.   Let us haste to hear it,
And call the noblest to the audience.
For me, with sorrow I embrace my fortune;
I have some rights of memory in this kingdom,
Which now to claim my vantage doth invite me.

HORATIO. Of that I shall have also cause to speak,
And from his mouth whose voice will draw on more.]

FORTINBRAS.   Let four captains
Bear Hamlet, like a soldier, to the stage;
For he was likely, had he been put on,
To have prov'd most royally: and, for his passage,
The soldiers' music and the rites of war
Speak loudly for him.

The miraculous words are another step, almost the last, in Hamlet's passionate pilgrimage. Renunciation has been followed by reconciliation; peace is imminent.

The war-like noises break the spell which the still, exalted face and poignant voice have woven. Hamlet straightens himself with an effort and walks toward Osric who stands at the left of the stage near Laertes' body. Osric drops on his knee and explains that the sounds betoken the arrival of Fortinbras and the ambassadors from England. Hamlet looks down at Osric and the ghost of a smile crosses his face at the memory of the flourish of feathers, the jests of less than an hour before. He turns again to Horatio who has followed him and stands now on his right, supporting him. His will still keeps him on his feet though he cries, in pain now, and weakening, his third ' O! I die, Horatio.' The poison is working on his body, yet his spirit is indomitable. His right arm hangs limp and helpless but he raises his left in salute to the on-coming king and starts to send him a message. In mid-sentence he stops, his words lost. His arm drops. He throws back his head a little and his face takes on an unearthly pallour. For a still, breathless moment he looks with living eyes on death itself. There is again a look of faint surprise, then of complete acceptance. ' The rest is silence.' He sways a little, his jaw drops, his head falls forward and he collapses into Horatio's arms.

Very gently Horatio lays him on the ground, and kneeling beside him crosses his hands on his breast. The trumpets blare. Fortinbras, followed by four captains, enters through the upper archway. Horatio rises and greets them, and the four soldiers come down the left stairway to where Hamlet lies. At the word of command they lift up Hamlet's body. As they stand at attention Fortinbras draws his sword in salute, the cannon roars and the lights black out.

Take up the bodies: such a sight as this
Becomes the field, but here shows much amiss.
Go, bid the soldiers shoot.